"Val, we have to make sure your inner demon isn't hungry," my cousin Micah said. "When was the last time you fed?"

Fed? I hated that word, hated the way it made me sound like one of the bloodsucking vampires I fought on San Antonio's dark streets. "Uh, last night. I lost control a bit."

"You can feed on Shade."

Whoa. No way. I liked him.

My cute little hellhound spoke inside my mind. THAT'S THE POINT, BABE.

I glared down at Fang. "I can't. It's dangerous."

"Really," Shade said softly, "I don't mind." He took my hand, grounding himself in this reality, in me, so that he no longer flickered through a dozen different dimensions. Because of that, I could see the shadow demon's features, though they were still partially hidden by his ever-present hood. Just as I remembered, he had shaggy blond hair, piercing blue eyes, and the face of an angel.

Lola, my inner demon, wanted him. So did I, for that matter.

Readers Raved About Val Shapiro and Fang
in
BITE ME,
Book One, *The Demon Underground* Series

" . . . this book takes me back to my Buffy days–yep, that kind of smart and sharp-edged humor. Love it."
The Bradford Bunch

Wicked fun . . . And a cute hellhound. Come on, I couldn't ask for more."
Cynthia Eden, author of *Everlasting Bad Boys*

"I can't wait to the next Demon Underground novel!!"
That Teen Can Blog

"I couldn't put it down."
Just Blinded Book Reviews

"Engaging for readers of all ages." **SciFiGuy**

"I can't wait to read more about Val and her trusty sidekicks."
Literary Escapism

" . . . a fun, exciting, action-packed tale that takes us into the dark side of society, but leaves us longing for more. I cannot wait for the next adventure . . . "
NovelTalk

"I absolutely adored Fang . . . !"
Bookluver Carol

Dedication

Many, many thanks to Karen Fox, Angel Smits, Jodi Anderson, Jude Willhoff, and Sharon Silva for their feedback, for sociable critique meetings I actually look forward to, and for unstinting support during some very tough times. That includes the rest of the Wyrd Sisters, too. You have no idea how much I appreciate your friendship every day.

I also want to acknowledge the general awesomeness of the Belles. Deb Dixon is a wonderful editor whose questions and suggestions greatly improved the book, and it's great working with Deb Smith and her enthusiasm for marketing and trying new things. Thanks for making it fun!

This is a work of fiction. Names, characters, places and incidents are either the products of the author's imagination or are used fictitiously. Any resemblance to actual persons (living or dead,) events or locations is entirely coincidental.

Bell Bridge Books
PO BOX 300921
Memphis, TN 38130
ISBN: 978-0-9843256-6-5

Bell Bridge Books is an Imprint of BelleBooks, Inc.

We at BelleBooks enjoy hearing from readers. You can contact us at the address above or at BelleBooks@BelleBooks.com

Visit our websites – www.BelleBooks.com and www.BellBridgeBooks.com.

10 9 8 7 6 5 4 3 2

Cover design: Debra Dixon
Interior design: Hank Smith
Photo credits: girl - © Jose Antonio Sánchez Reyes | Dreamstime.com
                 street - © Secondshot | Dreamstime.com

:Lr:01:

Try Me

Parker Blue

Bell Bridge Books

Chapter One

I watched from the trees at the edge of the Texas graveyard, too cowardly to face the people who grieved for the woman I'd murdered. They thought she'd been killed in a car accident. They thought her life had been cut short by the whim of fate. They were wrong.

But I didn't plan on telling them anything different. They didn't really know her, didn't really know what she'd become. Let them keep their illusions.

I shivered as a soft breeze with a hint of chill ruffled my hair. Someone sobbed, and it seemed totally weird that the night should feel so serene, the San Antonio cemetery still so lush and green even in November, when the people around the grave were so sad and depressed.

Once darkness fell, the mourners finally left. Still, I hesitated in the darker shadow of the trees, rooted in place. It's not like Detective Dan Sullivan and I had a solid romance thing going on, but we *had* been more than friends and vampire-hunting partners. Now he was giving me the cold shoulder . . . just because I'd separated his girlfriend's head from her body?

His *ex*-girlfriend, I reminded myself. She and Dan had broken up even *before* she started dining on people. And he'd said I was right to decapitate her in order to rescue the rest of us, including my step-dad and baby sister. But still.

I hadn't heard from Dan for several days. Now I watched from the gnarled oaks and scruffy mesquite trees at the edge of a Texas graveyard, too cowardly to face the friends and family who grieved for his ex, the woman I'd murdered. They thought she'd been killed in a car accident. They thought her life had been cut short by the whim of fate. They were wrong.

But I didn't plan on telling them anything different. They didn't really know her, didn't really know what she'd become. Let them keep their illusions.

I shivered as a soft breeze with a hint of chill ruffled my hair. Someone sobbed, and it seemed totally weird that the night should feel so serene, the San Antonio cemetery still so lush and green even in November, when the people around the grave were so sad and depressed.

Once darkness fell, the mourners finally left. Still, I hesitated in the darker shadow of the trees, rooted in place. With just Fang and me in the cemetery, everything felt . . . more normal. We were used to working outside the rules of society. Of being alone, and at ease, in the darkness.

Fang—part hellhound, part scruffy terrier, and all snark—nudged me with his nose. VAL SHAPIRO, HEAP BIG VAMPIRE SLAYER, AFRAID OF A DEAD BODY? he mocked. C'MON, DO WHAT YA HAVE TO, SO WE CAN GET OUT OF HERE.

Did I mention the hellhound part allowed him to read my thoughts and speak in my mind? I was okay with the snarky comments most of the time, but sometimes, it was annoying. Like now.

I nudged him back, but refused to rise to his bait. I hadn't hesitated because I was afraid. I hesitated because I wasn't sure why I was here. What could I possibly accomplish?

Sighing and hoping to get a clue, I walked over to her grave. As I approached, the cloying fragrance of the lilies overpowered the scent of freshly turned soil and choked the air out of my lungs. "Lily Ann Armstrong," one trailing floral ribbon read. "Beloved daughter."

I felt like gagging. Partially because of the nauseating flowers, but mostly because of the sentiment. Beloved daughter? *Depraved fiend* was more like it. Or evil bloodsucker.

Yet someone had loved her, had mourned her passing. But why was I here? Was I here to acknowledge the fact of her existence, to admit that I'd lopped her head off with one stroke of my blade?

Tell me, what could you say to the grave of a woman you'd decapitated? *Hey, sorry I murdered you, but you deserved it?*

Fang snorted. THAT WASN'T MURDER. YOU CAN'T KILL THE UNDEAD—YOU JUST COMPLETE THE PROCESS.

He had a point. They thought Lily had died a few days ago at the age of twenty-five, but in reality, she'd died months before, when she'd made the decision to become a vampire. I hadn't killed Lily—she'd done that to herself, done the unthinkable to stay forever young, forever powerful, forever evil. Yes, she'd deserved it, and I'd do it again in a heartbeat. After all, her hunger for power had put all of San Antonio in jeopardy, cost many lives, and almost cost me my family.

So why had I come? I'd never visited the graves of my other vampire kills. Why was this one different? Because my partner, Dan Sullivan, had once cared for her?

I didn't even know how I felt. Happy she was gone, sorry I hadn't caught her sooner . . . what?

Fang leaned against me, compassion in his big brown eyes. IT'S OKAY TO GRIEVE. BUT ARE YOU GRIEVING FOR HER . . . OR YOURSELF?

Good question. Because of Lily, I'd come into my power and unleashed Lola—the succubus lust demon inside me. I still felt mildly connected to the men I'd enthralled three nights ago, still fizzing with the energy I'd absorbed from them. The past three days, I'd felt more vibrantly alive than in my entire eighteen years of existence.

It was exhilarating . . . yet scary, too. I'd fought against letting my demon free my whole life, but because of Lily, I'd been forced to let the succubus loose to save the people I loved. Thanks to Lily, I now knew what I'd been fighting against, knew how tempting ultimate power was, how powerful it made me. It made me understand her in a way I hadn't before. She'd felt this seductive power, too, and had given in.

But I never wanted to be like her, never wanted to give in to the demon inside me. It meant a lifetime of battle between the two sides of my nature, but I was determined to come out on top.

So, yes, I grieved. For both of us.

THAT'S OKAY, Fang said, rubbing up against my leg. IT MAKES YOU HUMAN.

Whoa. For some reason, that really got me, and I felt a huge wave of relief wash through my body. Yes, I was human. Only one-eighth of me was demon. Not enough to make me a monster, no matter how my mother looked at me.

"Thanks," I said simply.

Fang grinned. NO PROBLEM. NOW, CAN WE GO KILL ANOTHER ONE?

I laughed, just as he'd intended. It was what the Special Crimes Unit hired us to do, what I was good at, my reason for existence. "Sure, let's—"

I broke off as Fang stared beyond me, wagging his tail. I turned around and smiled at the man who approached. Even in the dark I could sense his good looks. With dark wavy hair that curled around his ears, full lips, and a dancer's body, Micah Blackburn was the type of guy that girls drooled over. Everyone but me, that was. My succubus demon cancelled out his incubus, and he was the only guy I could be physically close to without having to worry about Lola getting all touchy-feely. He was kinda like the older brother I never had. We were probably related somewhere along the line, so I considered him my cousin.

Too bad I didn't look like him, though. He was a total hottie while I was . . . so not. Blah brown hair, blah brown eyes, average height. Ordinary—that's me. On the outside, anyway. Inside, I was totally *extra*ordinary. If I could figure out how to swap the inside for the outside, I'd do it in a nanosecond.

Micah smiled. "I thought you might be here."

"Why?" I hadn't known I was coming myself.

"Lieutenant Ramirez mentioned the funeral. I figured you'd feel the need for closure."

Closure. Muscles I hadn't realized were tense relaxed as I realized Micah had nailed it. I'd come for closure. And now, with the finality of her burial, I had it. I could let go of it all. "Yeah, I guess. Why did you track me down? Why didn't you just call?"

"I did."

"Oh, I forgot. I turned the phone off so it wouldn't ring in the middle of the funeral. "I pulled it out and checked it. Sure enough— two calls from Micah, none from Dan or Lt. Ramirez. Damn.

"What's the matter?" Micah asked.

I shrugged and plopped down on the grass and sat there cross-legged, staring at the ground to avoid his knowing eyes.

Micah joined me, sinking down and looking all loose-limbed and graceful. Wistfully, I wished that was one of the traits of being our kind of demon. But no, it was just Micah.

"Want to talk about it?" he asked.

"Not really." But I knew he'd bug me until I spilled my guts. As the leader of San Antonio's Demon Underground, Micah had an over-developed sense of responsibility for anyone in his organization. And that included me . . . and Fang.

Fang snuggled against me. YEP. MIGHT AS WELL SPILL IT NOW AND GET IT OVER WITH. IF YOU DON'T, I WILL.

The hellhound could read the mind of anyone who was part-demon or part-vampire, and project his thoughts into theirs if he chose. Usually, I was the only one he chose to share with. Lucky me.

HEY, Fang protested, DO YOU KNOW WHAT IT'S LIKE READING THE MIND OF MOST VAMPIRES AND DEMONS? LIKE WADING IN A CESSPOOL. NO THANKS.

Gee, I guess I should be flattered.

YOU BETCHA.

Micah stared into my face. "Val?"

I sighed. "It's nothing."

IT'S SOMETHING, Fang corrected, making it clear he was communicating to both of us. TELL HIM.

"Okay, okay. Ramirez told me to take a few days off after I . . . stopped . . . Lily."

"Because you killed Dan's former fiancée?"

"No, because I let Lola fully free for the first time."

Micah nodded. "Oh, of course."

"Yeah. He wasn't sure I could handle it." Heck, *I* wasn't sure I could handle it. And though Lola had been fully satisfied for the first time in my life, it didn't mean she was content to lie back and bask in the feeling. Far from it. Instead, she seemed to want more and more all the time. "You were right," I admitted. "I should have been feeding her a little bit of lust all along. It would've been a lot easier to handle now." For years, I hadn't let her feed at all. I'd starved her, then suddenly let her gorge to her heart's content. In hindsight, neither was a good decision.

Micah shook his head, looking exasperated. "I told you before, there is no Lola, no separate demon inside you. It's part of *you*."

"I know, I know. It's just easier to think of my demon nature as a separate person inside me." Someone to blame my urges on, someone else to take the fall for the lust I had a problem controlling. Too weird that I had men lusting after me all the time and I was still a virgin. "Leave me some illusions, will ya?"

"All right, but tell me what's wrong."

"No biggie. I got bored, tired of having nothing to do." When Micah continued waiting patiently, I admitted softly, "Okay, I've been waiting for Dan to call, just to reassure me he hasn't had second thoughts about me. That he doesn't think I'm a monster, and he doesn't blame me for enthralling him and everyone else." And to check out that spark, that closeness we'd felt immediately afterward. "He hasn't called."

YEAH, Fang said. ALL SHE DOES IS MOPE.

"Do not." I paced a lot, too.

So, I'd gotten on my Valkyrie motorcycle, plopped Fang in his seat on the back and driven off to blow the cobwebs out of my brain. Somehow, I'd ended up here, at the gravesite of the woman who still complicated my life even in her death.

Micah gave me a one-armed hug. "I thought Dan was fine with . . . Lola."

I leaned into the hug, and slipped my arms around his waist., laying my head on his shoulder, feeling warmth suffuse me at the rare contact with a person of the male persuasion. "I thought so, too. But maybe it was just a side-effect of the spell Lola cast over him."

"Maybe," Micah murmured. "But don't worry, he'll come around."

I wasn't so sure, but a demon girl could hope . . . "Thanks, I—"

Fang suddenly spun around, his eyes flashing purple. VAMPIRES, he snarled, and leapt toward the three onrushing forms.

Lola surged to the fore. I scrambled to my feet and whipped out one of the stakes I kept tucked in my jeans' back waistband. As the first vamp jumped at me, his hands outstretched and fangs gleaming, I stabbed him right in the heart. He dropped like a rock.

Fang had the female vamp engaged so I turned to check on Micah. He wasn't doing so well. He'd never made it off the ground and was pinned by a vamp who was sinking fangs into his neck. Terrified, I grabbed another stake. "Go fang yourself, buster." I plunged the stake into the fangbanger's back as hard as I could.

It was enough to pierce his heart and he dropped on top of Micah.

A LITTLE HELP HERE, Fang yelled.

He'd harried the female vamp and kept her occupied, but though he was part hellhound, she still outweighed him six to one. As she lifted her foot to kick him, I tackled her and punched her in the face as hard as I could. Her neck snapped back and she hit the ground. She looked surprised.

It felt good, so I dropped down on top of her, straddled her waist and hit her again. And again and again.

ENOUGH, Fang yelled in my mind. YOU WHUPPED HER GOOD. STOP ALREADY.

His sarcasm got to me. I stopped, fist upraised, and stared down at the vamp whose face was beaten, battered, and bloody. Repulsed, I let my arm drop. Had I done that?

Fang dropped a fallen branch by my hand. JUST KILL HER

ALREADY.

Yes, that was my job—taking out the bloodsuckers who preyed on humans. Not beating the crap out of them like the monster some thought me. Before the vamp could recover, I snatched up the branch and, using both hands, stabbed it down so hard I pinned her to the ground. She stiffened, then lay still, well and truly dead.

FEEL BETTER NOW?

Actually, I did. "Shut up," I muttered and felt the sizzle in my blood cool a bit. Lola had gotten her jollies with one kind of lust anyway, so she was happy. *Glad someone is,* I thought, annoyed at myself. I got to my feet to check on Micah.

He had rolled the vamp off of him and was sitting up, wide-eyed, holding a hand to his neck.

"You okay?" I asked.

Micah nodded. "Yes, thanks to the two of you." He removed his hand from his neck. The bite mark was very shallow, so the vamp hadn't gotten started, thank goodness. I wondered idly why they were here, then realized they had probably come to pay their respects to Lily, former leader of San Antonio's bad-ass vamps. San Antonio, land of the Alamo, cowboys, barbecue, and the undead. Well, they could pay their respects in person now—in hell.

Speaking of which . . . I pulled a GPS locator out of my pocket and activated it so one of the city's secret Special Crimes Unit pick-up units would come to dispose of the dead vamps. After I'd done my duty, I studied Micah more closely. Though it was rather dark, my enhanced senses allowed me to see him clearly. He looked really shocked.

"Never fought a vamp before?" I guessed.

He glanced up at me. "No. They're so much faster and stronger, I try to avoid it."

I glanced down at the dead undead who'd almost fanged Micah and was surprised to see how slight he was. Micah must outweigh the vamp by a good thirty pounds. Why hadn't he been able to fight the bloodsucker off?

As I helped Micah to his feet, he added, "I don't know how you do it—you're as good as they are. Rick must have been one great trainer. You're not even breathing hard."

True, my stepfather had been an excellent martial arts trainer, but speed and strength came naturally to me. There'd been no need to teach me *that*. "You mean, you're not as good as they are?"

He laughed without mirth. "Of course not. I'm only one-eighth incubus, like you. The only thing I could do is enthrall them . . . and only if they're female." He glanced at me curiously. "Why didn't you do that to the two males?"

Because I'd tried my whole life to avoid using my succubus powers to control men. I'd grown up with a mother who never forgave my part-demon father for enthralling her. "I didn't think about it, I just reacted." But . . . why hadn't Micah been able to fight off a baby vamp?

Fang frowned up at me. GOOD QUESTION.

My expression must have looked as odd as I felt, because Micah asked, "What is it? What's wrong?"

"Don't you . . . have super strength, reflexes, senses, and healing ability?"

He paused in brushing off his pants, looking surprised. "No. Do you?"

"Yeah, I thought you knew that. You mean that's *not* part of being a lust demon?"

"Not so far as I know."

Fang stared at me. HOLY CRAP, BATMAN. WHAT DOES THAT MEAN?

"I have no idea." My mind raced as I struggled to understand what Micah had revealed. Why *was* I so much stronger and faster than him?

"It's possible . . . " Micah hesitated.

"What? Tell me."

He looked apologetic. "I personally don't know of any, but it's possible that you are descended from more than one type of demon."

"*What?*" Stunned, I asked, "What other kind of demon?"

"I have no idea. We lost a lot of knowledge when we lost the *Encyclopedia Magicka.*"

IT'S NOT LOST, Fang said. VAL HAS IT.

It was Micah's turn to say, "*What?*"

"I have it," I confirmed. "I didn't know anyone was looking for it."

"All three books?"

I nodded. "My father gave them to me for my fifth birthday." *Right before he killed himself in despair over being a demon,* I didn't say out loud. .

Micah goggled at me. "So that's where they went. We've been

looking for those books for years, struggling in the dark, trying to find clues to our demon nature whenever we could. And you've had them all along?"

He looked indignant, but I held up my hands in surrender. "Hey, I didn't know he *stole* them. You can have them back, no problem." It was the least I could do after Micah had made me feel so welcome. Besides, they really belonged to him, since my father had probably stolen them from Micah's father.

He relaxed and ran a hand over his face. "I'm sorry, but you have no idea how much having those books would have helped us over the past thirteen years. It's the only known copy of the encyclopedia in existence."

Fang rolled his eyes. EVER HEAR OF A SCANNER? OR A COPY MACHINE?

Micah grinned ruefully. "Good point. But my father probably didn't want to make it too easy for others to steal—the information can be dangerous in the wrong hands."

"Dangerous how? You mean because it reveals our weaknesses?"

"Yes, but that's just the first volume. The other two . . . " He gave me a quizzical look. "Did you read the other two?"

"No—I didn't read much at all." I shrugged. "I figured they were just more books on magick, maybe a little more accurate than most." After all, I'd been around lots of them at Mom and Rick's New Age bookstore. And I wasn't much of a reader—action was more my thing.

"And you didn't feel any . . . *pull* from the books?"

"No. Should I?"

"I guess not. My father didn't explain that real well, but I definitely got the impression there was something dangerous about possessing volumes two and three. They're about the old magicks, ones no one uses anymore. I'll be glad to get them back, so I can keep them safe."

"I'll bring them over to you right away, I promise."

It dawned on me we were *chatting* there in the dark, in a cemetery, with Lily buried nearby in two pieces—her head and the rest of her—and the gape-eyed corpses of three vamps sprawled around us. I shrugged. No biggie. All in a day's work.

"I appreciate it." Micah snapped his fingers. "That reminds me. The reason I've been trying to find you is because I want to make sure you come to the social. You can bring the books to me then."

I grimaced. "I'm not feeling very social right now." And I didn't know many people in the Demon Underground.

"You should come. Eat, drink, get to know other part-demons like yourself."

"Why don't you guys just start a chat room? Or friend each other on Facebook?"

IT'S OKAY, Fang assured me. I'VE BEEN AND IT'S FUN. YOU CAN BE YOURSELF WITH NO BLOOD, MAYHEM, OR VAMPIRES BEATEN TO A BLOODY PULP.

I glared at him, but he ignored me.

Micah added, "Oh, and the New Blood Movement wants to discuss something with us, too, so some of them are coming as well."

I grimaced. I hadn't seen Alejandro or his vampire followers since I'd lopped Lily's head off and stained his pristine rug. He'd *said* he was cool with that, but . . .

Oh, well, might as well get it over with. "Uh, okay. When is it again?"

He checked his watch. "In about an hour, at the club. I've closed it to the public tonight."

"Okay, I'll come and bring the books. Maybe you can help me look through them to find out why I have these abilities and you don't."

Micah shook my hand. "It's a deal."

The SCU pick-up unit, disguised as an ambulance, drove up then. Micah left, and I helped the staff load the undead remains. Then I headed home to the townhouse I shared with Dan's sister, wondering what freaky thing would happen next. It had been a hell of a week, and the revelation that I might have *two* demons inside me made me tired and confused.

Fang nudged me. DON'T WORRY ABOUT IT, KIDDO. YOU'RE STILL VAL.

Yes, but until an hour ago, I'd thought I knew myself pretty well. Now I had no idea who . . . or what . . . or how many of me . . . I really was.

Chapter Two

Fang and I went to the townhouse to stock up again on stakes and holy water—just in case—and I put the heavy books of the encyclopedia in a backpack. My friend and landlord, Dan's sister, Gwen, a nurse, wasn't there to ask questions, thank goodness. She worked the night shift at the hospital.

My cell rang as we were about to head out, and I checked the number. Nope, not Dan. It was my stepfather. Sighing, I answered, "Hello, Rick."

"Hello, sweetheart. How's everything going?"

"Okay." Fang snorted, but I ignored him. "Everyone there okay?"

"Wonderful, thanks to you. Jen and I owe you our lives and—"

I cut him off. "You don't have to keep thanking me. Once was enough." Besides, that's what family did for each other.

"Sorry. I just meant that I've been talking to your mother, and she's grateful, too."

"Uh huh," I said noncommittally, as Fang rolled his eyes. We both believed Mom was happy that her husband and favorite daughter had been saved . . . but I wasn't so sure she was glad *I* was the one to do it. She'd always blamed me for being a bad influence on Jen. It's why she'd kicked me out of the house and made me live on my own the day I turned eighteen. I'd been lucky to connect with Fang, Dan, his sister, and a job with the San Antonio P.D.

"No, really," Rick said. "I'm calling to invite you to Thanksgiving dinner."

I hesitated. A week ago, I would have been thrilled to be invited back into the fold. But now . . . I wasn't sure. I stuck my hand in my pocket and hunched my shoulders. "I don't know. I'm still not sure I'm welcome." They were all fully human. I'd finally accepted that I'm not. Fully human, that is. The whole time I was growing up, Mom had made me feel like a freak. I wasn't sure I wanted to go back.

His voice softened. "Really, Val, she's mellowed. She's even hired one of Micah's people at the store."

"You mean she'll actually have another part-demon around Jen?" *Just as long as the part-demon isn't me, huh?.*

"Yeah, well, but Jen doesn't like him."

Fang snorted. THAT EXPLAINS A LOT. IF BABY SISTER DOESN'T LIKE HIM, MOM ASSUMES HE CAN'T BE A BAD INFLUENCE ON HER.

True. And it might deter Jen's unhealthy fascination with all things vamp and demony. Mom wasn't being altruistic—she was covering her butt. After seeing how naïve Jen was about Alejandro and the other vamps, I couldn't blame her. "I don't know, Rick. I might spend Thanksgiving with Micah and the others."

Rick sighed. "I know they probably feel more like family right now than we do."

"Not really, but at least they don't carp at me and blame me for everything wrong in their lives like Mom does."

"I understand, but Jen and I want you here, and your mother promised to behave."

I grimaced. Why couldn't she just want me to come home 'cause I'm her daughter, too? Selfishly, I wanted her to *want* me there.

But that obviously wasn't going to happen. "I don't—"

"Think about it, Val. Thanksgiving is three weeks away. Really, I think this could bring the two of you back together."

Fang eyed me. DON'T DO IT. YOU KNOW YOU'LL REGRET IT.

He was probably right, but Mom, Rick and Jen were the only human family I had. Hedging, I said, "I'll think about it."

"Good, good." Rick sounded relieved. "We'll count on you being here."

I made a noncommittal noise and changed the subject. "Hey, did Mom ever mention anything about my father being more than one kind of demon?"

"No." Rick sounded surprised. "Why?"

"No reason. I'm just, uh, trying to learn more about my uh . . . heritage, you know?"

"Sorry, she never mentioned anything else about him. Want me to ask her?"

"Sure, if you would." Mom was the only connection I had to my father's demon ancestry. If I have any close relatives on his side, they'd never made themselves known to me. But she might know.

"Okay, will do. Or you could ask her yourself . . . "

I grimaced. Yeah, right. Loads of fun, talking to Mom about her unwanted demon in-laws. "Hey, listen, gotta go. I have a thing."

"Okay, sweetheart. See you soon."

He hung up and Fang nosed me. DO YOU REALLY WANT TO SEE MOMMY DEAREST AGAIN?

"Not really." But there was something deep inside that longed to be a kid again, playing with my sister, training with Rick, baking cookies with Mom . . .

. . . BEING TREATED LIKE CRAP, LIKE YOU'RE SUB-HUMAN, BEING HIDDEN AWAY FROM THE WORLD LIKE YOU'RE A FREAK . . .

I winced. Fang was right. Unless I could somehow rip out the demon part of me, my mother was never going to love me like she did her fully human daughter. I sighed. It was her problem, not mine, and I'd learned to deal.

EVEN BETTER, YOU HAVE A NEW LIFE OF YOUR OWN. AND ME.

I laughed and hugged him. "True. Let's get going so we don't miss the party."

† • ‟

Fang and I cruised down to San Antonio's famous River Walk on my Valkyrie, looking forward to the restaurants and crowds and romantic atmosphere, relaxing in the balmy autumn evening. I parked the Valkyrie and Fang and I walked down the stone steps. Tourists and locals mixed freely on both sides of the narrow, jade-green river, strolling hand in hand, or chatting and laughing over meals under bright umbrellas. The little twinkling lights in the trees overhanging the river made it seem somehow magical . . . in a good way. The River Walk always seemed to me like a lost world in a bubble of its own, far removed from ordinary reality. Or at least, certainly something I never knew as ordinary.

But despite being in my favorite place, I couldn't help but speculate on what other kind of demon might be lurking within me. It was hard not to wonder . . . and worry.

RELAX, Fang said. MAYBE THERE'S MORE THAN ONE WAY TO BE A LUST DEMON. MAYBE YOUR PHYSICAL STRENGTH IS INHERITED FROM YOUR FAMILY AND NOT MICAH'S. NO BIG.

"Maybe not for you . . ." What if it was something else? Like there was a demon time bomb set to go off in my body or something.

OBSESS MUCH?

"Maybe I have good reason."

AND MAYBE YOU DON'T. DID YOU READ ABOUT ANYTHING LIKE THAT IN THE ENCYCLOPEDIA MAGICKA?

No, but I hadn't read that much of it, and I didn't remember reading about anyone having a mixture of demons inside them. What happened when two types of demons mingled?

YOU GET VAL SHAPIRO, Fang said. NOTHING WRONG WITH THAT.

I grinned down at the hellhound. He did know how to make me feel better.

Ignoring the "Closed" sign at Micah's place, Club Purgatory, Fang and I entered through the front. A man at the podium glanced at us then waved us in. "They're in the Ladies Lounge," he said.

Fang sniffed the air. THERE'S ANOTHER DOG HERE. COOL—SOMEONE MY OWN SIZE.

He bounded up the stairs, and I followed. The club looked so different with the lights turned up. Not as dark and mysterious. No crowds of swooning women watching Micah dance. Instead, the purgatory flame and devil theme seemed a little theatrical and hokey under the bright lights.

When I entered the lounge, I saw that someone—probably Micah's assistant, Tessa—had made an attempt to decorate for the party, with streamers, balloons, and floral centerpieces on all the tables. But thankfully, no stupid party hats. Could you imagine demons wearing pointy pieces of cardboard snugged with elastic under their chins? *Not.*

The room was full of people of all shapes, sizes, age, and ethnicity. All colors and creeds of human being could be part-demon. And most of them looked entirely normal . . . though a good sprinkling of them showed evidence of their mixed family trees.

I was used to them, now. I didn't even blink at the sight of small horns peeking from their hair, or purple skin, or vaporish clouds where their faces should be.

Fang immediately followed his nose to the other side of the room, and I smiled at Micah, who came to greet me. He glanced at the backpack. "You have the books?" he asked eagerly.

"Yep."

I handed them over. He unzipped the backpack and peered inside. "Excellent." He glanced around and beckoned Tessa over. She looked even more elfin than normal in this lighting. Not that she was an actual elf. At least, not so far as I knew. Tessa's claim to demon fame was subtle. She went into trances and uttered mysterious prophecies.

"Could you put these in the office and lock the door, please?" Micah asked.

Tessa smiled a greeting at me. "Sure." She hefted the backpack. "That's strange . . . I didn't know I'd be able to feel the magick."

"You can?" I asked in surprise.

"Yes. Can't you?"

"Uh, no. Guess I'm not sensitive enough."

Tessa shrugged and took off with the backpack, but now that I didn't have anything to hold onto, I wasn't quite sure what to do with my hands . . . or the rest of me. I hadn't attended many parties in my lonely life, so I stood there, feeling like a total loser.

Micah must have sensed my geekiness, because he gestured toward the bar. "There's food and drink over there. Have some, then mingle, get to know folks."

"Uh, are there some . . . manners or customs or whatever, that I should know?" I didn't want to screw up or anything. *Please, give me directions on how to navigate this foreign land.*

"One thing—in the Demon Underground, it's considered bad manners to ask someone what *kind* of demon they are. Unless they choose to tell you themselves, of course."

"Then how do you know the ones who look like regular humans really are part-demon?"

"To belong to the Demon Underground, they have to register with us and demonstrate their abilities, so I know their background."

"I don't remember registering."

"You didn't have to—your father did it for you, when you were born."

"Oh." That made sense.

A couple more people came in the door, and he waved me on. "Go, meet and mingle. Come see me afterward, and we'll go through the magick books. See if we can find out more about what other kind of demon might be in your background."

Easier said than done. I glanced around, but wasn't sure how to start mingling, since even Fang had deserted me. Thirsty, I decided to do as Micah suggested and headed for the bar to get a Coke. An attractive middle-aged Hispanic woman smiled at me as I picked up a glass. She looked like someone's mother, and I couldn't imagine what kind of racy demon she might house. She held out her hand. "Hi. You must be Val. I'm Maria Ramirez."

As I shook her hand, I wondered how she knew me. Then the

significance of her last name struck me. "The lieutenant's wife?" I asked.

"Yes—Juan has told me so much about you."

Juan? Sheesh, I hadn't thought of my boss having a first name. I laughed nervously. "All good, I hope."

She smiled. "Of course, though I understand you're going through a bit of a rough time right now. If you ever want to talk . . . "

I stared down into my Coke, not sure what to say. "Thanks. I'm good."

She patted my hand. "Well, give me a call if you change your mind. Juan can give you the number." Maria pointed to the far corner. "I think someone is trying to get your attention."

I glanced up and realized she was right. Someone stood up and waved at me. Deep hoodie hiding his inhuman face, gloves hiding his hands . . . it had to be Shade. Good—someone I knew. I smiled and waved back then glanced hesitantly at Maria, not wanting to seem rude.

"Go ahead," she said. "It'll do you good to be with people your own age."

I thanked her and headed toward the corner. As I neared the guy who'd waved at me, I asked uncertainly, "Shade?"

He tipped back his hood for a moment and I saw the dark ribbons of light swirling in the space where his face should be. Yep, it was Shade all right. You could only see a shadow demon's features if his skin was touching someone else's. Then he looked totally normal, or rather, totally hot. I was kind of surprised Shade hid under his hood here, but maybe his lack of ordinary human features made even part-demons uncomfortable.

He was sitting at a table with four other people, and they brought up another chair and scooted around to make space for me next to Shade. "Val, these are my friends," he said. He introduced them, and I tried to remember their names. The guy with the wavy blond hair and wide smile was Josh, and the quiet, brooding redhead was named Andrew. I reined Lola in tightly to keep her from flirting with the two guys. I turned toward the girls. The dark-haired Emo girl with the geeky clothes and glowing violet eyes asked to be called *Mood* and the other girl, Shawndra, had green hair, pale skin, and tons of piercings.

I felt a familiar canine nose nudge my knee, through my jeans. AND THIS, Fang said, IS PRINCESS.

I glanced down to see a beautiful little dog gazing up at me with her big, brown eyes. HELLO. I AM A PUREBRED CAVALIER KING

CHARLES SPANIEL. YOU MAY PET ME.

I raised my eyebrows at her diva attitude, but scratched her smooth, silky ears as directed.

"You found another part-hellhound dog?" I asked Fang. But the answer was obviously *Yes*. An ordinary canine would have shied away from demons and wouldn't have been able to speak in my mind. She's not *quite* purebred, I thought with amusement.

YEAH. ISN'T SHE GORGEOUS? Fang stared at her in admiration, obviously smitten.

"Stunning," I confirmed with a smirk.

Apparently satisfied by my recognition of her beauty, Princess laid down at Shade's feet, and Fang cuddled up next to her with a mental sigh of admiration.

Amused, I glanced at Shade. "Is she yours?"

I BELONG TO MYSELF, Princess said indignantly.

Oops. "I should have asked if Shade is your human servant," I said dryly.

Princess sniffed. THAT IS NOT AMUSING. HOWEVER, YES, I AM CURRENTLY RESIDING WITH THE SHADOW DEMON.

Shade spread his hands. "When I met Fang, I realized there might be more like him, so I went looking. I found Princess holding court in the county shelter. No one else dared adopt her." Though I couldn't see his face, I could hear the laughter in his voice.

YOU DIDN'T CHOOSE ME. I CHOSE *YOU*, Princess said.

Shade rubbed her head. "You did indeed." He sounded very pleased about it. I grinned, too, glad that it gave us something else in common.

"How come we haven't seen you around before?" Andrew asked me. He said it with a smile, but it sounded like more of a challenge.

Shawndra bumped him with her shoulder. "Hey, don't be rude." Her speech sounded clear, though I wondered how she managed with the piercings in her lips and tongue

Determined not to stare, I turned to Andrew and shrugged. "No biggie. I just didn't know you guys existed."

He scowled. "Now who's being rude?"

Huh? "No, I didn't mean it that way—"

Shade interrupted. "She just learned about the Demon Underground about a week or so ago. But she's one of us, now. Aren't you, Val?"

Was I? "I guess," I said doubtfully. Though I wondered how

many of them were surly, like Andrew. If only they were more like Josh, who seemed content to watch and smile. Mood glanced at him, too, and I was surprised to see the naked longing in her eyes. A longing that Josh seemed clueless about.

She flushed when I caught her at it, then leaned back in her chair, pretending to be bored. "Don't mind Andrew. He's been a jerk lately."

"That's not fair," Shawndra protested. "You know he has a good reason."

Mood gave them a lazy smile beneath glowing violet eyes. "Yeah, and I could help with that."

"No thanks," Andrew said. "I'll pass."

A murmur ran through the crowd. I turned to see Micah walking onto the stage with a microphone. Embarrassment flickered through me. The last time I'd seen him up there, the lights had been low, and he'd been dancing and getting the ladies in the audience all hot and bothered, feeding his incubus with their lust for him. But he was in street clothes now and obviously playing host and leader, not sexy dancer. I relaxed.

Once he had everyone's attention, Micah said, "Before I introduce our guest, I'd like to make an announcement. Thanks to Val Shapiro, the *Encyclopedia Magicka* has finally been returned to us."

Cheers erupted around the room and Andrew gave me a grim smile. "Good job, Val."

I felt my face warm as everyone turned to look at me.

As if he sensed my embarrassment, Micah continued. "But that's not why we're here tonight. I know we've spoken before about the New Blood Movement, and how they are trying to improve their reputation by creating blood banks where humans can donate blood and vampires can receive the sustenance they need without harming humans."

"Yeah, right," Andrew muttered. "Real altruistic."

Couldn't say I disagreed with him. In theory, the donations were as sterile as donating to a hospital's blood bank. But in reality, most donations were the lurid, fang-to-neck kind, with the human getting a real thrill along with it. Since vamps could enthrall a human's mind, they could make sure the human thoroughly enjoyed the process . . . and came back for more. A recipe for trouble, and sleazy at best.

But I had to admit the New Blood Movement was providing a service. At least it kept the bloodsuckers in line.

Most of them, anyway. Some, like the ones I'd staked earlier this evening, enjoyed the fear and terror of their victims too much to line up for snacks like drug addicts trading their highs for rehab meds.

Micah continued, "Alejandro is the leader of the New Blood Movement, and he's asked to speak to you tonight."

Alejandro strode in from the wings, handsome, confident, charismatic. Dressed all in black with long dark hair and caramel-colored skin, the vampire exuded magnetism. Strangely enough, he wasn't using his vampire nature to enthrall everyone. It just came naturally to him.

Alejandro accepted the mic from Micah and made a sweeping gesture with his other arm. "Thank you all for welcoming us," he said with just a trace of a Spanish accent.

Us? I realized then that there were vamps in the crowd, sort of mingling, but more hanging out in small clumps around the room.

"As Micah said, the New Blood Movement is designed to make it safe for humans to walk the streets of San Antonio without fearing those of my kind."

"What about the bloodsuckers who don't belong to your organization?" someone yelled.

Alejandro smiled. "An excellent question. Many of 'the lone ones,' as we call them, were misled by my former lieutenant, Lily, who betrayed us in the interest of obtaining power."

More muttering, and more than a few sidelong glances at me. I guess they all knew the story. Among San Antonio's vamps I was known as the notorious *Slayer*.

"Yes," Alejandro continued, "The Slayer eliminated the threat, and we are attempting to contact Lily's other followers to bring them within the fold. But there is one way in which you can help us."

"How?" someone shouted.

"Why would we want to?" came another voice.

Obviously, Alejandro had anticipated these questions, for he continued smoothly to explain how they planned to announce their existence to the world. The vamps had friends in high places who were prepared to put legislation in place to require all vampires to subscribe to the creed of the New Blood Movement. Those who did would be afforded protection under the law. Those who didn't would forfeit any rights they might have. In other words, the vamps in this part of the Lone Star State would be treated as extremists. They could either live as peaceful citizens or be hunted like terrorists.

Alejandro nodded at Micah. "Your leader, here, wants your

existence to remain a secret, but it doesn't have to be that way. You part-demons can choose to stand beside us vampires as we make this announcement. Together we can make sure the state of Texas extends the same legal protections to all of us in the . . . shall we say . . . in the 'alternate non-human lifestyles' community."

There was silence, along with a general uneasiness, as people digested this. I knew it was hard to believe in altruistic vampires, but I'd been inside the minds of the leaders of the Movement and knew they were telling the truth. I even admired them for it, though I wasn't so sure outing themselves—and us—would be as easy as they thought.

"Micah's right," a deep voice boomed. "We don't want to be exposed. And you vampires shouldn't push the issue. It's suicidal."

I could understand his viewpoint, too. If vampires came out of the closet, it was only a short leap for humans to confirm that demons existed as well. Imagine the terror, the ignorance, the Salem-like "demon trials." The whole point of the Demon Underground was to help demons blend into the human population quietly, help them find jobs and pass for human so they wouldn't be persecuted.

I heard nervous mutterings all the way around the room, and one guy jumped on stage to say it. "We don't want to be recognized as demons," he shouted. Huge, with a chest the size of a barrel and a face that looked as if it had seen one too many fights, the man-mountain thrust his pugnacious face into Alejandro's. "We aren't asking for special rights; just to be treated like everyone else. I see where you'd benefit, with all that free blood and all," he said in the deep voice that boomed out. "But what's in it for *us*? Sounds to me like you'll expose *us* to ridicule and discrimination."

Unperturbed, the vampire leader turned to face the distrustful audience. "Not at all. You're a peaceful people and have lived harmoniously among the general population for many years. It will not be difficult to convince people that you mean them no harm."

Yeah, right, I thought. *And we'd all frolic with bunnies and rainbows forever. Riiiight.*

"Ridiculous," one demon shouted. "Your daydreams will get us all killed." He shoved the vampire next to him.

The vampire shoved back, and soon vampires and demons were knocking over chairs, leaping to their feet, and tussling around the room.

Fang scooted farther under the table. I'M STAYING OUTTA THIS.

Good plan. In my mind, there were no bad guys here. They were all trying to do the right thing. Of course, Lola perked up at the violence and testosterone permeating the air, and for a moment I thought about letting her loose. It would be so easy to capture every man here, so easy to enthrall them, bend them to my will, be a hero, stop this violence . . .

. . . FEED ON ALL THEIR LOVELY SEXUAL ENERGY, Fang countered.

True. Lola's intentions weren't exactly altruistic. I sighed and forcibly reined her back in. After all, Micah could have easily done the same to the women in the room, and it was obvious he hadn't.

Oh, crap. In a demon-versus-vampire rumble, who would come out on top? I didn't want my friends, including Micah and Shade, to get hurt in this turf war. My stomach clenched. How could I stop this?

Chapter Three

Suddenly, I felt waves of calm and serenity flowing out to the crowd. I glanced up on stage and saw Alejandro standing there, his arms wide as he willed the rumble to calm. Mood jumped up on our table. Her eyes flashed a deep purple as she spread her arms to mirror him, receiving his waves of reassurance and amplifying them, sending them out to the crowd.

Though people quieted, they did it with resentment, even as they realized that peacemakers from both sides were making with the sweetness and light.

Once the tension in the room had calmed down, Alejandro and Micah both apologized to each other and asked the demons to reconsider the proposal when they'd calmed down.

Chastised, everyone gathered their things to leave. The other demons at our table had disappeared during the fray, but Shade offered Mood a hand to help her down from the table. "That was effective," he said.

She shrugged. "It's what I do."

Suddenly I remembered reading about mood demons in the *Encyclopedia Magicka*. They could enhance emotions, amplify them to people all around them. Thank goodness, Mood chose to amplify serenity instead of fear or terror. I looked at her with new respect.

Remembering Micah's request that I talk with him after the party, I hung around as he conferred earnestly with the brawny demon who'd jumped up on stage to yell at Alejandro. His name was Ludwig, someone said. Fang continued to woo Princess while we waited for the crowd to disperse.

Finally, when there were only a few demons left, I approached Micah. "You still okay with us browsing the encyclopedia together?" I asked. "I understand if you want to postpone it until later."

He shook his head tiredly. "No, that's okay. I'm good. Let's go to my office."

He beckoned to Tessa, and we followed him to his office. He unlocked the door, and I glanced around. "Where'd you put the books?" I asked Tessa.

She unlocked a drawer of Micah's plain wooden desk. "Right here . . ." She looked puzzled. The drawer was empty. "I know I put them here," Tessa insisted.

Swiftly, she pulled out Micah's chair and looked under the desk, then yanked open the other drawers and looked inside. "Where are the books?"

Oh, no . . .

All three of us searched every inch of the office. No luck.

Micah slumped in his chair and ran a hand over his face. "They're gone," he whispered in defeat. "Someone must have taken them."

"I'm so sorry," Tessa said, looking stricken. "I locked the door and the drawers. I thought it would be enough."

"It's not your fault," Micah assured her.

Fang appeared by my side. THIS IS SO NOT GOOD.

That was an understatement. "Who would take them?" I asked.

"I don't know. Someone who knew they were here," Micah said. "And, since I stupidly announced their existence to the entire audience, everyone knew."

Tessa nodded. "Including Alejandro and his vampires."

"You don't think one of them took the books, do you?" I'd just come to terms with the fact that not all vamps were bad. Then again, not all humans and demons were good, either. "Alejandro was on stage the whole time."

"But one of his people could have easily done it," Micah countered.

SO COULD ONE OF OUR PEOPLE, Fang reminded him.

Micah glared at him. "Whose side are you on?"

Fang sat back on his haunches and managed to look surprised. WHOA, DUDE. I'M JUST SAYING. YOU KNOW, POINTING OUT THE OBVIOUS.

"I know, I know," Micah said apologetically. "But everyone in the Underground knows how important the books are to *all* of us. I can't believe a vampire would take them."

I turned to Tessa. "Can you use your powers to find a clue?"

She shrugged. "I don't know. My gift doesn't work like that. If I touched the thief, a prophecy about the encyclopedia might emerge, but I can't control it. My powers decide what's important for that person . . . which usually isn't what's important to us."

Okay, she couldn't go around touching people and spouting fortunes without someone getting suspicious. I took a deep breath. "What do we do now?"

"We find the books," Micah said, as if it were obvious.

"And how do we go about doing that?" I asked.

He shrugged. "First, let's make a list of everyone who was present. Tessa and I can probably remember all of the demons. Do you know any of the vamps besides Alejandro?"

"Some of them." Certainly not all. "What are you going to do with the list? Question everyone?"

Tessa frowned. "Good point. Do you really want to tell your people the books are missing again, and that vamps might have stolen them?"

Micah looked thoughtful. "Maybe not." He glanced down at Fang. "*You* can read the minds of both demons and vampires."

YEAH, BUT ONLY WHAT THEY HAPPEN TO BE THINKING ABOUT AT THE TIME. IT'S NOT LIKE I CAN RUMMAGE AROUND IN THEIR BRAINS, DUDE.

I nodded. "And I can read the minds of vamps when they try to control me, but Alejandro's men know that, so they won't try it."

Micah looked at Fang. "How many demons know about your ability?"

MOST OF THEM. IT'S HOW THEY RECOGNIZE ME AS ONE OF THEM.

"Too bad," Micah said. "I was hoping to have Val casually mention the books then see what you can find in their heads."

I nodded. After all, it was partially my fault the encyclopedias were missing again. "We can still do that. And hey, if they steer clear, *that* will tell us something, too. But what if none of the demons took the books?"

"Then the thief must be one of Alejandro's people," Micah said, obviously liking that idea much better. "He says he wishes to cooperate with us. Maybe he'll agree to let you question his vampire lieutenants."

"Good plan," I had to admit. If the vamps tried to control me, I *could* rummage around in *their* brains.

"But Tessa has a good point," Micah added. "Let's try to keep it secret for awhile. If you could get into contact with as many of the people present tonight as possible, maybe we can eliminate some of them as suspects."

"Got any suggestions for how to do that?" I asked. "It's not like I know many of these demons, and I don't have a good reason to visit the New Blood Movement since Ramirez pulled me off duty." I was still temporarily on leave from the San Antonio police department's Special Crimes Unit, after slicing off Lily's head.

"I'll take care of getting you in touch with the demons," Micah said and eyed me speculatively. "Do you feel ready to go back to work?"

"Yes. I didn't have any problems tonight controlling Lola." Not many, anyway.

"Good. Then contact Lieutenant Ramirez and tell him so."

"What if he doesn't want to let me? Can I tell him we're searching for the books?"

Micah thought for a moment. "Yes, but ask him not to mention it to his wife. I trust Maria, but the fewer demons who know, the better."

"Okay. Fang, let's go."

ALL RIGHT, Fang exclaimed, whirling around in excitement. BACK IN THE GAME AGAIN.

Yeah. I was more than ready . . . sitting around for the past few days doing nothing had bored me out of my gourd. This would give me something to do.

NOT TO MENTION GIVE YOU THE CHANCE TO SEE DAN AGAIN, Fang said slyly.

You have no right to talk, I shot back at him. *After all, you have a girlfriend now.*

Fang strutted out the door. NOT YET, BUT I'M WORKING ON IT. PRINCESS IS ONE HOT LITTLE BITCH.

Chapter Four

On the way to the station, I had to listen to Fang yammer on and on about Princess—her beautiful hair, her gorgeous eyes, her wonderful coloring. You'd think it would be difficult to hear him talk inside my brain from the back of a small motorcycle, but noooo. I couldn't avoid the never-ending babble in my mind. It made me want to puke.

HEY, Fang protested. I HAVE TO LISTEN TO YOU MOON OVER DANNY BOY . . . AND I CAN'T TURN THAT OFF.

"I don't moon over Dan. And it's not my fault you hear all my thoughts." I couldn't shut him out, so the hellhound heard every single freakin' thing in my head. Then again, it was a small price to pay for the fuzzy mutt's devotion. We were best friends.

AWWW . . . YOU LIKE ME. YOU REALLY LIKE ME, Fang said as we pulled up to the station.

There was sarcasm in that remark, naturally, but also a bit of real feeling. He made me grin. I took off my helmet then pulled off the goggles that protected Fang's eyes. Rubbing his ears, I said, "Don't let it go to your head."

We walked into the police station, and I spoke to the woman at the desk. "Is Lieutenant Ramirez in?"

"Yes, but he's meeting with everyone in the Special Crimes Unit. You can wait in his office—"

"Well, I'm a Scuzzie, too, so I'll join them."

"No, wait—" the woman said, half-rising as if to stop me.

I kept on going. Ramirez was the only one who could tell me what to do. Not some chick who sat a desk all day and had never even seen a vampire or a part-demon.

It seemed like a strange time to have a meeting, in the middle of a night shift, but that probably meant it was really important. I needed to be there.

Fang and I headed toward the briefing room. The station was drab, shabby, and gray—very government issue. Not a lot of money went into keeping up the building, but the SCU did have some of the best toys around to keep their people safe—like vamp-proof vehicles coated in silver and special ambulances-slash "dead-undead" pickup units. At least they had their priorities straight.

I didn't want Ramirez to tell me to mind my own business in front of his all-human subordinates, so I just cracked the door in the back open a bit so I could hear. Fang sighed in disgust and flopped down beside me.

Peering in, I saw Dan and Lt. Ramirez at the front, talking to each other in low voices as twenty people or so muttered in the background. *Looks like the meeting hasn't started yet*, I told Fang.

Lt. Ramirez looked the same as always: whip-thin, care-worn, and über serious. As for Dan, he looked good—real good. Short brown hair, chiseled features, strong bod, the gleam of heroic manliness in his eyes. What's not to like?

Fang snorted. AND YOU MADE FUN OF MY FEELINGS FOR PRINCESS . . .

I ignored him as I concentrated on Dan. Three days ago, he'd sounded so positive and upbeat, so glad that I'd killed his former-fiancée-turned-evil-vampire. He'd even seemed willing to accept Lola. Had he changed his mind since then?

MAYBE HE FEELS EMBARRASSED THAT A GIRL SAVED HIS LIFE.

I hadn't thought about *that*. Was he really that narrow-minded? I'd saved Rick, Jen, and Fang that day, too. Dan hadn't seemed like the macho type who'd resent a chick saving his bacon.

Ramirez turned to the crowd. "All right, quiet down. There have been a lot of rumors flying around about Val Shapiro, and we're here to set them straight."

About *me*? What the heck? No wonder the woman at the desk had tried to stop me. Fang perked up, practically quivering with the indignation I could feel radiating from him. I grabbed the scruff of his neck to keep him from barging into the room. I wanted to hear this.

"What would you like to know?" Ramirez asked.

Detective Mike Fenton stood up. "We heard rumors about what went down at that nest of vampires. She chopped one's head off but let the rest of them bloodsuckers live."

I winced. I thought Mike and his partner, Hank Horowitz, had accepted me after I'd clobbered Hank in a fair fight. Maybe Fang was right, and men didn't like being beaten by a girl.

FANG IS *ALWAYS* RIGHT, came the hellhound's comment, right on cue. He shook off my restraining hand, promising he'd chill.

The muttering around the room showed that other detectives wondered about my loyalty, too.

Ramirez held up his hands. "The truth is this. The vamp Val killed was causing the rash of vampire attacks throughout the city and attempting to take over the Movement for her own purposes. Val stopped her. The other leaders of the Movement have no quarrel with us, and we have none with them. That's why she let them live."

"The only good vamp is a dead vamp," someone said.

How original.

Annoyed, Ramirez said, "The New Blood Movement has proven they will not take anyone's blood without consent. As I've told you before, the SCU is not authorized to kill vampires just because they are vampires. Not unless they attack an innocent."

More muttering, then someone else asked, "How do we know Shapiro isn't a bloodsucker herself?"

What? How the heck did they come up with that *lame idea?*

Ramirez looked annoyed. "Val is not a vampire—"

"Oh, yeah?" Horowitz stood up, interrupting the lieutenant. "She's wicked fast and her reflexes and healing are way better than any human's. That's not natural."

Beefy blond redneck.

"Just like a vamp," Fenton added.

Oh, crap. From their perspective, it did make sense to suspect me.

Dan frowned. "She's my partner. I'd know if she was a vampire. She's not—I've seen her outside in full daylight."

"Maybe she tricked you," Fenton insisted. "Because she's sure not human."

Narrow-minded little toad. The fact that he was right made it even worse. As anger rose within me, so did the lust demon. Lola was ticked. She urged me to let them have it, let them know just how violent and inhuman I really was.

Fang glanced at me. HOLD IT TOGETHER, VAL. THEY'RE NOT WORTH IT. THE MAJORITY OF YOU IS FULLY HUMAN. MORE THAN THEY ARE, THAT'S FOR SURE.

Fang made a lot of sense. But as the questions flew, so did the stupid theories. Dan and Ramirez were kind enough to keep my secret—no "hey, guys, our teenaged crime fighter is part demon!"—but everyone else's idiotic questions were royally ticking me off. My blood was bubbling, seeking an outlet, seeking a way to vent Lola's wrath.

When someone yelled, "What the hell *is* she?" I couldn't take it anymore.

I pushed open the door, Fang right behind me. "I'll tell you what she *is*. She's *pissed.*"

Fang barked for emphasis, making it clear he felt the same way.

They all turned to gape at me. Dan looked stunned. Even Ramirez looked a bit surprised. The rest stared, wondering, measuring, doubting . . . like I was some freak in a sideshow. But now that I had everyone's attention, I had no idea what to do with it.

GIVE 'EM WHAT FOR, Fang suggested.

Good idea. The demon energy within me popped and sizzled, looking for an outlet. I really wanted to punch one of them—or two or five—but restrained myself. Not a good idea. Instead, I put all that energy into motion and marched up to the front and glared at all of them.

Some avoided my eyes, but others glared right back, looking suspicious and distrusting.

Damn it, just when I thought I finally belonged somewhere. A few days ago, these men had welcomed me into their midst, helped me celebrate my eighteenth birthday, and accepted me as one of them. Now, the suspicion and uncertainty practically rolled off them in waves. I turned to Dan, hoping for a spark of compassion, but his expression was closed, unreadable. A void opened up somewhere inside me.

"Okay, Miss Pissy," Fenton snarled from the front row. "Tell us all about it."

Seeing he was wearing a silver cross on a chain, I leaned toward him, smiling. As he scowled back, I snaked out my hand and placed my hand against his necklace. He lunged for me, but a couple of other guys held him back. Too bad.

I held up my palm. "See? No burn. Not a vamp."

I thrust my unscathed hand at Fenton and he sneered, murder in his eyes.

"Then what are you?" someone asked. "Your eyes flashed a funny kind of purple just now. That's not normal."

I looked at Dan, but he shook his head, expressionless, refusing to give me any advice. My heart sank. Had he deserted me? I glanced at Ramirez and raised my eyebrow, silently asking if I should reveal my secret. His own wife was like me, part-demon.

He nodded slightly, looking annoyed but determined. "Go ahead," he said. When I nodded, he turned to the rest of the room. "What Val is about to tell you is confidential and, like the existence of vampires, is not to be discussed outside this department. If I learn that any one of you has talked about this with anyone else, I'll feed you to the vampires myself. Is that clear?"

The lieutenant's unyielding glare made it clear he was willing to go all Terminator on their butts if they didn't comply. They grimaced but nodded.

I took a deep breath, wondering how the heck to say this.

GET IT OVER WITH QUICK, Fang advised. LIKE PULLING OFF A BANDAGE.

Okay, here went nothing. "I'm one-eighth succubus," I blurted out and winced, expecting the worst.

The general consensus was a bewildered, "Huh?"

Thankfully, Ramirez came to my rescue. "A succubus is a type of female demon who is able to . . . attract men at will."

Well, that was a polite way of putting it.

"Wait, I read about them," Horowitz said.

Horowitz could read? Who knew?

"They're lust demons. They control men with their thoughts and suck them dry. They don't just steal a man's sex urge. They steal his brain."

Since everyone in the room except me and one female detective was of the male persuasion, they didn't look too happy about this. I wasn't thrilled with his negative interpretation either, and Lola sure wasn't. Forget trying to explain that lust was a two-way street, and brains weren't part of the equation. Lola surged to the forefront, and I struggled with her, battled with the thought of letting her loose and giving them a baleful demonstration of her power.

Thankfully, Ramirez took charge. "That's a little inaccurate. A succubus will *enthrall* a man and feed on the sexual energy he generates, but she won't necessarily harm him. In Val's case, it isn't a problem."

Fenton rose threateningly to his feet. "How do we know she's not controlling us *now?*" Others rose as well, agreeing with him.

"I'm not," I gritted out. Idiots.

"Oh yeah? Prove it."

Furious, I said, "You want proof? I'll show you the difference."

VAL, DON'T, Fang cried out.

Too late. The demon I'd tried so hard to control burst free and lashed out, instantly ensnaring every man in the room except Dan and Ramirez, and even they looked hypnotized.

Dan's sexual independence was a matter of snarky pride to me, and Ramirez was like a father figure. But the others? Let them see.

Invisible lines of force snapped into being, connecting me to the seven chakra energy centers in their bodies, strongest in the second chakra of sexuality. They wanted me, worshipped me, would do anything I wanted. But I wanted only one thing, and it wasn't about sex. "Sit down and shut up," I snapped.

They complied immediately. *"That's* what it feels like to have a succubus control you."

OKAY, YOU GOT 'EM, Fang said drily. SO WHAT ARE YOU GOING TO DO WITH 'EM?

Lola urged me to take advantage, whispering how mean they were, how they deserved to be shown what I could do, how wonderful it would be to soak up all that lovely energy . . .

No, I couldn't. It would be wrong. As the two sides of my nature slugged it out, the one woman detective in the room, a petite blond I'd never seen before, came up out of her seat and charged toward me. "You've made your point. Now stop," she ordered.

I tried, I really did, but my panic only fed Lola more.

Fang poked my leg with his nose. C'MON, VAL, GET IT TOGETHER.

As I struggled with Lola, the cop hauled her fist back and punched me in the face.

My head snapped back. Damn, that hurt. But it didn't help. In fact, it made it more difficult to control my raging demon. Fang growled at her, but the female cop ignored him and tried to hit me again. I caught her fist in my hand. "Don't," I managed to get out. "I'm . . . trying . . . to stop. You're . . . not helping."

Thankfully, she must have believed me or saw the war on my face, because her body relaxed, though her eyes continually darted between my face and the men. She didn't seem worried about Fang. A lot of vamps had made that mistake.

BUT SHE'S NO VAMP, Fang said. AND SHE'S RIGHT.

I know that. And the sound of Fang's calm voice in my head helped me get a grip. Slowly, carefully, I released my hooks in the men's chakras. For a moment, they sat there, stunned. Then all hell broke loose as they yelled out questions and curses.

Surprisingly, assistance came from an unlikely source. The female cop took a deep breath and bellowed, "Sit down and shut up." I don't think she realized she echoed what I had told them moments before . . . and I hadn't realized such a loud voice could come out of such a small body. Was she part-demon, too?

NO, Fang said. I CAN'T HEAR HER THOUGHTS. BUT SHE'S A FIRECRACKER, ISN'T SHE?

Yeah, I had to admit.

Dan looked at me grimly. Ramirez finally seemed to come out of his trance. "Stop it. *Now.*"

Most of the men quieted down, except for Horowitz. "No way—"

"You goaded her into it," the woman said. "Stop complaining. You wanted proof. She did what you asked."

Whoa. I hadn't expected *support.*

Some of them looked a little shame-faced, but mostly they looked confused and ticked off.

"Thanks," I told her.

The blonde turned her glare on me. "I didn't do it for *you.*"

Huh? This chick's abrupt attitude changes could give me mental whiplash.

Dan stepped forward. "Thank you, Detective Jones. Now, if you would all do as she suggested?" His words might be polite, but the steel behind them held a warning I wouldn't want to test.

The room quieted, and I felt like a target with a whole bunch of mental darts aimed at it.

Of course, someone had to say something. And equally of course, it was Horowitz. "Demon," he muttered. "No better than a damned vampire."

It hit me like a punch in the gut, especially when the others murmured in agreement and Dan didn't say anything else in my defense.

"That's enough, Horowitz," Lt. Ramirez said, his tone annoyed and biting.

Everyone's resentful expression settled on Ramirez. "There is a *huge* difference," the lieutenant said. "Demons are born—vampires are *made.* One encourages our natural passions, for good or bad—the other simply wants to use us for dinner.

"The vampire Val killed chose to be made into one of the undead, chose to try to rule San Antonio with fear and death. Val is only one-eighth demon. She was born with no choice in the matter, just as I had no choice in being born Hispanic, and you, Horowitz, had no choice in being born part village idiot." He ignored the snickers and continued. "The difference between her and the vampire is that *she* chose to use her nature to fight on our side, fight for the good and the right, the innocents. There is a *huge* difference," he repeated, glaring at the men in emphasis.

They wouldn't meet his gaze, and I knew they didn't believe him. Maybe the lieutenant's little speech should have made me feel better, but I knew something the rest of them didn't. The reason Ramirez was pro-demon was because his wife was part-demon as well.

The emptiness was back. I should feel more pain, but instead, I felt numb. Unfortunately, I was getting used to being thought of as a monster.

Ramirez waved Sergeant Jones, Dan, and me to a seat then stood with his feet apart and his hands clasped behind his back. Dan refused to look at me, and stared icily into thin air. Ramirez glanced around for a moment, as if weighing the tension in the room. To me, it felt as thick as mud.

"I'm glad this came out," he said. "We're lucky to have Val in the department. She's been staking the bad vamps for years—by herself, without help, protecting her human family—and she's the most effective weapon we have in our fight against murderous vamps in San Antonio. In fact, I'd like to hire more demons like her."

Explosions of disbelief sounded around the room. I managed to keep my mouth shut, subduing Lola, as Ramirez waved the men to silence. He pivoted and looked down at Dan. "Sullivan, you've worked with one fully human partner and one partner who is part-demon. Which do you prefer?"

Dan looked annoyed at being put on the spot, but said, "My first partner was a good man. He wasn't prepared for the full power of a vampire's evil, and so he was killed. Val, on the other hand, knows how vampires think, and she understands exactly how deadly they are; she *does* the killing, which keeps both of us alive."

Didn't exactly answer the question. *Gee, Dan, thanks for nothing.* His attitude was starting to tick me off.

"I believe there are more part-demons in San Antonio like her," Ramirez said.

The other detectives gaped at him.

Fang snorted. YEAH, RIGHT. AS IF HE DOESN'T KNOW.

Chill, Fang. You want him to expose the entire Demon Underground? His wife? They keep their identity a secret for a reason. There's a lot of ignorance and prejudice out there.

Oblivious to our mental conversation, Ramirez continued. "I'd like to seek them out, find more of them. I think they're our allies. We need every advantage we can get in this fight against murderous vampires."

He went on to explain his position, talking up the advantages and refusing to believe there was a negative side. His arguments were all thorough and convincing. He must have thought this through before today.

Finally, at the end, some of the guys looked ready to be persuaded . . . but not everyone. I was impressed. I hadn't figured on anyone agreeing with him, except maybe Dan. And speaking of Dan, he'd put in a few good words for me, but it felt more like he didn't really want to side with me against his buddies.

"In fact," Ramirez concluded, "you may be living next door to a part-demon and not even know it."

They didn't seem convinced, so he added, "There's another part-demon in this room, someone you probably don't suspect. Would he like to reveal himself?"

Who? I glanced at Fang. *Who else is a demon?*

HE'S TALKING ABOUT ME.

Sure enough, as everyone else glanced around the room, wondering who it could be, I saw Ramirez looking steadily at me.

He must be crazy. Look at how they reacted to *me*. I'd hate to see what they'd do if told that even man's best friend might be part-demon, too.

NAW, IT'S OKAY. I THINK I KNOW WHAT HE WANTS. AFTER ALL, I'M JUST A CUTE WITTLE DOGGIE-WOGGIE. Fang trotted forward and jumped up on the table at the front of the room, then barked to get everyone's attention and glanced at the lieutenant expectantly.

"Most of you know Fang," Ramirez said. "And you know he's Val's constant companion." Grudging nods of agreement. "But what you don't know is that Fang is part-demon, too. The preferred term is . . . 'part-hellhound.'"

At that, Fang sat down, wagged his tail, and let his tongue loll sideways out of his mouth, looking goofy. Everyone laughed at the joke.

Ramirez smiled. "Being part demon, he not only has the ability to take down vampires and the occasional human . . . " Ramirez glanced sideways at Fenton, who'd felt Fang's sharp teeth on his behind . . . "but he has the capability of understanding human speech. Fang, are you willing to demonstrate?"

Fang nodded, which made a lot of the chuckles stop.

"Fang, would you please—"

"Wait," Fenton said. "How do we know this isn't a set-up?" He jabbed a finger at me. "That she's just trained him really well?"

Of course he'd think that. Moron.

Ramirez smiled and gestured toward Fenton. "Then be my guest. *You* talk to him."

Fenton leaned forward and said, "Sit."

Since Fang was already sitting, he rolled his eyes. Everyone laughed again.

The back of Fenton's neck turned red. "Lay down." Fang did. "Roll over. Play dead."

With each command, Fang did exactly as he asked. I hated watching him act like a performing monkey and wondered how long he'd put up with it.

AS LONG AS IT TAKES TO CONVINCE THESE IDIOTS THAT I CAN UNDERSTAND THEM.

"Lift your right paw," Fenton commanded.

Fang stood, turned to the side and lifted his back right leg. I gaped. No, he wouldn't.

Everyone cracked up and Fenton said hastily, "No, no. The *front* paw."

Fang turned back to face him and raised his front paw, then flopped it up and down in a wave, looking cute and adorable.

A man toward the back asked, "Did you really bite Mike Fenton?"

Fang nodded as Ramirez said, "He deserved it at the time." True—he'd jumped me in a fair fight and made it *un*fair. Fang had only evened the odds.

"And what does Mike deserve now?" the man asked with a grin.

Fang whipped around and leaned forward, pointing his butt in Fenton's direction. He turned to look over his shoulder with a doggie grin then released an explosive sound and stench.

Everyone cracked up, even Fenton.

I shook my head. Male humor. Strange how releasing a little gas could bond them together. And make a part-demon look harmless and amusing. *Good job, Fang.*

YOU GOT IT, CUPCAKE. He turned around and bowed, first to the right, then to the left. If they didn't realize Fang could understand human speech by now, they had no business being in this unit.

Ramirez took advantage of the friendly mood to say, "Are you convinced *now?*"

Fenton held up his hands in surrender. "Okay, okay. No way could you fake that."

Lt. Ramirez thanked Fang then said to the detectives, "Open your minds. You're in this unit because you're able to accept the idea of evil in forms most people can't imagine. Now I'm asking you to accept Val, Fang, and the other part-demons like them, as allies. To believe they're only dangerous to our common enemy, which is not all vampires, just the law-breaking ones. We don't arrest citizens based on anything other than their actions, do we? That rule has to include *all* citizens of San Antonio, human, vampire, and part-demon. Think about it."

Then, wisely, he let them leave on a high note, since the laughter in the room had dissipated the tension. He asked me to follow him, and for Dan and Detective Jones to wait around. I gave Dan an angry, wistful look, but couldn't tell if he caught it.

Fang and I joined the lieutenant in his office, and before he could say anything, I blurted out, "Just now, enthralling them . . . was an accident. I didn't mean to do it. I couldn't control it."

Looking weary, Ramirez said, "I know. That's why I asked you to take a break from the unit until you got your power under control. I was afraid something like this would happen. The cat is out of the bag, now. Or, rather, the succubus."

Humor from Ramirez? Maybe I wasn't in such deep doo-doo as I feared. "I'm sorry. I didn't mean to—"

"I know you didn't," he said, interrupting. "I was going to let them know about your powers eventually, just not in this way. But I'm afraid now I'll have to insist you take time off until the effect of this episode has been forgotten a little. I can't have my entire unit being worried that you'll hypnotize them and make them bark like a dog."

NOTHING WRONG WITH BARKING, Fang protested.

"I can't," I said, feeling miserable. "Have you heard of the *Encyclopedia Magicka?*"

He nodded. "My wife mentioned it. Said it's been lost for over a decade."

"Well, not exactly. I had it." When he looked surprised, I added, "But I didn't know it was the only copy in existence and that my father had stolen it. I gave it back, honest."

"I'm glad to hear it, but I don't see how that pertains to the situation at hand."

"Because I gave it to Micah at the underground social and it was stolen again." I told Lt. Ramirez the whole story then concluded by explaining why I wanted to go back to work with the sanction of the SCU so Alejandro wouldn't get suspicious when I questioned his people. I needed to find the books before someone could use them to do harm.

Ramirez sighed and rubbed a hand over his face. "You make a good case. I'll have to change my plans."

He rose to stick his head out the door, and called in the other two. The blonde followed Dan in and Ramirez said, "I don't think you've met Detective Jones, have you, Val?"

"Not officially," I said. Though her fist had met my face.

Fang chortled.

I ignored him as Ramirez introduced us. "Nicole Jones, Val Shapiro."

We nodded warily at each other, and Ramirez gestured for the two of them to sit. They did, Dan taking the farthest chair, making Nicole sit next to me. What was up with *that*?

YEAH, Fang said. YOU BATHED THIS MORNING.

Ramirez leaned forward, clasping his hands together. "Detective Jones is new to the unit, and I'd like you two to train her before I assign her a new partner."

I glanced at her. Short, slight, blond . . . and fully human. What made the lieutenant think she could possibly take on a vamp and win?

Some of my doubt must have shown in my eyes, because Dan said curtly, "Nic can do it."

Nic? How was it Dan knew the pretty blonde well enough to call her by a nickname? "I already have two partners, and I don't need another one," I said bluntly.

YOU JUST DON'T WANT THE COMPETITION, Fang said with a smirk.

Dang, I hated how he could see right through me . . . and call me on it. I glanced at her doubtfully. "Besides, this job might be a bit too much for her."

"Nic can do it," Dan repeated. "And she has good reason—her brother was killed by one of Lily's followers."

"I'm sorry, I know how tough this has to be on you," I said to

Nicole. "But all the wanting in the world doesn't mean you can kill vampires." I should know—all the wanting in the world hadn't made me fully human.

"I'm better than I look," she said quietly. "Like you and your dog."

SHE'S GOT YOU THERE, Fang said.

Whose side are you on?

I'M JUST SAYING.

Well, stop. You're not helping.

"Jones is part of the unit," Ramirez said. "That's not up for negotiation."

I shook my head. "But you said you wanted to bring on more part-demons. Doesn't it make more sense to have me train them instead of her? Any other scuzzie can train her."

"But you're the only other female," Ramirez said softly. "You can help her, show her a few tricks."

"And you trained me," Dan added. "You're good at it, Val."

He looked so darned serious . . . no sign of a smile or anything to show that we'd kissed and meant something to each other not that long ago. Was this change Nicole's fault? Probably. No doubt the cute little blonde had wormed her way into Dan's life during the past few days. Imagine what would happen if she had more time to work on him?

"I'll be better at training demons," I insisted. "Who else could do it?" I gave Ramirez a steady glare, reminding him silently that I needed to interact with demons and vamps to find the books. Not some lightweight who'd probably faint at the first sight of fangs.

He nodded. "You're right. That is a better use for your talents. Okay, Sullivan, you take on Jones as your new partner, and Val and I will recruit some more part-demons for the SCU."

Wait. No, that's so not what I meant. I gaped at them all, wondering how to retract everything I'd just said without looking like a jealous fool.

YOU CAN'T, Fang confirmed. WERE YOU *TRYING* TO DRIVE DAN INTO HER ARMS? 'CAUSE THAT'S WHAT JUST HAPPENED.

Yeah. Talk about a royal screw-up . . .

Chapter Five

Dan stood and nodded. "Okay. Let's get to work, Nic."

They headed out the door and down the hall before I got my act together.

No, he couldn't leave like this. Heart in my throat, I blurted out, "Dan, wait."

He and Nicole turned to stare at me. *Now what, genius?* "Uh, can I talk to you, Dan? In private?"

"Is it really necessary, Val?"

Why did he look so annoyed, like I was some dumb kid hanging on his shirttail, or something? "Yes, it is." I had to find out what the heck was the matter with him. Fang trotted forward and poked him in the shin for emphasis.

He heaved a sigh. "Okay. Nic, you want to wait for me in the break room?"

She nodded and gave me an odd look I couldn't interpret, then left. I wanted to grab his arm, turn him away from her, but was afraid he'd pull away. Not wanting to test it, I said, "Let's go back to the briefing room, okay?"

Dan followed me to the room, which was empty as I suspected. Good. I glanced down at Fang who backed up, saying, HOW ABOUT I JUST WAIT OUTSIDE?

"Thanks." He could probably still hear my thoughts from there, but it was nice of him to give me the illusion of a little privacy.

The door shut behind Fang and I turned to face Dan. He stood there, arms crossed, annoyance on his face. "What was that all about?" he asked. "You're the best trainer we have. Do you want her to get killed?"

"No, of course not." I wouldn't wish that kind of death on anyone. "But I have a good reason for wanting to train demons instead." Such as finding a certain thief . . .

"Like what?"

I hunched my shoulders and glanced away from his hard stare. "I . . . can't tell you."

"More secrets, Val? Why can't you tell me?"

"This involves Micah—something I have to do for him. It's his secret, and I don't have permission to share it with you." I'd already shared too many of Micah's secrets with Dan. "But Ramirez knows about it."

Dan nodded. He understood honor and duty. "I thought—" He broke off and rubbed his neck with one hand.

"Thought what?"

"That you might be jealous of Nic," he said reluctantly.

Lola rose within me, jealous, possessive . . . her emotions focused into a single word: *Mine*. It reverberated throughout my body, demanding Dan's absolute obedience. Lola was like a genie in a bottle, desperately rocking to get out and sink her hooks into Dan.

Oh, crap. I *had* to keep her from popping the cork. Enslaving Dan each time I saw him was *not* the way to win him over. I closed my eyes and fought Lola to a standstill. Luckily, it seemed to be easier this time.

Once I had her under control, I opened my eyes to see Dan watching me warily. "Should I be?" I asked as calmly as I could.

Dan wouldn't meet my eyes. "You and I were partners, Val. Nothing more."

My throat choked up and I barely got out, "That's a lie and you know it. What's the matter with you, Dan?" I asked it softly, hoping he'd see reason, not think this way, not treat me like this.

"Nothing."

Yeah, right. "Don't give me that crap. You act like I have Ebola or something."

He stuck his hands in his pockets and shrugged. "I'm just keeping my distance."

"Why?" I hated that it came out more as a wail.

"Come on, Val. You know how it is. People bond during intense situations, but it's not based on anything real. It never lasts."

"You don't know that." When he did nothing but shrug, I added, "You said you were cool with what I am, that every man needs a little Lola in his life."

He sighed. "Yeah, but I still remember what it felt like to be totally owned by you. I still feel the pull, and I hate the fact that I can't trust my own emotions around you."

"Dan, I promise, I won't do it again——"

"You just did. Tonight, in this very room."

"I couldn't help it. They goaded me into it."

"And what happens when they goad you again? Or I do something that happens to tick you off? You're like a time bomb waiting to explode and I don't want to be in the blast zone again when it happens."

"I'm getting better, I swear it. Just let me——"

"No." He cut me off with a weary sigh. "It won't work. It would never have worked. I'm too old for you, you have your whole life ahead of you——"

"Cut the crap, Dan." He was pissing me off now. "Stop acting like you're doing this for me. Seven years difference isn't that much and you know it." It certainly hadn't stopped him before. "Tell the truth. This is really about that little blonde, isn't it?"

"Nic?"

"Of course, Nic. Who else is slobbering all over you?" I knew I sounded like a jealous idiot, but I couldn't help myself. I had to know what he thought.

"She's not——"

"Okay, slight exaggeration. But the timing seems awfully convenient. You meet her and all of a sudden you're dumping me. What does that tell you?"

"Nothing. It's a coincidence, nothing more."

"That's not how it looks from this angle. Are you going to date her?" The thought made my gut tighten.

His jaw tightened. "I don't know. I hadn't thought about it. But if I do, it's none of your business."

I pressed my lips together and nodded. None of my business. Guess that told me where I stood. "Got it." I was out, she was in. My eyes suddenly stung and I looked down so he wouldn't get the satisfaction of seeing me hurt.

"I need time, Val," he said softly. "I need to think about this. It's better if we don't see each other for awhile. Maybe this is a good thing."

Not trusting myself to speak, I nodded again then turned my back on him, hunching forward against the pain.

I heard him walk away and the door close behind him.

Soon after came the click of nails against the linoleum floor. Fang nudged me. YOU OKAY?

Hot tears spilled down my cheeks and I dropped to the floor and hugged him to me, burying my face in his wiry fur. "No," I choked out.

He licked my hand. HE DOESN'T DESERVE YOU.

Yeah, and he didn't deserve my tears either, the rotten insecure-with-my-power jerk. I raised my head and wiped away my tears. "I know." A world of possibilities waited for me out there, and I hadn't even started to discover them. Time to make like Magellan and explore.

I rubbed Fang's ears, silently thanking him for being there for me. "He was right about one thing, though."

WHAT?

"I do need to find a way to control Lola. I can't let her get the best of me again."

Fang snuggled closer. MICAH CAN HELP.

I hoped so. 'Cause if I didn't, I'd never be able to find a guy who loved me for myself . . . Lola and all.

Chapter Six

I decided to take the rest of the night off and actually sleep in the dark, like most people do. Unfortunately, that meant I woke up late morning just as Dan's sister came home from work. Gwen Sullivan, normally a bouncing bubble of fun, greeted me from the kitchen as Fang went out the doggie door of the townhouse. Now, though, the redhead looked a little tired after her nursing shift in the ER.

She opened the refrigerator and put some eggs and cheese on the counter. "Want an omelet?" she asked.

Gwen was a great cook—something I was so not—but she was also Dan's sister, and I wasn't sure I wanted to talk to her right now. "No, thanks." I grabbed a Coke, figuring I'd catch something to eat later.

"How are you doing, Val?" she persisted.

"Fine," I muttered without meeting her eyes.

"Really? That's not what I hear."

Surprised, I glanced up to see her watching me with a combination of sympathy and pity in her eyes. I'd love to unload on her—the only girlfriend I had—but sheesh, Dan was her brother and she didn't know about my inner demon. "You heard wrong," I said shortly, and headed toward my bedroom.

That didn't stop her. She followed me. "Dan told me what happened the other day." She paused in the doorway to my room, then added softly, "All of it. The succubus and everything."

Oh crap. I closed my eyes briefly then turned around to see her expression. What did she think of me?

"Hey, I'm cool," Gwen said softly, looking like she wished she could take my hurt away. "You can't help what you are. I told Dan that, too."

"It didn't do any good," I muttered.

Fang came trotting in then and looked back and forth between the two of us. HEY, WHAT'S GOING ON?

She knows.

ABOUT ME, TOO?

Gwen answered that herself by saying, "He told me about Fang, too. Makes sense. I wondered why he only ate people food, was so well-mannered, and seemed to always understand what we said. He's a lot smarter than any dog I've ever known."

She bent down to pet him and Fang accepted it as his due. DID I MENTION HOW MUCH I LIKE HER?

"I don't know about the well-mannered part," I said drily. "He's a bit of a smart-ass."

HEY, Fang objected. I AM NOT. I'M A WHOLE *LOT* OF SMART ASS.

I laughed and repeated it to Gwen. She chuckled, then said, "You're really good at that—changing the subject."

I tried to shrug it away, but Gwen wouldn't let me. "If you ever want to talk about it . . . "

My stomach churned at the thought. My emotions were still too raw, like an open wound. "Thanks, but I have help. My cousin Micah—" I stopped there, not knowing if Dan had told her about Micah and the Demon Underground. Again, it wasn't my secret to share.

"Okay, but can I make a suggestion?"

"Sure." Hey, if it would help remove some of this pain, I was willing to try anything.

"Think about who you are and who you want to be."

"Huh?"

She sank down onto my bed and asked, "Who is Val Shapiro? Are you just a bad-ass vampire hunter and a succubus? Is that all that defines you?"

I frowned and sat down beside her. "I don't get you."

She bumped my shoulder with hers. "What I'm asking is, what do you want to be when you grow up?"

Fang cocked his head, also waiting for my answer. "I, uh . . . I don't know. I never thought about it."

"Do you want to still be staking vamps when you're forty?"

"Probably not." I guess I figured I'd never live that long. "But what else can I do?"

"What do you want to do?" Gwen countered. "Do you have any other hobbies or interests?"

"Not really."

Gwen nodded and stood to look around my room, studying it like she was trying to find something. "So, you've lived here . . . what? Almost a month?"

"I guess. So?"

"So there's absolutely nothing personal here, nothing that screams 'Val.' It's all . . . generic."

I glanced around, noticing it did look kind of bare. Guess I didn't have the decorating gene. "Fang sometimes screams in my mind . . ."

Fang and Gwen snorted in unison. "Didn't you ask your parents for more of your things when you left?"

"What things? I have my furniture, my vampire doll, and some jewelry from Mom . . ." I stopped, realizing that sounded kind of lame. "I guess I'm just not the materialistic type."

Then again, the place did look kind of sterile, temporary. Especially compared to the decorating Gwen had done in the rest of the townhouse. She had lots of bright colors and funky doodads that really reflected her personality. What did this room say about mine?

She added gently, "I was hoping to learn more about you through the things you like to have around you." She glanced down at Fang. "The only thing I can tell from this room is that you like smart-ass terriers."

DAMN BETCHA, the terrier in question said.

Yeah, but how was I supposed to figure out what my style was?

WHY DON'T YOU ASK GWEN FOR HELP? SHE HAS A GREAT SENSE OF STYLE.

Out of the mouths of hellhounds . . . Out loud, I said, "I guess it wouldn't hurt to add a bit of color or something." Maybe then I'd actually want to stay here more often. "But will you help?"

Gwen grinned. "Of course. You know how much I love shopping."

I laughed. "Retail therapy?"

"Something like that. What decorating style do you like?"

What styles were there? "I like what you've done. It's fun."

She shook her head. "No, the point of this is not to copy my style, but to find one of your own. Define yourself your way. Define Val."

"Okay." I nodded decisively, liking the idea of having something to focus on besides how miserable I felt. And it even sounded fun.

OH, JOY, Fang muttered. SHOPPING. I'LL PASS.

Just as well. I had special identification for him that said he was a working police dog, but it was still a hassle to take him in and out of stores.

"Good," Gwen said with a little bounce. "Let's go on my next day off—"

A loud beep went off then, startling both of us. I hadn't had a cell long enough to get used to it. I glanced at the phone. It was a text message from Micah, asking if I could meet him in an hour. "I need to answer this."

"Okay," Gwen said and exited the room. "I'll still make breakfast if you want some. For Fang, too."

YES! the walking garbage disposal said.

I grinned. "Thanks, we'll take you up on that after all."

Over breakfast, we made plans to go shopping on her next day off, then Fang and I headed to Micah's office at Club Purgatory. I paused at his office door, feeling my stomach churn again. Micah had promised to help me control Lola, and I really wanted to, but I wasn't sure what he had in mind or if I'd like how he planned to do it.

Fang shoved me with his nose. C'MON, TAKE IT LIKE A MAN. At my wry look, he corrected himself. ER, I MEAN, LIKE A VAMPIRE SLAYER.

Sighing, I raised my hand to knock but Tessa opened the door before my knuckles met the wood. "Hi. We're just finishing up our list of the demons who were at the party. Go on in—I'll see you later."

She left and I saw Shade and Micah conferring at the computer at Micah's desk. "We're printing it out now," Micah said. When I glanced questioningly at Shade, Micah added, "I trust Shade completely."

Fang sniffed the air, looking disappointed. GUESS HE LEFT PRINCESS AT HOME.

As the three of them finished their discussion, I glanced around the room. Elegant, classy, and kind of minimal but comfy. Lots of wood and warm colors. I liked this style, too, and it was way different from Gwen's. I frowned. Figuring out what I really liked might be harder than it looked.

"I think that's it," Micah said, and printed out two copies of the list. He gave one to me, saying, "Here's who we remember being at the club that afternoon."

I glanced at the list. "Where should I start? Do you have anyone you suspect of stealing the books?"

Micah shook his head. "No, if there was, I wouldn't have let them in the Underground. So, you can start anywhere. Shade will help. Ramirez suggested you two team up as partners—you can train each other."

I got how I'd help Shade, but . . . "How will he help me?"

"He can help you with control."

"With Lola?" How could he do that? He was just as susceptible as any other man . . . except Micah, of course.

"Yes," Micah said. "I promised I'd help you learn to manage . . . Lola, but first we have to make sure your inner demon isn't hungry. It's best to start sated, not empty. When was the last time you fed?"

Fed? I hated that word, hated the way it made me sound like a bloodsucking vampire. "Uh, last night. I lost it a bit."

"If you do as I've suggested and feed gradually, you won't have that problem. You'll be in total control."

"I know," I muttered, feeling a little embarrassed in front of Shade. And Lola had perked up in the shadow demon's presence, which meant it was still too dangerous to be around him.

SHE'S NOT TOTALLY SATISFIED, Fang drawled, making it clear he was speaking to everyone in the room.

Tattletale.

But he ignored me as Micah said, "Okay, we'll help you satisfy your inner demon under safe conditions. You can feed on Shade."

Whoa. No way. I liked him.

THAT'S THE POINT, BABE.

I glared at Fang, but was glad he hadn't shared those thoughts with everyone. "I can't."

"It's okay," Micah said gently. "He volunteered."

"Really," Shade said softly, "I don't mind." He took my hand, grounding himself in this reality, in me, so that he no longer flickered through a dozen different dimensions. Because of that, I could see the shadow demon's features, though they were still partially hidden by his ever-present hood. Just as I remembered, he had shaggy blond hair, piercing blue eyes, and the face of an angel.

Lola wanted him. So did I, for that matter, but that was dangerous. For him, not me.

"Would it be easier if you could see me, or not?" Shade asked.

I gazed into his face, but the guy wasn't accustomed to having people see his expressions, so he wasn't used to having to hide his feelings. As a result, his face was too expressive, almost painfully so. Emotions paraded so clearly across his face that it was as if he'd written them there. Admiration, longing, hope . . . and that was before Lola reached out for him.

His seeming innocence took my breath away. I released his hand.

"Not, I think." It would feel too much like taking advantage.

He nodded, and Fang growled in my mind, BE NICE. HE'S MY FRIEND.

I am being nice. *Would you rather Lola stripped him bare?*

Fang harrumphed but didn't say anything more.

"Okay," Micah said. "Why don't the two of you sit down and relax? And Fang, if you could refrain from distracting them?"

YOU GOT IT, PAL. Fang settled down next to me and laid his head on his paws.

We parked in Micah's comfortable chairs and I glanced at Shade, seeing nothing but the swirling dark ribbons of light where his skin should have been. Weirdly, it made me feel better that I couldn't see his face. But at least I knew he didn't mind this, that he actually looked forward to it.

"Relax," Micah reminded me. "Let loose of that hold on yourself, just a little, and reach out for Shade."

Lola was straining to get at the juicy tidbit that was Shade, so I tried to do as Micah said. But it didn't quite work that way. Instead of coming out as a trickle, the dam burst and Lola surged out and lunged for Shade, sending greedy tentacles of pure lust whipping into him.

He gasped.

No—that wasn't what I wanted to do!

I tried to pull back, but Micah said, "No, let it go. Go with it, don't fight it."

I forced myself to do as he said, and amazingly, he was right. Now that I wasn't trying to rein Lola in, she was content to slow down, explore Shade and all his reactions.

My God, this was so different from before. I didn't feel like a puppet master or that he was my slave. Instead, I felt Shade react to Lola, felt the heat rise in his blood, the longing for me. He clenched the arms of his chair tight and his breathing intensified. The energy Lola craved rose within him and flowed steadily into the demon inside me, filling her, satisfying her totally.

Wow—I was enjoying this as much as he was. Was this normal? It kind of felt like watching an X-rated movie. I wasn't sure whether to be embarrassed or excited. I was definitely squirmy.

"You're doing fine, Val," Micah said soothingly. "Now, release him, slowly."

It was a whole lot easier to do than I expected, since Lola was thoroughly pleased now. She gave one last caress to his second chakra of sensuality and Shade shuddered. Lola withdrew, happy and content.

WAS IT GOOD FOR YOU, TOO? Fang drawled. BET SHADE WANTS A CIGARETTE RIGHT ABOUT NOW.

Shut up. I felt mortified enough without his help. "I'm so sorry, Shade. Are you okay?"

He shook his head. "Quite well, thank you," he said, though his voice sounded a little shaky. He released his death hold on the arms of the chairs, though, so I guess that was a good sign.

"You did fine," Micah said encouragingly. "With a little practice, you should be able to control it as well as I can. I bet you won't lack for volunteers, will she, Shade?"

"Definitely not," Shade said in a breathy voice.

I felt my neck turn hot. I wasn't used to this kind of attention.

"Okay," Micah said decisively. "Now that you're sated, let's try another exercise to help you control the lust demon inside you." He glanced at Shade and Fang and gestured to the door. "If you two wouldn't mind waiting outside? She needs as few distractions as possible."

They left, and Micah set a tall candle on the table in front of me and lit it.

"What's that for?"

"It's to help you find control."

"How?" Though I really wanted to learn how to control my demon, I still felt a little weird about what I'd done to Shade. Not that he seemed to mind, but I would like to manage the intensity better, so I wouldn't embarrass him in the future. How could a candle possibly help with that?

Micah dimmed the lights. "Stare into the flame."

I rolled my eyes at him. "You're kidding, right? Do you really think that will help?"

"I really do. And how do you know it won't unless you try it?"

"Okay, okay." I stared into the flame, thinking about bailing, but I'd stupidly agreed to do as Micah asked. And why was that again? Oh yeah, because it was supposed to help me with my so-called "gift." Though how staring into a small bit of fire would help control Lola, I had no idea.

"Try," Micah insisted, as if he'd read my mind. "Blank your mind and think of nothing."

I sighed and did as he said. But thinking of nothing was like trying *not* to think of a pink elephant. All you'd get was rosy pachyderms cavorting around in your head.

"Watch the flame," he said softly. "And go to a place inside you, a still quiet place where no one can reach you . . . not me, not Dan, not your mother, not even Lola."

Now there was an attractive thought. But was there such a place? I'd tried finding it before, but was too easily distracted. Now, though, now that I'd fed on Shade, Lola had receded far into the background. I searched deeper . . . and deeper still. Somewhere, in the quiet of my soul, I found a tiny spot that seemed isolated, calm . . . whole.

I slipped into it and just drifted there, drinking in the incredible beauty of aloneness, of feeling safe, protected, and very much at peace.

Sometime later, I heard Micah's voice as if from far away. "Val? Val, are you okay?"

I blinked and reluctantly withdrew from the safe place. As I focused on the candle, I realized it had burned down quite a bit while I visited Never Never Land. Clearing my suddenly clogged throat, I said, "Yeah, I'm okay. Really okay." I'd been in some Zen-like fugue or something.

I gave him a sheepish grin. "Guess you were right. Not a sign of Lola anywhere. But I'm not sure how it will help. It's not like I can carry a candle with me and ask every guy to wait while I stare into a flame and make like a yogi."

"I don't expect you to. Practice this alone until you can go to your space easily, and you'll eventually be able to slip into it whenever you want. It'll take time, but don't worry, I'll help and so will Shade. He'll let you know when to reel it in. That way you can search for the thief together while you teach him to hunt vampires."

I nodded. It made sense, and if it helped, I was willing to try it. But first I had to get over being squeamish about using Shade like that. "Did you talk to Ramirez about Shade joining the Special Crimes Unit?"

"Not yet. Two reasons. First, I'm not sure how he'll feel about interacting with the rest of the SCU. He has a built-in advantage, but I don't know if he's willing to use it."

Yeah, the boogie man factor could be a help in distracting the bad guys, but the good guys . . . not so much. "And second?"

"Second, he'll only be able to help you if he can keep from losing his temper. If not, you'll have to help control *him* because—"

A knock came at the door and Tessa peeked her head in. "Big problem, boss. One of your watchers at the downtown blood bank called in. Some vamps are going crazy and killing people. They need help."

Fear thrilled through me. My God, it was broad daylight. They'd never been this bold before. "I'm on it." Fang bounded into the room, looking ready for anything. But I wasn't so sure about Shade, who'd followed the hellhound in. "You up for this?" I asked him.

He nodded sharply. "Gotta learn sometime. Let's go."

Chapter Seven

Shade had his own motorcycle, a sweet blue Ducati that was practically a piece of art. He quickly pulled on gloves, leathers, and a black helmet with a dark-tinted visor. No wonder he rode a bike—he looked quite normal with all of his skin hidden.

I tried to help Fang with his goggles, but he said, NO TIME. LET'S ROCK AND ROLL, BABE.

Ooookay. I saw Micah jump into his car somewhere behind us but we left him in a nanosecond as we took off. We weaved in and out of traffic, Shade having no problem keeping up with me. I normally wouldn't take the risk—it was the other drivers I was worried about, not me—but the fact that vamps were attacking during the daytime scared the crap out of me. What did it mean? Nothing good, I was sure.

We arrived together at the blood bank. Fang jumped off and Shade did, too, not bothering to take off any of his gear as he headed for the door.

Not good. He wasn't trained. I swung off the bike and caught up to him at the hotel-turned-blood-bank. Grabbing his arm, I said, "Stay out of the way. You don't know how to deal with them yet."

"I can help," Shade insisted. "If only as a healer."

No time to argue. "Okay, but don't fight. I don't want to have to worry about protecting you." Or having him lose his temper, though come to think of it, Micah had never actually explained why.

"Got it," he said.

I opened the door to a madhouse. Normally, the waiting area was quiet, with people patiently waiting their turn to donate. But now, there was total mayhem. There were about a dozen people in the room, most of them screaming as blood stained the white tiled floors. Talk about sensory overload. I had to pause to assess the situation.

One vamp was down and staked, and two more were causing

major problems as people tried either to shield them or kill them. The rivalry made sense. If the vampires had gone crazy and someone had tried to stop them by staking a bloodsucker or two, now the suckees were trying to protect the other vamps. Vampires tend to enthrall their willing meal tickets.

My eyes swiveled as a handsome and familiar form stepped into view. Good God, Dan was here. How'd he get here so fast? He was off-duty; he worked nights, like me. He, along with a demon who must be one of Micah's informants, were trying to flank a female vamp over by the cookies and orange juice without stepping on the humans passed out and bleeding on the floor.

In another group near me, I saw someone—Nicole—trying to get hysterical humans out the door.

"Help her," I told Shade.

On the other side of the lobby, a male vamp was crouched down on the floor, mad-eyed and glaring like a cornered animal, his fangs sunk into the neck of a limp teen girl.

Fang me! The girl was one of the blood bank's fresh-faced human volunteers, Brittany. I was shocked into immobility, shocked that I knew both the victim and the vamp. The vamp was Lorenzo—the one who had invited Dan and me to play in his fantasy woodland bower at the blood bank. What the hell was the matter with him?

Fury shone through his eyes as he held her like a broken doll. Her arms and legs splayed awkwardly, and blood dripped down her neck as he continued to suck.

"Lorenzo, stop!" I yelled. I was afraid to approach too closely, sick at the thought that he might tear her throat out. Brittany thought the New Blood Movement was all noble and courageous. Wonder what she thought now . . .

If she could think. Was she even still alive?

Lorenzo scrabbled back into a corner with his prize, like a lion guarding its prey.

"Wait, Lorenzo," I pleaded, following cautiously. "Think about what you're doing." He was supposed to be one of the good guys. "You don't want this. Alejandro wouldn't like it."

THERE'S NO REASONING WITH HIM, Fang said. LORENZO'S NOT HOME ANYMORE.

"What do you mean?"

HE'S STARK, STARING BONKERS. A WHOLE SIX PACK SHY OF A CASE.

"Okay, buddy, if you want something to bite, bite me." I beckoned him with both hands, but he ignored me. I took a step forward and he clutched Brittany tighter.

Damn. What should I do? The screaming and jostling behind me scraped across my nerves. I jerked a vial of holy water out of my pocket, uncorked it and let it fly. The water hit the flesh on his arm and sizzled. He screamed, and Fang attacked his other arm, but the vamp still wouldn't let go of the girl.

TURN LOLA LOOSE, Fang shouted in my mind.

I hesitated only a moment then threw my arms out toward Lorenzo, trying with all my might to focus the succubus on him and only him. Since she'd fed earlier, it worked. I could feel her need slam into him, take total control of his body, and make him mine to command.

"Stop," I yelled. "Let Brittany go."

Though I could feel the madness churning within Lorenzo, Lola had a lock on him that he couldn't break. He froze, released the girl, and waited for my next order. Good, Lorenzo was taken care of.

But no time to worry about Brittany. First, I had to take care of the other vamp before more people were hurt. I spun around and saw that Dan and the demon had the female vamp cornered behind the refreshments table, but couldn't quite get to her. Or maybe the fact that she was female kept them from attacking.

I'd never seen her before. She looked preppy and well-fed, not the typical grunge-vamp types I saw on the streets. She also looked confused, uncertain, fangs dripping blood on her sweater and pencil skirt. But her vulnerable appearance wouldn't stop *me*.

"Need help?" I asked Dan, coming up beside him

"No. I can handle this. Call for back-up."

"I am back-up, you idiot."

But as he turned to say something, she leapt over the table and took off like a bat out of hell, zipping past him and heading for the door at a dead run. I spun to follow her, but she bowled over a middle-aged woman like she wasn't even there. And when Nicole and Shade made the mistake of getting in the vamp's way, she grabbed a chair and jabbed it into them.

Oh crap, they both went down. I couldn't stop to see how they were—I took off after her through the blood bank's lobby, afraid of how much more damage she could do. She was fast, but her high heels and her confusion slowed her down. Fang was faster. He scrabbled across the tile like mad then took a flying leap and hit her square in the back before she could make it out the front door. She went down and I was on top of her, pulling a stake.

Dan caught up with me. "You should have let her go. It's daylight outside. She'd fry."

"Something's wrong with these vamps. They should be holed up, far away from any possibility of coming into contact with a stray sunbeam."

I glanced down at the vamp. She wasn't fighting back—it was more like she was clawing at something just in front of her face. Though I had her pinned, it was like she didn't even see me.

Dan grabbed her head, the silver in his bracelet blistering the side of her face. "What are you waiting for? Stake her, or I'll drag her outside."

I lifted a stake. The blood bank's main door burst open. "Slayer, hold!"

I stopped. Not because of the command, but because of who it had come from. Alejandro stood there, looking menacing yet concerned with his cape draped over him to keep the sunlight at bay.

"Why?"

He took a graceful step to the side, out of the light, and lowered his cape. "Wait, please. She is one of mine."

"She's sure not acting like it," I snapped.

"I can take care of her." He knelt next to her and touched the tips of his fingers to her forehead. She relaxed and lay still, as if she had fainted.

Dan and I let her go and rose to our feet. "How'd you do that?" I asked Alejandro.

He waved a hand dismissively. "She is one of mine, so she is under the command of my touch."

WHOA, Fang said. YOU LEARN SOMETHING NEW EVERY DAY.

Yep.

"Did you order this massacre, bloodsucker?" Dan growled.

Gently, Alejandro said, "I am not your enemy."

"He's right," I told Dan. "He's obviously trying to help."

Dan made a sound of disgust. "Oh yeah? Tell them that." His abrupt gesture encompassed the carnage in the room . . . the moans, the fallen, the blood.

Alejandro glanced around, looking appalled. "What happened here?"

Dan thrust an impatient hand through his hair. "Three of your minions—Roger, Lorenzo and the girl—"

"Corina."

"—came out of the elevator and started attacking people. They called the SCU, but no one's on shift yet. We've never had vampires attack humans during the daytime, before." Dan looked at me. "How did you get here so fast?"

"Micah," I said, without explaining more. He knew Micah had demons working undercover at the blood banks. Dan nodded, and the watcher in question inclined his head at me then did his best to melt into the background to help with the wounded. "Why were *you* here?" I asked.

"I was showing my new partner—" He broke off and looked around wildly then blanched when he saw her lying unmoving on the floor. "Nic!"

Her shoulder was impaled on one leg of the chair. As Dan dropped beside her, the SCU pick-up unit came in, bringing medics with them. "Help her," Dan ordered one of them then went to assist the other victims.

"Check on Brittany, too," I said, and pointed to the girl, who lay still and pale.

I glanced around for Shade, my heart suddenly in my throat. He was sitting up against a wall, holding his helmeted head in his hands, the visor cracked from the force of the vamp's blow. Even a part-demon who seemed to be all shadow had a physical body that could bleed.

HE'S ALL RIGHT, Fang assured me.

Relieved, I turned back to Alejandro, who stepped over strewn bodies to look down at the vamp who'd been staked. "How could this have happened?" he asked wearily. "Roger was such an avid supporter of the Movement. As were Lorenzo and Corina."

"That's what I'd like to know," I said, my voice hard.

Alejandro shook his head and moved over to stand beside Brittany and the medic. "Sorry, she's gone," the medic said, then closed her eyes and glared at Alejandro.

The vamp leader stared down at Brittany, looking extremely saddened. Taking a deep breath, he gestured at Lorenzo, who was staring at me as if I were a lake in the middle of a parched desert. "Do you have him enthralled?"

"It seemed like the thing to do," I drawled, trying not to sound defensive. Strange, though, I hadn't realized I was still controlling him.

Alejandro knelt and placed his fingers against Lorenzo's forehead. He slumped like Corina had. Lola let him go without a peep. I turned to Alejandro. "What will you do with them?"

"Confine them until we can learn what happened. They do not appear to be themselves."

"Oh, yeah? Who are they, then? What have they turned into?"

I don't know what I expected him to answer, but it wasn't with a thoughtful look and a murmured, "I don't know."

As the SCU medics began loading up patients, I said, "Unless you want a whole lot of trouble from the general public, you might want to change the memories of the survivors."

Alejandro nodded, concentrated a moment, then was done. Spooky how easy that had been for him.

Dan followed the guys carrying Nic out the door. Dang, was it my fault she was hurt? If only I'd helped him train her, even a little—

VAL, COME HERE, Fang said urgently. SOMETHING'S WRONG WITH SHADE.

I whirled around and saw that Shade was on his hands and knees with his visor open, vomiting on the floor. I hurried over and blocked everyone else's view of his face. "Are you all right?"

"Huh?" Shade asked.

HE'S CONFUSED. HE MAY HAVE A CONCUSSION.

One of the medics came over and said, "Let's get that helmet off him."

Fang and I both moved to shield Shade and I said, "No, you can't." I couldn't let him see Shade as he really was.

Fang nudged me. YOU COULD HOLD HIS HAND AND HE'D LOOK NORMAL.

Maybe, but only as long as I was holding it. As soon as I let go or they took off with him, his secret would be out.

Surprised, the medic asked, "Why not?"

Ah, hell. Which was worse . . . revealing his secret to the SCU guys or letting him go untreated with possible life-threatening injuries?

Fang growled. I DON'T LIKE EITHER ONE OF THOSE OPTIONS. PICK DOOR NUMBER THREE.

I agreed. "Trust me," I told the medic. "I'll make sure he's taken care of." But what else could I do? Oh yes, I knew—

Micah strode in. "What happened?" he demanded of Alejandro. "Why did they attack?"

The only clue to the vamp leader's reaction was the tightening of his lips. "I have no idea. But I shall get to the bottom of it." He paused, then said deliberately, "Are you certain one of *your* people did not cause this?"

Just what we needed—more testosterone. Micah bristled, but before he could sling his own accusation, I said, "Micah, Shade's hurt. Do you know of any doctors who can treat him?"

Micah looked horrified as he studied Shade's hunched body. He lowered his voice so only I could hear. "No. Our only healer is . . . Shade himself."

"Well, I know one more possibility," I said.

Without another glance at Alejandro or the rest of the mess, Micah and the demon informant got Shade to Micah's Lexus and laid him gently in the back seat. Fang and the demon crowded into the seat beside him. They promised to watch him closely and keep him comfortable.

"Follow me," I said, and took off on my Valkyrie as soon as Micah started his engine.

I prayed like hell Gwen was as open-minded as she seemed. She was our only hope.

Chapter Eight

When I got to the townhouse, I scanned the parking lot. Good—Gwen's car sat in its usual spot.

Micah parked beside me and rolled down the window. "Why are we *here?*"

"Gwen is a nurse at the ER," I explained. "She can help."

"She's *human*," Micah protested, and the other demon looked a little skeptical.

"Yes, but she's Dan's sister—she knows what I am, knows what Fang is, and has seen the results of the vamps' attacks. She's cool."

Micah glanced uncertainly at the other demon. Now that there was less going on, I registered that the watcher was young, with milky-white skin, short wavy dark hair, and fine features with piercing blue eyes . . . almost inhumanly pretty. I didn't remember seeing him before.

Fang added, VAL'S RIGHT—GWEN'S COOL. AND WHAT OTHER CHOICE DO WE HAVE?

"I guess one of us could keep skin contact with him, so she won't see him in his demon state," Micah said.

I shook my head. "Not sure that's such a good idea. She needs to know he's not entirely human to help him."

"You could compel her," Micah told his informant.

Really? What kind of demon was he?

A DREAM DEMON, Fang said. HE CAN ENTER PEOPLE'S DREAMS AND CHANGE THEM, OR MAKE THEM BELIEVE THAT A REAL EXPERIENCE WAS A DREAM. OH, AND HIS NAME IS KYLE.

I quirked an eyebrow at my hellhound. *Sometimes you're helpful to have around.*

MAKE THAT ALWAYS, AND I'LL AGREE WITH YOU.

Micah thought for a moment. "All right, we'll chance your friend. Val, can you get the door?"

"Sure."

I opened the door of the townhouse and saw Gwen exercising along with a DVD, wearing loose yoga pants and a tank top.

"Gwen, I need your help."

She continued to exercise and turned toward me. "Can it wait—" She stopped when she saw Micah and Kyle helping Shade through the front door. "What's going on?"

"This is a friend of mine," I blurted out. "He was hit in the head and needs medical care." I gestured the guys down the hall. "Take him to my room, first door on the right." Fang led the way.

Gwen turned off the DVD and followed us, looking confused and concerned. "If he's hurt, you should take him to the emergency room," she said as the guys laid Shade down on my bed, his helmet and gloves still on.

"Can't. He's . . . different."

Gwen looked wary. "Different how?"

"Don't worry, he won't hurt you. But he has special . . . abilities that make him . . . " Ah, hell. How could I explain this? Forget it—let her see for herself. "Can you help him off with his helmet?" I asked Micah and Kyle.

They started to do as I asked, but Gwen pushed Kyle aside. "No, let me look first." She lifted up his cracked visor before we could stop her and gasped, then jumped backward away from the bed. "What the . . . ?"

"It's okay," I soothed her. I stripped off one of Shade's gloves and held his hand, skin to skin so the dark ribbons of light would stop pulsing across his face. "Look again."

She moved forward cautiously and peered into the visor, sighing in relief when she could see his face. "What did you do?" she asked me, then shook her head. "Never mind."

Gwen probed Shade's forehead carefully with her fingers then nodded at Micah and Kyle. "Take the helmet off, gently."

They did as she asked. Shade looked totally pale, with a bruise and lump forming at the top of his forehead. She checked his eyes, checked him over for other injuries, and fired questions at him.

Shade admitted he had lost consciousness for a short period of time and felt dizzy, nauseous and tired.

At Fang's prompting, I added, "He threw up, too, and seems really confused."

Gwen nodded decisively. "It looks like he has an MTBI."

"A what?" Medical terminology was so not my thing.

"Mild traumatic brain injury," Gwen explained.

Alarm rang through me and I jerked back.

Some of my panic must have shown on my face, for Gwen shook her head and laid her hand reassuringly on mine. "Sorry for the jargon. It just means he has a mild concussion." She glanced down at the bed where Shade had reverted to his swirly personality now that I was no longer holding his hand. "At least, that's what I'd say of a human."

All of a sudden, Shade's appearance flipped back into that of a human for a second then back again to swirly shadow demon.

"Whoa, that's not normal," Kyle said.

"What *is* normal for him?" Gwen asked.

"Normally he looks fully human only when someone is touching him skin to skin," I explained.

He blitzed off and on again, like a television on the fritz.

Gwen backed away, holding up her hands. "I have no idea how to treat this. I don't even understand it."

Kyle laid a hand on Micah's shoulder. "What about the encyclopedia? Maybe it will explain."

Oh yeah, the books. I glanced at Fang, remembering our mission. *What is Kyle thinking about the books?*

Fang cocked his head and stared at Kyle. ONLY THAT THEY MIGHT HELP. HE DIDN'T STEAL THEM.

Seeing that Micah was floundering for an answer that wouldn't admit the books were missing, I said, "I don't remember reading anything medical about shadow demons, but maybe Tessa can check."

Micah nodded, thanking me with his eyes. "I'll ask her." He turned to address Gwen. "He's mostly human. Can you treat him as you would a human and hope the rest of him follows?"

Gwen stared down at Shade uncertainly, looking a bit creeped out by his blinking in and out. It kind of freaked me out, too, so I grabbed his hand to bring him wholly into this reality. "Please?" I asked her. "He's a healer himself . . . he's the one who healed Dan's shoulder."

Gwen looked surprised. "When?"

"A couple of weeks ago. Didn't Dan tell you?"

One corner of her mouth turned up in a wry grin. "He never tells me when he's hurt. Doesn't want to worry his baby sister, I guess."

I nodded. That definitely sounded like the macho kind of thing Dan would do. "He owes Micah a favor for it," I hinted.

"Well, Dan will have to pay back his own favor," she said briskly.

"This one's on me."

Shade raised his head slightly. "Thank you," he whispered. "I will be in your debt."

"Don't be silly," Gwen said. "This is my job." She pushed him gently back down on the bed and asked him, "Do you have any clues how to treat yourself?"

A ghost of a smile flickered across his face. "Micah's suggestion is sound. "

"Well, there isn't a whole lot I'd do anyway. Let's put some ice on that bump, give him lots of fluids and rest, and monitor him to make sure he doesn't get worse."

Shade looked apologetic. "I feel less sick when someone keeps me grounded in this reality."

Micah nodded. "I'll make sure someone stays with you."

Fang poked me. MICAH ASKED ME TO PASS ON A MESSAGE TO YOU AND SHADE. HE FIGURES IF HE SENDS PEOPLE TO VISIT SHADE WHO WERE AT THE PARTY, SHADE CAN DISCUSS THE BOOKS AND I CAN READ THEIR MIND TO SEE IF THEY'RE GUILTY.

Good idea.

Shade jerked and glanced at Fang then nodded. Hmm, maybe I should coach the shadow demon a bit on how to hide his feelings, or he'd give us away.

YEAH, Fang agreed. HEY, IF SHADE'S GONNA STAY HERE, MAYBE YOU COULD BRING PRINCESS OVER SO SHE CAN HELP WITH THE MIND-READING WHILE I'M NOT HERE.

I glanced at Fang. *And you have a totally innocent motive, right?*

HELL NO. I WANNA MAKE SOME TIME WITH MY WOMAN.

I resisted the urge to laugh out loud. It was a good idea anyway. "Gwen, would it be okay if Shade stayed here for awhile? And brought his dog? She's small and very well-mannered."

"Uh, sure," Gwen said.

"Thank you," Shade said and winced as if the act of speaking had been painful.

Gwen looked sympathetic. "We could also give you something for the pain. Can you take acetaminophen?"

"Yes. But I'll need twice the normal dosage for it to be effective."

"Okay." Gwen glanced at me. "Can you help me find it, Val?"

"Sure." But I knew she didn't really need help. I followed her out of the room and as soon as we were out of Shade's earshot, I said, "I'm sorry. I know I should've asked you first if it was okay . . .

especially with all the people that will be traipsing through here. Is it a problem for Shade to stay here? I'll sleep on the couch."

She rummaged in her medicine cabinet and tossed me a grin. "Not if all his friends are as hot as these guys. There's a whole shopping mall of eye candy in there."

"Not all his friends are," I said, smiling. "And some are actually women. So what's the problem?"

She grabbed the bottle she was looking for and grimaced. "It's my overprotective brother. I just wanted to warn you that Dan won't like it."

We were still close enough for Fang to overhear our conversation from the other room. WHO CARES? he asked.

Unfortunately, I cared. That must be what that sinking feeling meant in the pit of my stomach. But Dan was already so unhappy with me that one more thing shouldn't make a difference. However, I did need to let Gwen know what was really going on before she consented to this. Quickly, I had Fang relay my intention to Micah. "I know Dan won't like it. And he'll like what I'm about to tell you even less."

Micah came to join us in the living room and we explained to Gwen about the missing encyclopedia and our intention to use this as an opportunity to find the thief.

"There should be no danger to you," Micah assured Gwen. "If Fang or Princess learn the thief's identity, they won't confront him. They'll let Shade know and he can call one of us."

Gwen nodded thoughtfully. "And will there be any danger to Shade while he's convalescing?"

"There shouldn't be," Micah assured her. "The thief won't know his identity has been compromised."

"But since people will have to keep in contact with him to keep him from getting sick, they'll be able to see his expression. And he hasn't learned yet to keep his expression from giving his thoughts away," I reminded Micah.

"Good point. I'll ask Fang and Princess not to tell him until after the thief leaves. Even if the thief does suspect, the hellhounds should be able to protect him. And Shade isn't totally without defenses himself. He must have been caught off guard to get this hurt."

Yeah, the incredible speed of a crazed vampire would do that to you. Plus Shade had been distracted by helping innocents. "How long will Shade need to rest?" I asked Gwen.

She shrugged. "In a human, I'd say they should take it easy for a week or two, limiting their activity and not doing anything strenuous to see how it goes. But I have no idea how that will translate to Shade."

"Neither will anyone else," Micah said. "I'll ask Shade to continue playing sick until we've interviewed everyone. Will that be a problem for you?" he asked Gwen.

"No. And what my big brother doesn't know can't hurt him."

"He does live in the complex," I reminded her. "And he comes to visit you a lot. He's bound to find out sooner or later."

Gwen shrugged. "He hasn't been by much lately." I winced, knowing that was because of me. Gwen laid a hand on my arm. "But that's okay. I'll deal with him when it happens."

Better her than me.

Micah thanked her, holding her hand in both of his own. His sincerity made her glow with pleasure. When she left to take the painkiller to Shade, Micah lowered his voice. "I'm doing this only to rule my people out. I still think it was one of Alejandro's. After all, the books give a great deal of information about our strengths and weaknesses. Think how much leverage that would give them in ensuring we do as they wish."

"Good point. And it's time I check that out." It was dark by now, so maybe Alejandro was receiving visitors. He'd given me his personal number after I helped him out with Lily. Relieved to have something I could actually *do,* I called him.

He answered right away. "How may I help you, Ms. Shapiro?"

Whoa. Don't think anyone had ever called me that before. Weird. "Considering everything that just happened, is this a bad time?"

He sighed. "It is not a good one, but I am certain you have questions for me."

Yes, and about more than he thought. "Can I come talk to you? I don't want to do this over the phone."

"Of course. I am at home and shall instruct the guards to let you pass. You already have the combination to the gates," he added drily.

Uh, yeah. A small matter of breaking and entering. But it had been in a good cause and ended well for everyone. "Okay, I'm coming right over."

When I turned off the phone, Micah said, "Can you leave Fang here with Shade while I pick up Princess and some of his things? I'll arrange for people to stay with him in shifts."

"Sure." As an invited guest, so to speak, I shouldn't be in any danger at the vamp mansion. I tossed a thought to Fang to let him know what was going on, then let Gwen know I was leaving for awhile.

Sheesh, I'd wanted friends, but now I was going to have a constant parade of them through my *bedroom*, for heaven's sake. I hadn't realized how much stress having real friends could be. More people to help . . . and protect.

I felt relieved at being able to escape, and guilty for feeling that way. Then again, we all did what we could. I wasn't much help at a sick bed, but questioning bloodsuckers was right up my alley. And if I got to pound on a few, that would be even better.

GOOD, Fang said. GO KICK ONE FOR ME.

Chapter Nine

One of Alejandro's lieutenants, the cowboy vamp, Austin, answered the door at the mansion and grinned at me. "Well, hello, darlin'," he said, tipping back his Stetson. "Coming through the front door this time?"

I shrugged. "Thought I'd try something different."

"And are you aimin' to expose more corruption in our fine organization this day?"

He seemed so amused, I wasn't quite sure how to take him. True, he had no personal reason to dislike me, but I had killed a few of his kind. "It's possible," I said briefly. "How are Lorenzo and Corina doing?"

His smile died. "They're still a mite bit troubled," he admitted.

"Sorry to hear that. Uh, Alejandro is expecting me."

"Sure thing. This way."

He took me to the study and waved me to a seat. "He'll be right along."

I nodded and he left the room. I glanced around, noticing that Alejandro had removed the rug I'd soaked with Lily's blood and replaced it with a blood-red one. Good planning. The rest of the study was about the same—all old-fashioned and masculine looking.

I was only alone for a few minutes before Alejandro came in and shut the door softly behind him. He seated himself at his desk, looking wiped. "What may I do for you?"

"Do you *really* have *no* idea what happened at the blood bank? Why your people . . . " I hesitated, not certain how to finish that sentence politely.

Alejandro did it for me. "Went mad?"

Well, yeah. I nodded.

He sighed. "Not yet. When I allow them to awake from my thrall, they are not present in their own minds."

Whatever that meant. "Do you think that'll change?"

"I hope so." Alejandro leaned forward, clasping his hands on his desk and staring into my eyes. "But that is not why you've come. Tell me, what would you have of me?"

"The other night, at the social event . . ."

"Of course. Have you come to talk to me about the demons' reaction?"

"Uh, no. Something else. But this is in confidence . . . "

He nodded.

Taking a deep breath, I said, "Something went missing that evening."

"*What* went missing?"

"I can't tell you."

"And how does that concern me?" From the steel in his voice, I had a feeling he knew what I was about to say.

"It was stolen during the chaos." His expression turned hard and I assured him, "Micah is investigating all of *his* people, but I was hoping you'd let me question those of yours who were there, too."

"And would you take their word alone for their innocence?" he asked, his tone dangerous.

"Would *you*?" I countered. After all, Lily had been one of his lieutenants, yet he hadn't suspected her disloyalty.

"I suppose not."

"If they try to control me, I can read their minds. Can you ask them to do that?"

"They won't be happy." He gave me a wry look. "After what happened, they fear you and the demon inside you. But if you promise to only ask about that one thing and not reveal anything else you learn in their minds, I will agree."

"You got it," I agreed. "I'm only interested in finding out about the—about that one thing."

"And if one of them admits to having this item that's missing, what then?"

"I'll ask them to return it," I said innocently. Of course, if they refused, all bets were off. I didn't say it aloud but Alejandro was no dummy. He caught the gist.

He sighed again. "Very well. I shall call all of them to me so you may question them."

Wow, I didn't know he had those kind of powers. "You can do that?"

He gave me an odd look, then tapped the cell phone lying on his desk. "With this, yes."

Oh. Duh. Feeling stupid, I said, "Okay, thanks."

Some were already at the mansion, and others were out and about, so Alejandro had Austin contact them all—only about a dozen.

The first was another one of Alejandro's lieutenants, Luis. He wasn't as nice as Austin. In fact, I'd bet he' d been a snobby aristocrat before he was turned. Dark-skinned, with a thin goatee and long hair clubbed back into a ponytail, he could out-snoot anyone I'd ever met. He regarded me with a sneer when Alejandro asked him to try to control me.

I expected some reluctance, but instead, he viciously slammed his mind into mine and tried to take over. It didn't work, of course. Now that he'd done that, I could read his mind. But I'd promised not to go fishing, so I simply asked, "What did you do the night of the social at the Demon Underground?"

I received quick images of the fight, his pleasure in slamming Ludwig against the wall, and his disappointment when Alejandro made him stop. And he made sure I knew he was disgusted with Micah's wimpiness in not outing the demons. He also blamed him for Lorenzo and Carina's condition, though he had no evidence or proof.

Unfortunately, he knew nothing of the books. Too bad. He was dangerous. One of Alejandro's less likable underlings. I wouldn't mind taking him down. "Thank you," I said. "That's all I needed."

Alejandro gave him a warning glance. "When the others arrive, have them come in, but do not mention why. Do you understand?"

Luis sneered again but gave his boss a curt nod and left without a word.

The others provided no surprise. Their answers were mostly the same. Though they were uneasy about sharing their thoughts with me, they had no knowledge of the missing books. Crap. With the vamps eliminated, that meant the thief was probably a demon. Micah was not going to be happy.

When the last of his people left, Alejandro said, "I take it you did not find what you were looking for?"

"No, but they all seemed pretty ticked off at the demons for not wanting to be outed along with you." They wanted to spread the wealth of any possible fallout. Couldn't blame them for that.

"It's a sore spot," he conceded. "In hindsight, I realize I should have let Micah know of my plans first, to smooth the way."

Yeah, Alejandro's love of the dramatic had put him in trouble this time. "Well, you might want to work on calming some of them down unless you want a war on your hands."

He nodded wearily. "There is only one you have not yet tested. Myself."

I didn't need to. The vamp leader had been within my sight the entire time. "That won't be necessary," I said, hoping he'd think it was because I trusted him.

He raised an eyebrow but didn't comment. Instead, he surprised me by asking, "How would you like to come work for the New Blood Movement?"

"Huh?" I responded stupidly.

He leaned forward. "Thanks to you, I have an opening for a new lieutenant in my organization. Your ability would come in very handy to smoke out any other traitors, ensure everyone who joins the movement is genuine, protect our interests among the demons and with the humans in the SCU."

Okay, I *still* felt stupid, 'cause I sure couldn't figure out why he was asking *me*. "You do realize that I work for the SCU, right? That I'm called the Slayer because I kill people like you?"

"Not people like me," he said with a smile. "People like those vampires who are not in my organization. And the fact that you called us *people* is very telling."

It was? I didn't know how to respond to that, so I said nothing.

"I'll double whatever the SCU is paying you."

"I don't do it for the money," I protested.

"I know, but having some extra cash doesn't hurt. What do you say?"

I wanted to blurt out an instant "no," but his offer was a little tempting. Not have to work with Dan, or be treated like a freak anymore by the normal humans . . . ?

No, if I went to work for Alejandro I'd be shunned as a murderer by his vamps and as a traitor by the demons and the San Antonio police department. How was that any better?

But before I could respond either way, he added, "Why don't you think about it and get back to me?"

I couldn't see myself working for him in any future I could envision, but there was no sense in turning him down right away. It wouldn't hurt to let him think I was considering it. "Okay. And thank you very much for letting me question your people about the . . .

missing item," I said, trying to be diplomatic for a change. Micah would be proud of me.

The leader of the New Blood Movement inclined his head. "This was but a small favor. I am still in your debt."

Okay. Not sure how he kept score, but I wasn't going to argue when the outcome was to my advantage. He rose to walk me to the front door. At first I wondered if it was to ensure I didn't wander places I shouldn't, but no, he was probably just doing the gentlemanly thing.

He opened the door to escort me out, but halted as Austin hurried into the hallway waving a cell phone. "There's something wrong at the Fort Sam blood bank."

Oh, crap. Another blood bank, another vamp gone mad? "What kind of trouble?" I asked.

But Alejandro said, "Let's go," and practically flew to the limo parked in the driveway. Austin jumped in the driver's seat and they took off.

Worried about who might get hurt, I jumped on the back of my motorcycle and zoomed after them. The blood bank was just outside Fort Sam Houston, in another of San Antonio's old hotels that had been converted to a new purpose. On my bike, I might be able to get there faster than Alejandro.

I did get there first, but a teenaged preppy type was guarding the door, holding her arms outstretched in front of it. "I'm sorry, the blood bank is closed tonight," she told a man who was trying to get in. She looked a bit freaked out. Whatever was going on in there, a human volunteer like her shouldn't have to deal with it. Look what had happened to Brittany . . .

The man tried to push his way past, but she was determined to stop him. Before he could get too physical, I let Lola loose and she wrapped her wiles around him. Just like that, he was mine to command. I had a crazy urge to wave my hand in front of his face and intone, "These are not the droids you want," but stopped myself. Fang's love for pop culture references was a bad influence.

Instead, I said, "The blood bank is closed. Go home." I could feel him enjoying Lola's caress. Eeeww.

Obediently, he left. I wished I could wipe away the feel of his mind. The girl thanked me, but seemed determined to keep me out as well. Too bad I couldn't use Lola on *her*. Not wanting to hurt her, I flashed my SCU badge and said, "Police." When she still hesitated, I added, "Alejandro is right behind me."

His name acted like an "Open sesame," and she let me pass without further argument. Inside, it wasn't as bad as I feared. The place was totally trashed, but there were no bodies and no pools of blood. Only two guys facing off about ten feet apart, one short and bald, with fangs bared. They were both breathing hard and looked like they'd been fighting for some time. Strangely, there were scorch marks on the wall . . . and on the bloodsucker. I recognized the non-vamp— Andrew, the surly redheaded demon from the party.

"You killed Veronica," Andrew yelled, and his eyes flashed purple as he punched straight out from his shoulder toward the vamp, a small fireball sizzling from his fist.

Baldy ducked, and the fireball splashed against the marble wall, singeing it.

"Andrew, stop," I yelled. He was a fire demon with a bad temper . . . two things that did not go well together.

The vamp darted a sneering glance at me. "Slayer," he said with contempt. "Come to help your friend? It figures."

"No, I've come to stop the two of you from making asses of yourselves. Looks like I'm too late."

Andrew snarled and clenched his hand into a fist again, turning toward me.

"I'd reconsider, Andrew, if I were you."

I let Lola loose, just enough to remind them what I could do. "Do you really want me to turn you both into mindless love slaves?"

Both guys backed off, but they didn't look happy about it. I relaxed a little. Maybe this wouldn't be as bad as I thought. "What's going on? Who started this?" I asked.

"He started it," Andrew muttered.

The bald vamp pointed at Andrew. "I caught your friend here spying on us."

I shrugged. "So?"

The bloodsucker looked startled. "So? What do you mean, *so?* He was *spying.*"

I shook my head and placed my hands on my hips. "Let me get this straight. You ask the demons to come out of the closet with you, ask them to trust you with their biggest secrets, then expect them not to come check you out and see how you operate?"

Both guys looked a little surprised. "Yeah," Andrew said to the vamp, with a smirk. "Ditto what she said." Though he was willing to go along with my story, I suspected there was more to this fight than he wanted to admit.

I turned on him. "And you—you say you want to keep our existence a secret, yet you practically set this whole hotel on fire?"

Andrew and the vamp both looked sheepish now. Geez, I felt like the grown-up in this situation. How messed up was that? I shook my head. "If you want the other side to take you seriously, you both need to practice what you preach."

The bald guy started to protest but a voice behind me cut him off. "That's enough, Vincent," Alejandro said. "You are both culpable in this matter."

I turned around and saw Alejandro watching, with Austin lounging against the wall and cleaning his nails with the tip of a knife. "How long have you been there?" I asked.

Alejandro smiled. "Long enough to see that the Slayer doesn't always resort to killing or enthrallment to win the day."

I *had* done well, hadn't I? It was kind of nice to settle things with reason for a change. Dang, where was Fang when I needed an "Attagirl?"

Austin gestured casually with his knife. "So, is there any other unresolved business between you two boys?"

Andrew looked mulish. "I—"

The door to the back rooms burst open and two male vamps surged out, looking wild. They headed straight for Andrew and me. What the—? They had the crazed looks I'd seen on Lorenzo's face. I yanked Andrew out of the way and was about to pull a stake when Alejandro yelled, "Stop them from attacking the demons!"

Austin and Vincent flew past me and slammed into the two unhinged vamps. In a blur of motion, they each pinned a vamp to the wall and held them there while Alejandro flew to their sides to place his fingers against the temples of the wild vamps, one after the other. They slumped to the ground.

"Yours, I take it?" I asked drily.

Alejandro gazed at the two sprawled vamps, his expression sad. "Yes."

"What's the matter with them?" Vincent asked.

"The same thing that happened to Corina and Lorenzo," Alejandro said softly.

Austin shook his head. "This is not good."

An understatement, but it could have been much worse. We were lucky Alejandro was on the scene. "Vamps suddenly turning into rabid animals at two different blood banks?" I said. "Does that suggest a pattern to you?"

"It does," Alejandro said. Glancing at Austin, he added, "Close the blood banks down. All of them."

Austin tipped his hat. "You got it, boss."

I glanced around. Vincent was dragging one of the zonked-out vamps to the limo outside, and Andrew was nowhere to be seen. He must have sneaked out. Probably off to tell Micah his version of events before I could. Well, good luck with that.

"Close down the blood banks?" I asked. "You think the problem is in the donated blood?"

"It appears that way. I shall do a thorough investigation."

"Uh, how are you going to get your blood supplies in the meantime?" Would the lack of donations doom the New Blood Movement and their lofty goal of not sucking on *unwilling* humans?

"Let me worry about that. I assure you, we will not harm anyone. I won't allow it."

Yeah, right. "I believe that's what you *intend* to do, but how long can you go on this way? And can you speak for *all* of your people?"

"Yes. And we shall go on as long as we need to until we can find out what kind of tainted blood is causing this madness and stop it."

His tone was uncompromising, final. Instead of arguing with him, I went back to another subject. "Did you hear Andrew accuse Vincent of killing someone?"

Alejandro sighed. "Yes. And, before you ask, we shall question Vincent together. While we wait, tell me, have you considered my job offer?"

Only for a fleeting moment. "Uh, you were serious about that?" I asked.

"Very."

"Um, I don't think so. I'm happy with where I am." Well, not happy, precisely, but at least it had to be better than working with the vamps, no matter how nice Alejandro and Austin were.

He nodded, looking disappointed but not surprised. "Very well, but the offer is still open if you should ever change your mind."

Thankfully I didn't have to answer that because the bald vamp came back in. Turning to him, Alejandro said, "Vincent, please try to control Ms. Shapiro's mind."

Vincent looked uncertainly at me, but when I nodded, he did as

Alejandro asked, so I was able to read his mind. "Go ahead and ask him," I told Alejandro.

"What happened here between you and the fire demon?" Alejandro asked.

Vincent shrugged. "I was seeing clients and noticed the redhead had been sitting here for hours, but hadn't been called to donate. I asked the receptionist, and she said he was waiting for someone. It seemed suspicious so I asked him what he was doing here. He became angry and attacked me, accusing me of killing someone named Veronica. All I did was defend myself."

Vincent was telling the truth. "And *did* you kill this Veronica?" I asked.

"No," he said, sounding bewildered. "I've never killed anyone."

I nodded at Alejandro. He was telling the truth about that, too. Then again, the fact that he was still here while Andrew had sneaked out probably would have made me believe him instead of Andrew, anyway. I released his mind.

"Thank you, Vincent," Alejandro said. "Please wait in the limo with Austin."

When Vincent left, I said, "I'm sure Andrew was acting on his own—I'll let Micah know what happened."

"Thank you. And please assure him that I will do everything I can to find out what is causing this madness in my people. Obviously, something is tainting the blood they drink, and I must test it, find out what it is."

"Do you have someone who can do that?" I could ask Gwen for a lab recommendation, but that might be stretching the limits of what she'd be able . . . or willing . . . to do.

"I do. The Movement has friends in many places."

Good to know. "Do you think this is deliberate?"

"Yes, I do. Someone is targeting our blood banks. The only question is, who? And why?"

"Who has reason to? Maybe those free-agent vamps who want to keep killing humans?"

He thought for a moment, then said, "It's unlikely. They would be more likely to *steal* our supply of blood than poison it." He raised an eyebrow at me. "With Micah's people present at both blood bank incidents, it leaves me to wonder . . . "

I winced. "I know it looks suspicious, but Micah is *not* behind this." Though that didn't mean all of his demons were guilt-free. "I know the demon at the first incident didn't start that trouble. We'll make sure to question the fire demon about the confrontation here."

"It can't be a mere coincidence that these blood bank attacks began so soon after Micah's gathering, where we announced our intention to reveal ourselves to the world."

He was right. The fact that Andrew had been at the party when the encyclopedia had been stolen wasn't lost on me either. Did the books have something in them that showed how to poison vampires through the blood they drank? I didn't remember reading anything about that, but I hadn't read the whole set of books, either.

I knew this much: So far the evidence hinted that a demon was responsible for drugging or poisoning—whatever you wanted to call it—the vamps. "We have been questioning our own kind, just like I've been questioning your guys," I assured him.

Alejandro's eyes narrowed. "You're questioning everyone about an item that was stolen . . . right after Micah announced the *Encyclopedia Magicka* had been returned. *That's* what's missing, isn't it?"

The surprise on my face must have answered for me. Alejandro said, "Of course. It must list the strengths and weaknesses of my people, including something that can poison their blood. That's a very dangerous weapon to leave in anyone's hands, much less an enemy's."

"Yes, we know. We haven't let anyone else know it's missing, and we're doing everything we can to find out who took it and why. I know you don't have any reason to believe me, but—"

"On the contrary, I do have reason to believe you." At my surprised look, he added, "You are the one person respected and trusted by both sides. A part-demon who fights evil, a vampire slayer who can discriminate between the good and the bad . . . you are our best hope to avoid a war between my people and yours."

That sounded way too much like, "Obi Wan, you're our only hope." I gulped. Crap—I was no Jedi Knight. Good thing Fang wasn't here. He'd be laughing his butt off.

Alejandro smiled at my shell-shocked look. "I know it is a great deal of responsibility to lay on your shoulders, but won't you help us?"

Find the missing encyclopedia, catch the person responsible for the blood poisoning, and avert an inter-species war? Oh sure, piece of cake.

Chapter Ten

Even reluctant heroes needed to sleep and eat once in awhile, and it was time for me to do both. When I got home, I found Shade asleep on the couch, with Fang and Princess sacked out on the floor beneath the coffee table. The female demon watching Shade told me he'd insisted on leaving my bed free for me. I didn't see any sense in arguing with her and Gwen was in bed too, so I grabbed something to eat, texted Micah with my suspicions about Andrew, then crashed.

When I woke, it was to the delicious smell of frying sausage and the sound of laughter. I dressed, grabbed my phone, and followed my nose to the kitchen. Shade sat at the table along with two of his demon friends—Mood and Josh. Mood had her hand on Shade's to keep him grounded. Though Shade was normally pale—which came with being all blond and gorgeous and working at night—he wasn't as white as he'd looked yesterday, so I guessed he was feeling better.

Gwen was dishing out the sausage with her famous banana pecan pancakes and maple honey butter. Oh, my. "Any of those left?" I asked hopefully. Gwen's cooking was the best I'd ever tasted.

"Sure," she said with a grin. "We're all having seconds now, so there's plenty."

I grabbed a chair and a plate then took a bite and closed my eyes in pure bliss. *Heaven.*

It's about time you joined the living, Fang said as he came in through the doggie door with Princess.

Hey, someone has to work to keep us in pancakes and sausage, I shot back, ridiculously pleased to see the little mutt. I scratched his ears and asked out loud, "Have you eaten?"

"Don't let him tell you he hasn't," Gwen said with a laugh. "He and Princess pigged out already."

Princess sniffed. I am not a pig. I am a purebred Cavalier King Charles Spaniel.

Shade stifled a laugh and leaned down to assure her she was a beautiful dog.

Feeling guilty, I said, "Gwen, how much do I owe you for all of this food? I can't expect you to foot the cost for me and all of my friends . . . and cook for us, too."

She waved it away. "Don't worry about it. Your cousin Micah thought of that already. He sent over some money for groceries. Plus you *know* I love to cook. It's fun to have so many appreciative mouths to feed."

The mouths she spoke of were full of pancakes and sausage, so they all grunted, made yummy noises, and nodded to prove their appreciation.

Fang snorted. TALK ABOUT PIGS . . .

"See?" Gwen said with a laugh. "It also gives me a chance to make some of my favorite things."

Well, if she was cool with it, who was I to bite the hand that fed me?

Fang groaned mentally.

Okay, okay. I'm not up to your standard of humor, Fang, but come on, admit it, you missed me.

ALWAYS, BABE, he assured me.

But there was something in his tone . . . something that sounded like guilt. He'd probably been too wrapped up in his new girlfriend to notice I was gone. I was happy for him, I really was, but couldn't help but feel a little jealous at the loss of some of his affection.

NEVER, he asserted, licking my hand. YOU AND I ARE A TEAM. BESIDES, HOW COULD YOU FUNCTION WITHOUT ME?

I probably couldn't. Smiling, I asked him, *Any leads on who took the books?*

NOPE. NOT A CLUE.

Has Shade asked Mood and Josh about that night?

NOT YET. THERE HASN'T BEEN A GOOD TIME TO BRING IT UP.

Okay, then I would. And it seemed like a good time to learn more about Andrew, since they all seemed to be such good friends. *Tell Shade to guard his expression.*

Shade jerked a little and looked at Fang, then nodded at me. Oh great. We'd have to work on that. Josh and Mood had been very careful to keep in contact with him at all times, so his naked emotions were on full display.

HE'S DOING BETTER, Fang said defensively as Shade froze his expression into a mask of fierce concentration and focused on his breakfast.

I knew that, and I hadn't meant to be snarky. Fang accepted my apology but before I could ask them anything, my phone rang—Micah calling to return my text from last night.

I haven't been able to find Andrew," he said. "Are you sure he's the thief?"

"Pretty sure."

"I take it you can't talk now?"

'Not really." Not freely, anyway. I had to be careful what I said around his best buds.

"Okay, I'll keep looking. Call me when you can."

"Will do, I said and Micah hung up.

"That was Micah," I told everyone. "He's looking for Andrew. Do you know where the fire demon hangs out?"

Josh shrugged. "Rivercenter Mall, mostly. Why?"

No sense in lying. They'd find out the truth sooner or later anyway. "I ran into him last night," I said, trying to sound casual. "He tried to flash-fry a vampire. One of Alejandro's gang. An *innocent* vamp."

Mood looked surprised. "He did? Why?"

"I was hoping you could tell me why. He said something about a 'Veronica?'"

"Oh," Mood said. She and Josh suddenly looked sad. "She was his sister."

The operative word being *was*. A motive, maybe? "Killed by a vamp?" I asked, pretty confident I knew the answer.

"No," Mood said, surprising me. "She died of ovarian cancer. She was only twenty."

Geez, that shocked me.

"Cancer happens to people of all ages," Gwen said softly.

Fang added, SHADE ASKED ME TO TELL YOU THAT A FIRE DEMON'S NATURE MAKES CANCER WORSE, SPEEDS THE GROWTH OF THE CELLS. VERONICA WENT VERY FAST.

Everyone looked depressed. Dang, not my intention. "I'm sorry. I didn't realize."

Mood nodded. "Andrew has . . . anger issues. He was probably acting out of grief, needing someone to take out his rage on."

I hated to ask, when they were obviously so upset, but still, I needed to probe. "Maybe the *Encyclopedia Magicka* will be able to help demons like her in the future."

I cast a glance at Fang. *How are they reacting to my mention of the books?*

NO GUILT THERE. MOOD IS CONCENTRATING ON SOMETHING, AND JOSH IS WITHDRAWN AND QUIET—ZONED OUT.

Crap. Though Mood had been busy calming the crowd during the time the books had been stolen, I'd hoped Josh had noticed something odd with Andrew.

"Don't you know if the books will help?" Mood asked. "You read them, didn't you?"

"Not really," I said. "Stupidly, I didn't know how important they were. I didn't read much of them."

They were the only gifts my suicidal father had left to me, so I'd kept them. But the fear that I might turn out like him had made me reluctant to read much about our kind—only what I needed to survive.

Then, realizing Mood didn't know the books were missing, I added, "I figure they're better off in Micah's hands."

Mood smiled. "Yes, they're safe with him."

Fang snorted, and I shoved him with my foot in warning.

Shade touched my arm. "Can I speak to you privately?"

"Sure. Let's go to my room."

Mood smirked, and I felt strangely flustered. Should I explain? I couldn't tell them he probably just wanted to find out what I'd learned. Should I tell them I didn't think of Shade in that way?

BUT MAYBE YOU DO, Fang said, and I swear he smirked, too.

I glanced at Shade and saw his feelings for me written all over his face. *My* face heated, and I felt warm all over. Oh, crap.

JUST GO, OR YOU'LL MAKE IT WORSE, Fang said, sounding exasperated.

Grabbing Shade's hand, I pulled him toward my bedroom so we could talk. I heard everyone else laugh behind me and Mood sang softly, "Shade and Val sitting in a tree . . . "

"Oh, yeah. So grown up," I called back and was met with more laughter.

I pulled Shade into my bedroom and suddenly felt awkward. I'd never noticed before how big the bed was, how boring my room was, or how big Shade looked in it. Though I kept hold of his hand to ground him in this reality, I deliberately glanced down and to the side. "Uh, we need to work on your control of your facial expressions . . ."

"I have been," Shade said. "I've been practicing. That expression on my face just now? It says, 'I adore you, Val.' Fooled everyone, didn't it?"

Huh? I raised my head to look at him and saw amusement and fondness on his face. Oh. He'd been acting, to throw them off as to the real reason he'd asked to talk to me in private. Feeling my face heat even more, I said. "I'm sorry. I didn't mean that you're in love with me or anything. I was just . . . " Acting like a complete fool.

AND DOING AN EXCELLENT JOB OF IT, Fang agreed from the other room.

Grrr. *Go away for a little while, would you? I don't listen in on you and Princess.*

OKAY, OKAY, Fang said, sounding disappointed. I'LL TUNE OUT. JUST BE NICE TO THE GUY. HE'S MY FRIEND.

I will. He's my friend, too.

"It's okay," Shade assured me, sinking down onto the bed. "I think I am a little bit in love with you."

Oh, wow. No one had ever said that to me before. Tears stung my eyelids, and emotion clogged my throat. I plopped down on the bed next to him, still holding his hand. "I-I—" I didn't know what to say.

"I didn't mean to weird you out or anything, but I thought you should know." When I didn't say anything, he added softly, "You don't have to say it back."

Hell, the way I was feeling now, emotions all mixed up and kind of sappy, maybe I *did* feel the same way. "Are you sure it's not just Lola?"

He shook his head. "You and Lola are a package deal. How could someone love only part of you?"

My family had no problem with separating the two of us . . . and Lola was definitely *persona non grata* there. "Good question," I muttered.

"Poor Val . . ." Shade put his arms around me and hugged me to him.

Oh, wow. This was so great. He smelled really good, and his warm arms made me feel protected and safe.

Lola stirred, wanting more of Shade . . . a lot more. I snapped her back, desperately trying to remember how the candle flame had helped me find an inner space where I could be free of her. I started to pull away, but Shade stopped me.

"It's okay," he whispered. "Remember, Micah said to use me to help keep Lola under control. It's better if you do it now and don't wait until she's so hungry that you have no control." He laid down on my bed and pulled me down beside him, looking all sexy, longing, and hopeful. "Let go, Val."

Lola wanted him bad, and I had to admit the rest of me did, too. But it was hard to let loose when I was a whole lot more used to holding back. I laid in the circle of his arms like a stiff pole.

Oops, bad choice of words. Desperately, I said, "I thought you wanted to ask me what Fang found out about your friends."

He kissed me on the forehead. "I'm guessing he cleared Mood and Josh, but you're not so sure about Andrew." He followed up with a snuggle and kiss just below my ear.

Lust and longing shot through me, but still I managed to keep a lid on Lola. "If you knew that, why did you want to speak to me?"

He chuckled into my neck. "For this. You need to satisfy Lola, and I'm here to let you."

Oh. He continued to place soft kisses in strategic places, and I felt myself melt in his arms, feeling all gooey and warm, yet dizzy with emotion. He was right. What would it hurt? "But you're injured," I protested half-heartedly.

He kissed my lips softly. "We aren't going to do anything but kiss," he promised me. "I know you won't take too much energy. I trust you."

I could see in his eyes that he meant exactly what he said. His faith both humbled and seduced me. Convinced he really meant it, I relaxed and kissed him back, letting Lola emerge, slow and easy. I felt my energy flow into him everywhere we touched body to body, smooth and thick as sweet syrup. He gasped and his whole body quivered with desire. For me.

Our kiss broken, I held on to him as if he were my lifeline and let the energy ebb and flow through us, enjoying the waves of sensation as much as Lola did, as we explored his nerve-endings psychically, stroking and pleasuring here . . . there . . . everywhere. His desire fed back to me, filling the empty wells of my demon self, making me strong and whole. I felt fully in control, confident and assured . . . and very, *very* turned on.

But Shade had asked for only this, no more, so I resisted the urge to strip off our clothes and offer up my virginity. Though I wanted very much to lose it right then, I was also too conscious of the people in the kitchen just down the hallway, wondering exactly what we were doing in here.

But when Shade grasped my butt in both hands and clutched me to him, I lost it. Pure lust shot through me, directly into him, where we were pressed together at the hips. I arched into him and Shade stiffened, then gasped and shuddered, his fingers digging into the soft flesh of my backside.

He relaxed, then lay still, leaving me feeling like I still wanted something, but wasn't quite sure what it was. Lola knew, though, and drank up all that lovely energy he offered us. Well, not all. I had enough control to take only what I needed, not so much that it would leave him totally depleted.

"I'm sorry," he muttered into my neck. "I didn't mean to—"

"It's okay," I assured him. "That's what's supposed to happen, I think."

"But you—you're not satisfied."

"Sure I am. I let Lola drink her fill."

He raised up to search my face. "That's not what I meant—"

I cut him off. "It's enough." Especially the way he looked at me, all sleepy, satisfied, and worshipful. That was Lola's doing. Feeding on him with his consent was one thing.. Letting him confuse his reaction to Lola with falling in love with me was quite another. I couldn't trust the way he felt and couldn't let myself get the two confused either.

I smoothed his hair back from his brow where his bruise still lingered. "How's your head doing?"

"It's fine," he said impatiently. "Val—"

My bedroom door burst open then and we both jumped. Crap—I should have locked it. Dan stood there, but his face wasn't as easy to read as Shade's. All I could see was he'd shut down.

Fang barreled in after him. SORRY, VAL, WE COULDN'T TELL HE WAS GOING TO DO THIS.

Don't worry about it.

Gwen, Mood, and Josh peered in behind him, and I tried to untangle myself from Shade with as much dignity as I could. Thank heavens we were both still clothed. Before anyone could say anything, I went on the offensive. "What do you want?" I asked Dan.

"I came over to see my sister, and I find her place filled with . . . " He fought for words and finally said," . . . your *friends*." He gestured, looking disgusted at finding Shade in my bed in all his swirly glory.

Well, I was beyond feeling embarrassed and heading straight for totally pissed. "Demons, you mean. Gwen knows what they are."

"She *what*? She shouldn't know a damned thing about them."

"Why not?" I challenged. "You told her about vampires and me—without my knowledge or consent, by the way."

"That's different. She lives with you—she had a right to know."

"Yes, she did, just as she has the right to know my friends are demons as well. Are you saying I can't have my friends over to my own place?"

Dan gaped at me, not knowing what to say.

Gwen touched his arm. "She's right, Dan. And she brought them only because Shade really needed my help. He was injured."

"Just like Nicole," I added. "But he couldn't go to the hospital the way she could, so I had to get some help for him."

"But why my sister?"

"Because last time I looked she had way more medical training than anyone else I know. And she's a kind and generous person." *Unlike someone else I could name.* "And though Shade can heal others, he can't heal himself. Remember that, Dan?" I pressed. "Maybe you should take a moment to recall how this demon healed you when you really needed it."

Dan relaxed a little and ran a hand over his face. "You're right. Shade deserves treatment just as much as anyone else. And I understand why you brought him here, to Gwen. I'd probably do the same thing in your shoes."

Whoa. That was quite a concession. I glanced at Mood to see if she was controlling him, but she shook her head. I guess Dan could be reasonable.

"But that doesn't mean I like it," he added.

"You don't have to," Gwen said, looking mulish. "I'm a big girl now and I can make decisions for myself. You don't have to play the protective big brother all the time, you know."

Dan spread his hands helplessly. "I can't help it. It's what I do."

Gwen laughed. "I know."

I did, too. It was what had made me fall for him in the first place—his hero complex. Unfortunately, it was also what made him so frustrating to deal with sometimes. Especially when it came to women. Speaking of that . . . "How's Nicole?"

He sighed. "She's very lucky she wasn't hurt worse. She's out of danger now." He glanced at Shade. "She said you tried to protect her, to push her out of the way. You probably saved her life."

Shade shrugged, his expression inscrutably swirly now that no one was touching him. "You would have done the same."

All too true.

Dan shrugged. "Thanks just the same."

Gwen patted Dan's shoulder. "You're tired and not thinking

straight. Why don't you go home and get some sleep? We'll talk tomorrow."

"Okay, good idea." Dan glanced around him once more at all the demons in Gwen's townhouse—and in my bedroom, specifically. He started to say something, then shook his head and left.

The tension dissipated. Mood grasped Shade's hand and led him and Josh back into the kitchen.

I glanced at Gwen to see how she was taking the whole scene.

She looked concerned . . . for me. "I'll talk to Dan later, let him know he was being a jerk." She cocked her head. "This attitude of his isn't really directed at you, you know. He gets all big brotherly overprotective when he thinks I'm in danger."

Or when Nicole has been hurt, apparently. I nodded, not really caring at the moment. I didn't want to think or worry about any of this anymore. Remembering something Gwen had said before, I asked, "Didn't you mention something yesterday about going shopping with me?"

She perked up. "I did. And I have the day off. Want to go?"

"Sure. But I need to shower and change first."

SHOPPING? Fang said incredulously. WE HAVE A THIEF TO CATCH AND YOU'RE GOING *SHOPPING*?

Yep. I guess you missed the part where Josh said Andrew hangs out at the Rivercenter Mall?

OH, Fang said, sounding impressed. WELL, AREN'T *YOU* THE CLEVER GIRL?

Why, yes, I thought at him, not bothering to hide my smugness. I was riding the crest of Shade's appreciation for me, even if Lola was part of it. *And don't you forget it, either.*

Chapter Eleven

Gwen offered to drive, and as I got in her car, she said, "I'm guessing you want to go to the Rivercenter Mall?"

Busted. I shot her a guilty look. "I forget how smart you are."

She laughed. "No, I'm not, but I do know how Dan thinks when he's working a case. I figure you aren't too much different." She pulled out of the parking spot. "But you have to promise me one thing."

"What?"

"If you can't find Andrew, you'll still spend time really shopping."

"Okay. That actually sounds fun."

It didn't take too long to get to Rivercenter. Located downtown on the River Walk, the four-story, glass-walled mall was nestled between a couple of high-end hotels, including the historic Menger. The glass could have made it look cold and modern, but it didn't. That's because one arm of the San Antonio River dead-ended inside the mall. Surrounded by the food court, with plants and brightly colored umbrellas outside, the area looked comfy and inviting.

If Andrew was hanging out somewhere in the mall, it was probably there, the most popular social spot. We cruised the area but didn't see the redheaded fire demon. I did, however, spot someone who looked familiar—the green-haired girl I'd met at Micah's party. She was chatting with some friends, so I steered Gwen in that direction.

I walked by and pretended I'd just recognized her. "Oh, hi. Shawndra, right? I'm Val. We met at Micah's party."

She smiled and nodded, but cast nervous glances at her companions—they must be fully human and not aware that Shawndra wasn't. I wasn't in a mood to be too sympathetic. "Say, Shawndra, have you seen Andrew? I heard he hangs out here."

She shook her head. "Haven't seen him in days."

"Do you know where he might be?"

"No. He's been kind of weird ever since his sister died. Can't blame him, y'know?"

I nodded. "Well, Micah's looking for him, so if you see Andrew or know where he might be, let Micah know."

"Okay," she said, but wouldn't meet my eyes.

She knew something, but I couldn't press the issue here and now.

"Thanks." Gwen and I had only gone a few feet when Shawndra caught up to us.

She leaned in close and lowered her voice. "Tell Micah that Veronica and her boyfriend got kinda cozy with the vamps toward the end. Andrew wasn't very happy about it."

That made sense. "Thanks. Do you know—"

"Sorry, gotta go," she said and scooted off before I could question her more.

I started to follow her, but Gwen stopped me with a hand on my arm. "Not a good time," she murmured.

Yeah, I knew that. But it was frustrating to get information in little bits and pieces like this. What did this mean? Was it even important?

Gwen put an arm around my waist. "Okay, Val. Job over. Time to have fun. You promised."

I thought about protesting, but she was right—I had promised. "Okay." Besides, the next obvious step was to talk to Alejandro again, and he wouldn't be available until the sun went down. I did text Micah, though, to let him know what little I'd learned. I grinned at Gwen. "Let's go shopping."

"Great. First stop, Macy's." As we headed upstairs, Gwen said, "Let's not worry about what styles are called and just figure out what you like. First, what kind of feeling do you want in your bedroom?"

"I'm not sure what you mean."

"Well, what do you want to feel when you're in there? Warm and comfortable? Cool and relaxed? Or hot and sexy?"

"Definitely *not* hot and sexy." Lola didn't need any encouragement.

"Okay, then how *do* you want to feel when you're at home alone in your room? Think about it for a few minutes."

I didn't realize choosing a style and colors would be so complicated. "I don't know ... I guess I want ... a sanctuary. Somewhere quiet and relaxing where I can go and just chill."

"Okay, what do you find calm and relaxing? What kind of place?"

That was easy. "The River Walk." It's where I went to unwind.

"Good." She beamed at me. "Now we're getting somewhere." She pulled me toward the bedding department and helped me figure out what I liked and didn't like. Nothing seemed quite right, though, until Gwen said, "I think I found something you might like. It's on sale, too." She pulled out a duvet cover in a beautiful shade of silvery grayish blue with a cracked pattern of a lighter ice blue. Very soothing. I loved it and could definitely imagine myself relaxing under its palette of watery colors.

We paired it with chocolate brown and soon had pillows, curtains, and a rug that matched. I couldn't wait to get home and put it all together. "A chic, sophisticated look," Gwen called it.

Me, sophisticated? Who knew?

I checked out and gulped at the final total. But I hadn't spent much of my salary since Ramirez had hired me for the San Antonio P.D., so my checking account could handle it. Gwen and I loaded up with the bags of my purchases and, feeling like a pack mule, I said, "Thanks for your help with this. I appreciate it."

"No problem. Once we get your bedroom decorated, we'll work on your clothes."

I didn't trust that gleam in her eye. I glanced down at my jeans and sweatshirt. "What's wrong—"

"Val!" someone yelled.

I glanced around and saw my perky, blond, half-sister hurrying toward me, beaming. "Val, you're *shopping*," Jennifer said, as if it were an earth-shattering event.

As she almost strangled me with a hug, and her ponytail whacked me in the face, I said, "Yeah, Gwen talked me into it."

Behind Jen, I heard an exasperated, "Jennifer, I told you not to run through the mall like that." It was Mom, and she came to an abrupt halt when she saw me. Surprise and chagrin crossed her face, then she came forward more slowly. "Hello, Val." There was a lot less tension in her face than I was accustomed to. Had kicking me out made her happier?

"Hi, Mom." My pleasure in seeing my sister—back to normal after the recent events, in which Lily had held her hostage at Alejandro's house—dimmed. Gwen nudged me. Oh yeah, introductions. "This is my roommate, Gwen, Dan's sister. Gwen, this is my little sister, Jen, and my mom, Sharon."

They all made polite noises and Jen said brightly, "What are you shopping for? Christmas? Are all those bags yours?"

"All just for me," I said, feeling selfish. Mom and Jen always shopped early for the holidays, but I was the last-minute type. "Gwen was helping pick out some things to decorate my room. It's kind of boring and blah."

"Cool," Jen said. She peered inside the largest bag. "Oh, sweet. Aren't these colors sweet, Mom?"

Jen was trying a little too hard, but I appreciated the effort.

Mom dutifully looked in the bag. "Yes, very nice," she said. But what I heard in her tone was, *I'm only being polite to please my real daughter.*

Strange how Mom could make me feel like a kid, and unwanted, again, all with a few simple words. Wait—she could only make me feel that way if I let her. And I was determined not to let her. I had a place of my own now . . . a job, friends. I didn't need her anymore.

"We were just going to go to lunch," Jen said brightly. "Why don't you join us?"

Crap. Eating lunch with a churning stomach didn't sound like fun. I glanced at Mom.

She smiled politely and said, "Yes, why don't you?"

Well, at least she was trying to be pleasant. Guess if she was making the effort, I could, too. Otherwise, I wouldn't get to see Jen or Rick much. I glanced at Gwen. She knew my history, and though she looked sympathetic, she was obviously leaving the choice up to me.

"Okay," I said. "Where do you want to go?"

We decided to eat at Chili's, and headed in that direction. Jen, thinking she was being subtle, drew Gwen slightly ahead, babbling away and asking her questions.

"How have you been?" Mom asked in a carefully neutral tone.

Just as cautiously, I said, "Fine. I have a great job, great friends."

"I knew you'd land on your feet."

She did? She really thought I'd be okay? Well, that was a small consolation for her kicking me out of the house. Very small. "Uh, how about you and Rick?"

"Fine. We're doing fine."

Sheesh, could this be any more awkward? "And Jen? Is she doing better now?" No longer trying to be like me, no longer scaring the heck out of her parents by consorting with vampires?

"Yes. And you?" Mom asked tightly. "Are you learning to control your . . . self better?"

What had happened to make her sound all pissed off again? Her gaze darted toward a group of guys up ahead. They were watching us, laughing too loud, and strutting.

Oh. Mom thought my inner demon had caused this masculine showmanship. But after feeding on Shade this morning, Lola had no interest in a bunch of young idiots. At first I was a bit ticked that Mom automatically assumed I was to blame, then realized she had no reason to believe differently. Sighing, I said, "Stop here a minute."

"Why?" But she did as I asked. Gwen and Jen kept on going.

The heads of the ratty pack swiveled away from me. They ogled Gwen and Jen instead.

"See, I'm not the only one who can generate lust." Gwen and Jen could do that all on their own, no succubus required.

Mom nodded. "I see." As we started walking again, she added softly, "I'm sorry for making an assumption."

Whoa. Mom, apologizing? *That* was a first. Maybe we could actually have a civil conversation? I nodded to accept her apology, and we proceeded in silence to Chili's.

Once we got there, Jen did most of the talking over lunch, asking me about my decorating, grilling Gwen about her job, and raving about some Christmas dance she had coming up next month and the dress she'd bought for it. Everyone was very polite and careful not to mention anything remotely weird. All very normal.

Stepford Wife normal, anyway. It may have looked ordinary from the outside, but inside, it felt rather surreal, like I was caught in one of those old Nick At Night *Brady Bunch* reruns. Only Marsha never had to stake a vampire or battle her inner succubus. As I pushed my half-eaten burger and fries around the plate, I wondered if maybe Mom and Jen thought that if they didn't mention my world, it would cease to exist. *Good luck with that.*

A worse thought occurred to me. Maybe they were avoiding the topic because they were ashamed of me, of my job with the SCU. After all, it had almost gotten Jen killed.

Nope, wrong. Jen had almost gotten *herself* killed by being stupid enough to hang around vampires when she wasn't equipped to deal with them. But Mom probably blamed me. I felt an urge to poke at the sore spot to see what would happen. Sure, it might open the wound wider, but I needed to know how they really felt.

When we were all finished eating, Gwen excused herself to use the restroom. Once she was gone, I blurted out, "Gwen knows what I am."

Silence fell, and Mom looked uncomfortable.

"We figured," Jen said.

Okay, so that wasn't why they were avoiding the topic. "Any ill effects from Lily's control of you?" I asked Jen.

Mom winced but Jennifer shook her head, her blond ponytail bouncing. "Not a one. Of course, I'm smart enough not to do *that* again."

Yeah, avoiding vampires was probably best all around. For people like her, anyway . . . normal people. "I hope so," I said, grinning. Jen was still her old self and didn't seem to have changed around me at all. Maybe she was being discreet, for Mom's sake.

"So, what are you doing with your free time these days?" I asked Jen. In other words, how much of a leash did Mom and Rick keep on her?

Jen shrugged. "Oh, you know. Just school stuff and working at the store."

A pretty tight leash, then. "Is Rick running the store all alone today?" They usually liked to have two people there.

"No." Jen grimaced. "The dark and broody one is there with him."

I raised my eyebrows. "Who?"

"You know," she said. "A de—" She broke off and cast a guilty glance around the restaurant. "I mean, someone like you."

Oh, that's right. Rick had mentioned that Mom had relented enough to let him hire a part-demon, in thanks for what Micah's people had done to help free Jen and Rick from Lily. "I assume he has a name?" I asked.

"Joshua," Mom said. "Do you know him?"

Hmm, not what I'd expected. Sounded to me like Andrew. "I know a Josh, but I don't think of him as all that broody." Introspective, maybe. Quiet. If it was the same guy, Jen and I must see people differently.

"Sheesh," Jen said. "All he does is mope around, and when he doesn't act like the end of the world is coming any moment, he looks angry at everyone."

"He's polite to the customers," Mom said, defending him.

Jen rolled her eyes. I gathered he wasn't all that friendly to *her*. Maybe her vanity was hurt. Or not. My little sister wasn't exactly the self-absorbed type. "Might be a different Josh," I said. It wasn't an uncommon name.

"Probably," Jen said wryly. "If you knew this one, you'd probably throw him to the vamps the first time he opened his mouth."

"Jennifer," Mom said, low and tight as she glanced around the restaurant. "Don't say that word."

What word? Oh . . . vamps.

Jen cast her eyes down. "Sorry, I wasn't thinking."

Gwen came back then and sat down, looking surprised at the tension at the table.

"It's okay," I told my little sister. "After all, they're coming out of the closet, so many people know about them."

Mom compressed her lips together but didn't say anything. Perversely wanting her to say what she was really thinking, I deliberately brought up the subject everyone at the table had been avoiding. "I'm doing much better at controlling my inner demon, Mom. Micah is helping me." So was Shade, of course, but I decided not to explain exactly *how* he was helping me.

My mother opened her mouth as if she wanted to say something, then glanced at Gwen and shut it again. Ah, it must be the stranger's presence that was causing her to be so polite. Persisting, I said, "But I do have a question. Did Rick ask you about my father's background?"

"No. What about him?" she asked, squirming. Obviously, it wasn't something Mom liked to talk about.

"Do you know if he has some other kind of demon in his gene pool?"

Startled, she asked, "Like what?"

"I don't know. Something strong, that heals quickly and is super fast." *Something like me.*

"No. Aren't those skills . . . part of what you are?"

"Not so far as Micah knows. Did my father have these abilities?" She ought to know—she'd lived with him for a year or so, before the divorce.

Mom frowned, thinking. "Not that I recall."

"Then where did I get them?" I asked softly. A sudden thought occurred to me. "Do you have any demons in your side of the family, maybe way back, like a great-great grandfather or something?" Maybe it was dormant in her and Jen and came out in me because of Lola.

Mom looked appalled. "Of course not. There's nothing like *that* in my family at all."

Ouch. "Nothing except me," I reminded her. "Or did you forget I'm part of your family, too?"

"Mom didn't mean it that way," Jen protested.

For some reason, it ticked me off that she defended Mom. Gwen looked decidedly uncomfortable. I felt a little bad about that, but heck, she was part of a family. She knew what family baggage was like. I let loose. "The hell she didn't."

"I didn't," Mom confirmed. "I didn't mean to—"

"You never mean to," I snapped back. "Yet you always manage to treat me like I'm a total stranger, a freak, not a real member of the family." Why the heck were my eyes suddenly stinging, anyway?

Mom covered my hand with hers. "Val, I'm sorry. There's some truth in what you say."

"I know," I muttered as I pulled back my hand and wiped at my eyes.

"But you have to understand I've managed your . . . situation . . . in a way I thought was best for everyone."

I closed my eyes, blocking out the view of everyone's expressions—Mom's earnest, Jen's anxious, and Gwen's compassionate. I sought for that calm quiet place deep inside me, but it was elusive today, too obscured by the emotions roiling inside me.

One side of me said, "Mom's really trying." But the other side retorted, "Yeah, but it's easy for her, now that she's gotten me out of her house."

The question was, what did *I* want? : That was easy—I wanted to do my job; meaning find the person who'd stolen the *Encyclopedia Magicka* and, apparently, was using its spells to turn San Antonio's most peaceful vampires into raving killers; find out what other kind of demon was inside me; and be at peace with my family, and myself.

I was still working on the first one, and nowhere near accomplishing the second. However, I realized my question about Mom's side of the family was off-base. If Mom and Jen had been part-demon, Fang would have been able to read their minds. So that wasn't the answer.

As for the third, I guessed if Mom could try to mend our relationship, so could I.

"Are you okay, Val?" Jen asked tentatively.

No. I was frustrated and a bit confused. But I opened my eyes. "Just peachy. Let's change the subject."

"You're still going to come for Thanksgiving, aren't you?" she pressed.

Mom's expression was neutral once more, so I couldn't tell how she felt. Did I really want to go, knowing it wouldn't be anything but tense, knowing I'd feel like an outsider in my former home? "I'm not sure," I hedged.

"Please come," Mom said. "It'll be like old times. When you were a kid. We'll eat too much, Rick will watch football, and we'll play games until we fall asleep."

It sounded good, but I doubted it could ever be that way again. "Can I bring Fang?" If I was going to endure this Thanksgiving, I at least wanted to have my best friend there.

"Sure," Jen said brightly. "I'll lock the cat up in my room while he's there."

"Okay, then, I'll come."

"Great," Mom said. "Bring anyone you like. In fact, why don't you invite Dan?"

I looked toward Gwen for help, but she slid her gaze back to me, tossing the conversational ball into my court.

I sighed. "Dan's just my partner at work, Mom, nothing else. And we're not even *that*, anymore."

"Oh." Mom looked surprised. "I thought you and he . . . " She trailed off, apparently unsure how to finish that sentence.

I couldn't let her think I'd been dumped and was all hurt and everything. "No, I'm kinda seeing someone else." Though "seeing" might be the wrong word when referring to Shade. I cast a glance at Gwen, silently hoping she'd back me on this.

"Really?" Jen asked eagerly. "Who?"

"His name's Shade. You haven't met him."

Mom smiled politely. "Then please bring him."

Sheesh, if they thought I was freaky, how would they react to Shade? "I don't know, Mom. He's a member of the Underground, too."

"I assumed that."

Jen bounced a little in her chair. "Promise you'll invite him, Val. I want to meet him."

Gwen nodded, like she was actually encouraging this madness.

Ooookay. It looked like I was the only one who saw the potential for a disastrous Shapiro family holiday. I took a deep breath. "Okay, I'll ask." After all, attending Thanksgiving dinner with my family and Shade had to be easier than our most recent family get-together, where I'd infiltrated a vampire's lair and beheaded a rogue bloodsucker to save the life of everyone I loved, right? Right?

Chapter Twelve

After lunch, Gwen and I gathered up all my shopping bags and said our goodbyes. Once Mom and Jen were out of sight, I muttered, "Good grief, can you really imagine Shade at the same table as my mother? She'll freak."

Gwen smiled. "I don't think you give her enough credit. She's trying."

Maybe. "But Shade and I aren't really dating." I'd made that up to keep from sounding like a loser.

"You will be soon," Gwen said with a grin. "Besides, with Shade and Fang both there, two friends will have your back."

"Good point." And if I put it that way to Shade, I wouldn't have to deal with the whole they-think-you're-my-boyfriend thing, either. "I'll play it by ear."

Gwen and I wandered the mall again then swung back through the food court, but still didn't see Andrew. His suspicious behavior made me think more and more that he *was* the thief. If he was using the magick to poison vampires, I had to find him before he got more innocent bystanders killed. I kept thinking of Brittany.

When we got home, we found a whole pack of demons waiting for us—Mood and Josh, plus Micah and three demons I didn't know. Josh looked as calm as always. But . . . why did it take so many people to stay with Shade? One would do it.

MICAH CAME TO SEE YOU, Fang said. THE REST ARE HOPING FOR LUNCH—I CAN HEAR THEIR STOMACHS GRUMBLING. BUNCHA MOOCHES.

Princess looked indignant. I AM NOT A MOOCH.

OF COURSE NOT, SWEET THING, Fang assured her. I WAS TALKING ABOUT THE HUMAN DEMONS, NOT US CANINES.

I grinned at Gwen. "I think your reputation as a cook has

preceded you. But you don't have to feed this hungry crowd, you know."

They all protested and Gwen laughed, dropping the rest of my shopping bags at the front door. "No problem. I can whip something up in a hurry."

Micah shook his head ruefully. "Now I understand why everyone was so eager to see Shade. Looks like I'll have to give you more money for groceries." He smiled. "And I guess I'll need to taste your cooking, too."

Demons tended to crave the sensual pleasures, including good food. No surprise.

"You shouldn't have to pay for everything," I protested. "Let them earn it. I'll put them to work."

The group seemed willing to help, so I asked them to decorate my bedroom, under Mood's direction, while Gwen cooked. Though Princess insisted she wasn't a *mooch*, she chose to stay in the kitchen, sneaking scraps.

I drew Micah and Shade into the living room, and Fang followed. Now that no one was touching him, Shade turned all swirly again. I felt a little shy about touching him after what had happened earlier in the bedroom, but people had been touching him all day, to keep him grounded. He wouldn't think I was coming on to him or anything, would he? But how would Lola react? Would she try to suck more out of him than he was willing to give?

Fang practically rolled his eyes. JUST DO IT ALREADY.

Feeling my cheeks warm, I tentatively laid my hand on top of Shade's. Lola was a little interested, but she was still sated, so she didn't try to attack him or anything. Relieved, I asked, "How are you doing? Feeling better?"

"Yes, much better. But . . . it's probably a good idea for you to keep touching me. Just in case."

I looked away. "Uh, are you still blitzing in and out?"

"I don't know. People won't stop touching me long enough to find out."

"Well, let's try it." I took my hand away and we watched him for a few moments. So far, so good.

Micah glanced at me. "Even if he *is* better, we need to keep using him as an excuse to invite demons here to help take care of him, until we've questioned everyone. Your roommate's reputation as a chef will help that along. Our kind can't resist great food."

I chuckled. "If your wallet can take it."

"Don't worry about that. I'm more concerned about finding the *Encyclopedia Magicka*."

Lowering my voice, I said, "I didn't have any luck tracking Andrew today. How about you?"

Micah shook his head. "Not yet. But I haven't stopped looking, and I've put the word out. *Someone* has to know where he is."

Shade's features flickered in and out once again. But it wasn't as strong as before, and he had lasted longer this time—progress. "Still not totally there," I said, and laid my hand on his again.

Shade smiled wanly. "Yeah. It kind of feels like motion sickness. I think I'll lie down for awhile here on the couch."

"Good," Micah said. "And we'll continue to keep someone with you over the next few days while we question everyone. Though I still think the thief has to be one of Alejandro's people."

I shook my head. "I don't think so. I tested everyone who was there that night, and none of them took the books."

"Everyone Alejandro *said* was there," Micah corrected. "How do you know he wasn't lying?"

I didn't, really. Had I missed something? Should I have read Alejandro's mind, too?

Fang nudged me. I'M SURE YOU DID EVERYTHING YOU COULD. BUT MICAH DOESN'T WANT IT TO BE ONE OF HIS PEOPLE.

Yeah, I know. And Alejandro had offered to let me read his mind. Why would he do that if he had anything to hide?

"We need to keep testing *everyone*," I emphasized. "Maybe someone helped Andrew, or knows where he hid the books." I glanced at Fang. "Have you read these three new demons?"

YEP. VERDICT, *NOT GUILTY.*

I figured, but had to ask. I glanced at Micah. "When I was reading the vamps, I did learn something."

"What?"

"They think one of your people, maybe the whole Demon Underground, is responsible for the vamps going mad."

Micah looked bewildered. "Why?"

"Because of everyone's reaction at the social. They think you're trying to make the New Blood Movement unstable so you can prevent them from coming out on a national level. To keep the demons hidden and underground."

"That's ridiculous. We don't operate like that."

"Maybe *you* don't, but can you say that for all of your people?" I asked. "After all, Andrew did try to roast himself a bloodsucker."

Micah sighed and shook his head. "All it takes is one stupid kid to mess things up. We really need to find Andrew, make him apologize. The last thing I want is a war with the vampires."

"Well, if one of the demons did steal the books to learn their weaknesses and make them go crazy, avoiding a smackdown might be kind of difficult."

Fang snorted. KIND OF.

Micah gazed thoughtfully at me. "How do you think we can smooth this over with Alejandro?"

Startled, I asked, "Why are you asking me?"

"Because you know him better than anyone. And he respects you."

Sheesh. How'd I go from vampire slayer to vampire *buddy*?

BY BEING FAIR, Fang said. BY NOT GOING OFF HALF-COCKED AND SEEING EVERYTHING IN BLACK AND WHITE. BY NOT BEING ANDREW.

"Okay, okay. Let me think." If I were Alejandro, what would I want? "Maybe if you convince the underground to come out with them. Or find out what's causing the vamps to go crazy and find a way to stop it."

Fang spoke up. OR GIVE THEM ANDREW'S HEAD ON A PLATTER.

A little extreme, maybe. But it worked for me.

Micah frowned. "I can try to meet with them again, and ask everyone to keep an open mind, but I'm not sure that's something I want to do. As for helping them to find out what's causing their problem, how could I do that?"

FIND THE BOOKS, Fang suggested.

Micah glared at him. "That's assuming one of my people has stolen them and is using them to injure Alejandro's people."

WELL, IT KIND OF LOOKS THAT WAY, DOESN'T IT? Fang retorted. AND IF YOU WEREN'T BEING SUCH AN OSTRICH, YOU'D GET YOUR HEAD OUT OF THE SAND AND SEE IT, TOO.

I grinned to myself, glad to see I wasn't the only one to catch the sharp side of Fang's tongue.

"All right," Micah said. "I'll keep an open mind. Let's say that's true. Let's say one of my people is trying to injure the vamps. What could he or she be doing? And how?"

"Blood," Shade said from where he was lying on the couch.

We looked down at him in surprise. I'd almost forgotten he was there.

"It's in the blood somehow," he explained.

I nodded. "Probably. But shouldn't we figure out what's in it first, then how they got it in there?"

Micah nodded. "But what could it be?"

I shrugged. "Well, the only way I know to hurt them but not kill them is with holy water or silver."

"That could be it," Micah said. "Maybe someone injected holy water or silver nitrate into the blood . . . and the pain made them crazy."

"That's possible," I conceded. "You might be able to test for silver nitrate, but how about holy water?"

"The volume of water in the blood sample might show that. We'll figure something out." Sounding more excited now, Micah asked, "Do you think you could get some of the blood from the banks where the two incidents occurred? We have a lab technician who can test the samples for us."

"I'll try." But I wasn't sure how Alejandro would take such a request. He might be a bit touchy after everything that had happened.

"Good."

The demons trooped back in then and insisted I come look at my bedroom. Cool. Since I didn't have to put it together, I'd have the surprise of seeing my bedroom completely done.

They all followed me to the bedroom and when I stepped in, my mouth dropped open. It didn't look like the same room at all. The icy blue and chocolate brown looked fabulous together. Very soothing and inviting. "Wow. You even moved the furniture."

"Yes," Mood said, beaming. "Don't you think it makes the room look bigger?"

"Yeah, it does. You're a genius." I looked at Fang. "What do you think?"

WHAT DO I LOOK LIKE, A DECORATOR? But he added, I'M COLOR BLIND. PARTIALLY, ANYWAY.

"You have to live here, too," I reminded him. "So I want to know what you think."

He jumped up on the bed, pawed at the spread, then turned around three times before he laid down. SOFT. I LIKE.

"He approves," I said, laughing.

"Great," Mood said, and I'd never seen the Emo girl look so . . .

un-Emo. "Now all you need is a few accessories in brown and blue, maybe a little silver. And what do you think about putting a headboard on the bed, maybe painting the walls a nice shade of—"

"Whoa, whoa," I said, putting out my hands to stop the words gushing from her mouth. "Give me some time to get used to this, first. I'm not sure my bank account can afford too much more this month."

Mood stuck her hands in her pockets and hunched her shoulders up to her ears in an apologetic shrug. "Sorry. I guess I got carried away."

"Oh, no," I assured her. "I want to hear your ideas."

Micah looked bemused. "I had no idea you were knowledgeable about decorating, Mood."

She shrugged. "I watch HGTV."

"Me, too," Gwen said from somewhere behind her. "Don't you love all their ideas?" As Mood enthusiastically agreed, Gwen poked her head in further. "Wow, the room does look great. And I agree with everything Mood said."

I laughed. "Well, good. You two can be my own personal decorators."

"You've got a deal," Mood said.

Gwen nodded. "But right now, I'm everyone else's personal chef. You guys hungry?"

They all were, of course, so Gwen fed them quesadillas with homemade salsa and guacamole, even fixing plates for Fang and Princess. I hadn't eaten much of my lunch, so I ate, too. Over the food, I casually brought up the subject of Andrew's whereabouts.

Mood glanced at Micah apprehensively. "Why are you looking for him?"

"Nothing bad," the Demon Underground leader assured them. "I just want to help him get his demon under control so he doesn't hurt anyone. You heard about the incident at the blood bank?"

They all exchanged glances and nodded.

"Well, he was obviously out of control. I want to help him find it again so he doesn't hurt himself or anyone else."

Gwen looked apprehensive. "How do you control a fire demon?"

Good question.

"With another demon," Micah explained. "We can usually find a way to contain someone who has gone rogue, without hurting them."

"And if you can't?" Gwen persisted. "What happens then? I see enough people in the ER as it is."

"Then he becomes just like a bad vampire," Shade said softly. "He's a menace to society, and to us."

"You mean you'd turn him over to the SCU?" Gwen asked.

"If we have to," Micah said. He glanced at me. "I doubt it'll come to that."

YEAH, Fang agreed. MICAH WILL PROBABLY USE YOU AS HIS OWN PRIVATE ENFORCER.

Made sense. And I had absolutely no problem with that.

The others looked appalled.

"Think about it," Micah urged. "If someone is that blatantly using their powers, harming normals, what would that do to us?"

"It would put us in danger, too," Shade said. "Jeopardize everything the Underground has been working toward."

HOO, BOY, Fang chimed in, obviously talking to all the demons at the table. TALK ABOUT A WITCH HUNT.

The others nodded slowly. Mood spoke up. "Well, I don't think Andrew is out of control, but I also don't know where he is. We've been looking for him, too."

Another guy put in, "Yeah. We've looked everywhere he normally hangs out."

The doorbell rang and Mood glanced at her watch. "It's not the next shift. They're not due for another hour."

I laughed. "Maybe they came early to check out Gwen's cooking. I'll get it."

But when I opened the door, my mouth dropped open. Andrew. All by himself, looking surly and defensive.

"Can I come in?" he asked.

"Of course." But now I was totally confused.

Fang snorted. YOU AIN'T THE ONLY ONE, BABE.

He followed me into the kitchen, and everyone looked as shocked as I felt. Gwen, wisely, made herself scarce.

"I hear you're looking for me," Andrew said, crossing his arms defiantly across his chest.

"I was," Micah confirmed. "Won't you sit down?"

"Naw. I'll stand."

"Would you rather speak in private?" Micah asked quietly.

Andrew snorted. "Nothing stays private around here for long."

Especially with Fang and Princess around.

HEY, the hellhound protested. YOU AND MICAH TOLD ME TO SNOOP. Princess didn't deign to respond.

I know. Sorry.

"All right, then," Micah said soothingly. "Why don't you tell me what happened at the blood bank?"

Andrew gestured curtly at me. "Didn't *she* tell you?"

"Yes, but I want to hear your side of the story."

Andrew sighed and dropped sullenly into a chair, the one Gwen had vacated. "It wasn't my fault. I was there, doing my watcher thing like you told me. I was keeping my cool, checking everything out and not bothering anyone, then this bloodsucker came up and called me a spy."

"Well, you were," I reminded him.

Fang shoved me with his shoulder. MICAH SAID TO TELL YOU YOU'RE NOT HELPING.

I shrugged an apology at Micah. *Tell Micah to ask Andrew about the blood poisoning and the books.*

DON'T WORRY. HE'LL GET TO IT.

"Yeah, I was spying," Andrew said. "But he didn't have to be such an a-hole about it. He really got in my face."

"Did he have a reason for it beyond the spying? Say, a threat to his blood supply?"

"Like how?" Andrew asked, confused.

NO CLUE ABOUT THE POISONING, Fang confirmed.

"Never mind," Micah said. "So what did you do?"

Andrew shrugged one shoulder. "What do you expect? I didn't want some dude breathing stale blood in my face. I shoved him away." He paused, staring down at his clasped hands. "Then he flashed his fangs at me and hit me and I . . . hit back."

Yeah, with fire.

HE'S TELLING THE TRUTH, Fang told us privately. HE WAS BLIND WITH RAGE, BECAUSE HE SOMEHOW BLAMES ALL VAMPS FOR HIS SISTER'S DEATH.

"I see," Micah said with a sigh. "We'll have to help you with your anger issues."

Andrew glared at him. "Oh, yeah, how? Is there something in that encyclopedia that tells you how to do that? I'd like to see it."

"Why?" Micah asked.

Andrew leaned forward, his gaze angry and intent . . . on me. "You've had the books all this time. Is there something there that told how to save my sister? How to keep me from dying like her?"

What? "No. I mean, I don't know." Maybe there was. I didn't

remember reading about fire demons.

"Then show me," Andrew insisted. "Show me what it says about my kind."

I spread my hands helplessly, feeling guilty. "I don't have them." I thought *Andrew* did.

NOPE, Fang said, sounding disappointed. HE DOESN'T HAVE THEM EITHER.

So that's why Andrew had come here—he wanted to read the encyclopedia himself. And that bombshell just blew all our suspicions to smithereens.

But . . . if Andrew didn't have the books, who did?

Chapter Thirteen

Andrew swiveled to glare at Micah. "Well? How about it? Can I see the books?"

"I don't have them on me," Micah said calmly. "And I'm afraid I can't loan them out to anyone until I'm certain we have a secure copy. But as soon as I learn anything about your kind, I'll let you know."

"Forget it," Andrew snarled. "I want to see them *now*."

Micah's expression turned stony. "That won't be possible."

"Why? Because there's something there you don't want me to know?"

"Of course not."

"Then prove it. Let me see them."

"I can't."

Andrew made a disgusted sound. "You mean you won't."

"Why can't he see them?" Mood asked, looking puzzled.

Micah squirmed. But before he could come up with another excuse, Princess said, BECAUSE THEY WERE STOLEN THE NIGHT OF THE PARTY. NOW GO AWAY. YOU ARE ANNOYING ME.

Everyone bent down to stare at the spaniel under the table. "That was supposed to be a secret," Shade said gently.

Princess huffed and tossed her head. WHO CARES ABOUT YOUR SILLY SECRETS? Her nose in the air, she pushed past the table legs and trotted off into the other room.

Hasn't your girlfriend learned the meaning of discretion? I asked Fang silently.

He somehow managed to look embarrassed. NOT REALLY. SHE'S A CUTIE, BUT NOT EXACTLY THE BRIGHTEST POOCH IN THE PACK. AND SHE HASN'T INTERACTED THAT MUCH WITH HUMANS, EITHER.

Plus she was a tad self-centered, but I decided not to mention that part.

Questions erupted around the table, and Micah held his hands up, looking annoyed. "All right, yes, they were stolen, but we're trying to find the thief. I wanted to keep it quiet until we found the books. Can I count on all of you to keep this to yourselves until we find him or her?"

Most everyone around the table nodded, but Andrew still looked ready to blow. "It was probably one of those bloodsuckers. They were there that night."

"We are questioning everyone who was there," Micah assured him. "But we were trying to do it discreetly."

Andrew's eyes narrowed. "Is that why you wanted to find me? You think I stole the books? I can't believe this." And before anyone could stop him, he threw his chair back and stormed out the door.

WELL, SO MUCH FOR GETTING HIM TO APOLOGIZE TO THE VAMPS, Fang said.

Not that I'd held out much hope for that, anyway.

Everyone else looked accusingly at Micah.

"He doesn't suspect any of his people," I assured them. "But I read the minds of the vamps who were there and cleared all of them, so I insisted we cover all the bases by checking all of you, too." Let them blame me instead of their leader.

"Well, I didn't do it," Mood said.

Micah smiled at her. "We know. We've cleared everyone here. But we haven't talked to the rest of the people at the party yet."

"I can't believe it was one of us," Mood said. "We have so much to gain by letting you maintain control of the books. Maybe it was someone else, someone who wasn't at the party but snuck into the office and took them."

"But how would they know I had them and was planning on bringing them that night?" I asked. "I didn't tell anyone except Micah and Fang."

They all looked at Fang.

He snorted. YEAH, RIGHT. WHAT WOULD I DO WITH BOOKS I CAN'T EVEN READ? BESIDES, ONE OTHER PERSON KNEW—TESSA. SHE HID THE BOOKS, REMEMBER?

They all thought for a moment. "Tessa?" one of the guys said. "No way."

"Why would she?" Micah asked. "She knew she'd have access to them from me."

Yeah, I couldn't see Tessa as any kind of thief. "No one else knew they were there."

Mood thought for a moment. "Maybe the books put off some kind of magick signature or something, that someone could follow."

I shook my head. "One that only activated when I brought them to the club? Doesn't make sense."

Mood shrugged. "Just trying to figure out how they could have gone missing. They didn't steal themselves. Or, at least, I assume they didn't."

Hey, with magick, who knew? "I'm betting on a person taking them," I said with a smile.

"But *why* would someone steal them?" Mood asked. "And why are you keeping it a secret?"

Micah sighed. "Because we suspect something the thief read in the book may be responsible for the vampires going mad and killing people."

Josh looked confused. "Vampires need a reason to kill people?"

"These ones do," I insisted. "The New Blood Movement is trying too hard to convince humans they're harmless. They wouldn't deliberately kill anyone unless they were driven insane."

"What about the other vamps?" Shade asked. "They'd have reason—they hate the Movement. And none of the independent ones have been affected."

Micah nodded slowly. "A good point. But again, how would they know the books were there?"

Josh shrugged. "Cell phone. One of the other vamps called them and told them after the announcement."

"That's possible," I conceded. "Anyone at the party could have called someone else . . . vampire, demon, or human."

Crap. That also widened my pool of suspects exponentially. Well, if I was going to spend all my time tracking down the thief, maybe some of them could help with the rest of it. "Okay, let's assume a bad vamp somehow found out about the books and took them." Especially since I could tell they really liked that idea. "I'll check that out, but we have another problem. The Movement blames us for their people going bonkers."

Micah held up his hands to halt the protests and counter-accusations. "We really need to keep on their good side."

"Why?" Josh demanded as Mood shook her head.

"Because we want to convince them not to come out and reveal themselves to the world. We can't do that if we're enemies. Besides, we're *not* responsible and I, for one, don't want to take the rap for it."

THEY'RE BUYING IT, Fang said with a grin.

Because it was true. I opened my mouth to explain about the blood, but Fang pushed against my leg. LET SHADE DO IT. I glanced questioningly down at the hellhound and he gave a doggie shrug. IT'LL SOUND BETTER COMING FROM HIM. THEY ALREADY ACCEPT HIM AS A PART OF THE GROUP. YOU'RE STILL . . . ON PROBATION.

Okay, that was fair.

"If we help them find the cause of the madness, they'll owe us," Shade said. He went on to explain that we assumed it was the blood they drank that caused the problem.

Theories flew about the room, but basically it came down to the same two potential causes we came up with—silver or holy water.

"Val is going to get some of the blood to test," Micah explained. "Then we'll see if we can find out who's causing this."

"But you're gonna still check out the vamps who aren't in the Movement, right?" Mood asked me. "They have to be guilty."

"Sure, I'll check them out," I said, "but I hope you're wrong."

"Why?"

"Because if the bad vamps have the books and they list the weaknesses of the demons as well, we could be in deep doo-doo."

ॐ • ॐ

I took a long nap that afternoon, knowing I was probably going to be busy all night. It was kind of nice to wake up in my newly decorated bedroom with Fang snuggled up next to me. Here, I could pretend for awhile that nothing was wrong and all was right with the world.

I scratched his ears. "Hey, you stayed with me," I said softly. "Princess losing her charms?"

He snuggled closer. NAW. BUT SOMETIMES SHE'S A BIT TOO HIGH MAINTENANCE. BESIDES, YOU NEED ME TONIGHT AND I NEEDED A LITTLE SHUT-EYE, TOO.

Good. The best way to learn where the bad vamps were hanging out was to attend the SCU briefing, and I didn't want to do it alone. I opened my bedroom door to let Fang out to use the doggie door and came face to face with Shade.

All he said was, "Hi," but to me, it sounded like a whole lot more. Like, I'm soooo glad to see you. Like, you are the hottest thing on two legs. Like, let's get naked together.

I gulped, and was *really* glad I couldn't see his expression right now. It would probably make me feel more self-conscious and dorky than I already did. As it was, I felt my face turn hot and Lola stirred, wanting to reach out and take some of that yummy goodness.

I pulled her back with an effort. "Hi," I responded, feeling oh-so cool and sophisticated. Not.

He reached out to take my hand but I pretended not to see it as I took a step back and closed the door partway. "I need to get ready for work."

"Oh. Sorry. I thought you might need to, uh, take the edge off first."

Cuddle up to Shade's hot bod, lie there with his arms around me, let our wanting and need flow back and forth between us? Sounded like heaven, but sheesh, I hadn't even brushed my teeth yet. And for some reason, the thought of using him again made me a little uneasy. "No, I'm good."

He nodded and left as Fang came trotting back in through the door. I closed it and the terrier jumped up on the bed. WHAT WAS THAT ALL ABOUT?

"Nothing. Shade just wanted to . . . you know."

SO WHY DIDN'T YOU 'YOU KNOW'? 'YOU KNOW' CAN BE GOOD FOR YOU.

I shrugged, not really wanting to discuss it with anyone of the male persuasion. But, knowing Fang would bug me until I relented, I said, "Because . . . he wants it too much."

WELL, HE IS A GUY.

"Yeah, but . . . is it me he wants, or Lola?" There, I'd said it, exposed my insecurities to ridicule.

AH, THE AGE-OLD QUESTION, Fang said, amusement in his voice. DOES HE WANT YOU FOR YOU, OR FOR YOUR BODY?

"Well, yeah."

DOES IT MATTER? Fang asked. YOU LIKE IT, HE LIKES IT. SO WHY NOT DO IT? HUMANS HAVE TO COMPLICATE EVERYTHING.

I glanced down at the terrier. "Because it *is* more complicated for humans, Fang." It wasn't just about whether I wanted to feel all hot and sexy with him again, because I did, but was Lola something he could become addicted to? How did I even feel about Shade? Was I ready to lose my virginity with him? 'Cause that was sure the way it was heading. If Lola made me want every guy who came along, how could I trust *any* of my feelings? And until I figured it out, I didn't want to commit myself to anything. Not even asking him to Thanksgiving dinner.

Not wanting to prolong this conversation either, I said, "I'm going to shower."

COWARD, Fang called after me.

"Whatever."

I got ready for work—jeans, long-sleeved T-shirt with a vest over it to hide the stakes in my back waistband—and headed out on the Valkyrie in the cool night air. Fang rode behind me in his goggles. We got to the station a little early and I didn't feel like facing the other scuzzies right away, so I took the time to call Alejandro.

After Luis made me wait for awhile, Alejandro came on the line. "Yes, Ms. Shapiro, how may I help you?"

No sense in beating around the bush. "The demons feel bad about what's happening with your people. They know you suspect them, so to prove they're innocent, they'd like to help."

"Help how?"

"By trying to find out what's causing your guys to go wacko. Unless you know already?"

"We haven't yet found the cause, no." He paused for a moment. "Help would not come amiss. What do you have in mind?"

"Well, since we all figure it's in the blood they drank at the blood bank, we wondered if we could get a sample of it. Maybe we can help you test it, find out what's causing it."

"We are doing that ourselves."

"So? It couldn't hurt to have two sets of eyes looking at it. Maybe we'd think of something you wouldn't."

Alejandro sighed. "Very well. We don't know which batches are contaminated and which are free of poison, but I shall send someone to drop off a representative sample. Where shall I send it?"

I thought for a moment. "Send it to Micah at Club Purgatory. He'll know what to do."

"I shall. The sooner we learn how the blood was poisoned, the better off we'll all be."

"You got that right."

He hung up and I breathed a heavy sigh. Time to face the scuzzies. "Ready for this?"

Fang had managed to get his goggles off by himself and bristled with action. "YEAH. ANYONE WHO WANTS TO MESS WITH YOU WILL HAVE TO COME THROUGH ME FIRST.

I laughed. "I can always count on you." We were a few minutes late, so I was able to slip in the back with only a few wary glances. Lt. Ramirez was leading the session and he nodded at me but didn't greet me by name, thank goodness. I took notes on the latest vampiric activity then darted out as soon as it was over so I wouldn't have to face any of them. *Yes, I know. I'm a coward,* I told Fang.

NAW. I CALL IT SMART.

For that, I picked Fang up and kissed him on his cute fuzzy nose.

HEY, WATCH IT, he protested. SOMEONE COULD SEE. But since he licked my nose as he said it, I didn't take him too seriously. I set him back down and we headed back to the Valkyrie.

My phone beeped—a text message from Micah. *There's a problem at the club. Can you come right away?*

Crap. What now? *On my way,* I texted back. Fang and I jumped on the bike, not even stopping to put on his goggles.

ANY IDEA WHAT'S UP? Fang asked as I took off.

"No. But it can't be good."

It seemed to take forever to get there, though it couldn't have been more than fifteen or twenty minutes. Everything out front at Club Purgatory seemed normal so I decided to go in the back through the loading dock. Ludwig was standing guard outside, his arms folded. "Micah called me," I said, before he could ask.

He nodded and opened the door. Just inside where all the deliveries were made, Micah and Kyle were holding a low, tense conversation. "What's going on?" I asked.

Micah turned to me, looking worried. "Shawndra was attacked and dumped off here on the loading dock."

"Oh, crap. Is she okay?"

"She'll be fine," Kyle assured me, though Micah looked totally pissed.

"Do you think this has something to do with the encyclopedia?" I asked.

Micah scowled. "I'm sure of it. They left a page of it in her pocket, with a message for you."

"Huh?"

Micah showed it to me. Scrawled in blood-red letters across the page was a warning: *Slayer, back off. Or else.*

Chapter Fourteen

I grabbed the encyclopedia page from Micah and scanned the text behind the handwriting. "This talks about an eco-demon. You think that means something?"

"Oh, I'm sure of it," Micah bit out. "Shawndra is an eco-demon."

"Plants and stuff? What's demonic about that?"

Fang butted in. SHE CAN EITHER MAKE PLANTS GROW . . . OR WITHER AND DIE.

Oh. "So how was she injured? Did this tell how?"

"Yes. The page tells us if it can injure plants, it can injure Shawndra. The creep dumped something toxic on her—probably weed killer—and dumped her off here, where she went into convulsions."

"Where is she now?"

"In the shower in my office," Micah said. "Tessa is helping her. She seemed to get better as soon as we got the worst of the chemicals off her. Thankfully, he only got her arm. Tessa thinks she'll be all right."

Ludwig stuck his head in the door. "Hey, there are two others who want to see you. And a delivery." He opened the door wider to show Dan and Luis standing there. Oh great. Neither one was exactly part of the Val Shapiro fan club.

"Let them in," Micah said. "Kyle, if you'd take the delivery?"

Dan and Luis came in, keeping their distance from each other. "Did Lt. Ramirez send you?" Micah asked Dan. Dan nodded, and Micah turned to me. "I sent him a message at the same time I did you, Val, before I knew how serious this incident was."

Micah turned to Luis, who was holding a cooler in one hand as if it would give him an STD or something. "How may I help you?"

Luis set the cooler on the ground and straightened his jacket, brushing invisible lint from his sleeve. "This is the package you requested from Alejandro," he said, managing to sound offended by being reduced to a lowly messenger.

"Ah, yes. Thank you. We'll see if we can help you learn anything."

Luis raised one eyebrow in disbelief, then turned to go. Kyle passed him on his way in with a small box in his hands, asking, "Where do you want the silver nitrate, boss?"

Luis spun, quick as a snake and pinned Kyle up against the wall, the vamp's arm across the demon's throat and his fangs bared. "What need have you of silver nitrate in a *bar*, demon boy?"

I whipped out a stake and shoved the pointed end against Luis's back, just enough to let him know it was poised against his heart but not enough to penetrate—yet. Though the poor dream demon had managed to keep his grip on the package, he looked terrified, unable to croak out an answer. That made me even more pissed at Luis. "Let him go, or your ass is ash, buster."

"Wait, wait," Micah said, his hands outspread in a calming motion. "The silver nitrate will be used to test the blood you gave us, to see if that's what's causing the madness. That's all." When Luis did nothing but glare at Micah, he added, "We can't test for it if we don't know what it looks like in the blood . . . and you obviously can't handle the stuff to test it yourself, can you?"

"We're on your side, asshole," I muttered. "Let go."

Somehow, my harsh words seemed to do more to convince Luis than Micah's appeasing ones. Luis let go of Kyle and backed off, his hands raised and his fangs retracted. He turned toward Micah, but stopped abruptly when he saw Dan watching him with narrowed eyes and a loaded crossbow. And Fang, of course, was snarling at him, eyes purple with demonic anger.

"Gimme a reason, bloodsucker," Dan muttered.

YEAH, JUST A LITTLE ONE, Fang begged.

Luis quirked his lips in something that was either a snarl or a contemptuous smile. "Call off your dogs."

Fang snorted with disgust, whether at Luis's lousy joke or at the cease and desist order, I wasn't sure.

"Please," Micah said to Dan and me.

I put the stake away as Dan lowered the crossbow, pale with some indefinable emotion. Kyle practically quivered with fear, but still managed to spit out, "You *ever* try to sink your fangs into my neck, bloodsucker, and you'll regret it."

"Faugh," Luis said with a look of disgust. "Demon blood. Wouldn't touch it."

"Enough, gentlemen," Micah said. "It was simply a misunderstanding. Kyle, if you wouldn't mind giving me the box . . . ?"

Kyle pretended to a bravery he didn't have to bring Micah the small package. "Thank you," Micah said. "Why don't you go see how Shawndra is doing?"

Nodding, Kyle beat feet out of there.

Micah's expression hardened. "Now, if you are done jumping to conclusions and scaring the hell out of my employees . . . ?"

Luis sneered. "If I find that you are lying about the silver nitrate, not even Alejandro's will shall keep you safe."

THEN BULLY FOR US. WE'RE TELLING THE TRUTH, Fang answered for all of us.

Luis gave Micah a curt nod and clicked his heels in what could have been a bow, if an abbreviated one, then left. The tension left with him, thank goodness.

When he was gone, Dan said, "What the hell was that all about? That wasn't why you texted Lt. Ramirez, was it?"

"No," Micah said with a sigh. "*That* was unfortunate timing. The reason I called for help is because one of my people was injured."

Dan disarmed the crossbow. "Vamp?"

Micah shrugged. "I'm not sure." He glanced at me, mimed opening a book, and cocked an eyebrow at Dan.

Evidently he wanted to know if Dan knew about the encyclopedia. I shook my head. Not that I knew of.

Dan caught the byplay. "What's going on here? What are you keeping from me?"

"None of your business," I said, still annoyed with him. "It's Micah's concern, not yours."

Micah made calming motions with his hands. "And I'll be happy to tell you what's going on. But not here. Let's go to my office and I'll explain."

There, Tessa and Kyle were hovering over a sleeping Shawndra wrapped in a robe, with wet green hair. I'd thought it was dyed, but now that I knew she was an eco-demon, I wondered if it was natural.

"How's she doing?" Micah asked softly.

"Better," Tessa said. "Once we washed the chemicals off her, she stopped convulsing. Kyle put her in dreamland, but I don't know if she needs additional medical treatment. Her skin looks burned. We can't go to a hospital . . ."

Yeah, and we couldn't call Shade. He was supposed to be

recovering. "Right." I pulled out my cell phone, looking for my roomie's cell number. "Call Gwen. She probably hasn't left for work yet." I handed Tessa my phone with Gwen's number on it.

Dan snatched my phone before Tessa could dial. "First, tell me what the hell is going on. You demons have dragged my sister into enough of your messes, don't you think?

AND YOU HAD THE HOTS FOR THIS MENTAL CASE? Fang asked me in disbelief. WHAT WERE YOU THINKING?

Well, when he wasn't all pissed and suspicious, he was pretty cute. And a great partner, besides. But right now, I could do without all the macho crap. Taking a deep calming breath, I said, "All Tessa is going to do is ask your sister how to treat Shawndra." It seemed to appease him, so I took my phone back and handed it to Tessa.

Dan's eyes narrowed. "What's wrong with her?"

"That's not important. What is important is that someone tried to harm her, deliberately. They knew what would hurt her the most, poisoned her, then dropped her here as a message."

Dan raised his eyebrow in a familiar questioning gesture.

I shrugged. "The message told me to back off. I think I'm getting too close to finding something that someone doesn't want found out."

"You going to?" he asked.

I glanced at Micah. "I don't see how I can." I had to find out who was doing this and stop them before more people were hurt.

Dan nodded as if he expected nothing less. "And what are you close to finding out?"

Heck, why not tell him? It seemed everyone else knew anyway. So, we told him about the theft of the books.

As Dan mulled it over, Tessa reported that Gwen recommended an antihistamine in case the problem was an allergic reaction and a lotion she could get at the drugstore.

After Tessa left, Dan said, "And Luis just happened to be on the scene right after the demon girl was dropped off?" He raised an eyebrow. "Convenient."

I shrugged. "A coincidence. I already cleared him."

Kyle gave Dan an odd look. "You were on the scene right after she was dropped off, too," he said, shifting his body between Dan's and the sleeping girl's.

Dan glared at the dream demon. "What are you saying? You think I'm responsible for this?"

Kyle didn't seem as afraid of the human as he'd been of the

vampire. "I'm saying we haven't cleared *you*. How do we know you didn't take the encyclopedia?"

"I wasn't even there."

"No, but someone could have told you the books were there. And you're a detective. You were probably just waiting for Val to move the books so you could grab them."

"Why would I want them?" Dan asked incredulously.

Kyle rolled his eyes. "Oh, I dunno. Maybe because you hate and fear vampires and demons and want to clean up San Antonio and make it safe for your kind?"

Dan gaped at him for a moment. He couldn't deny none of it was true. "Oh, come on. You can't believe that. It's ridiculous. Ramirez sent me. Tell him, Micah."

Micah rubbed his hand over his face. "Kyle has a point, you know. And if he thought of it, others will, too. I hadn't considered a normal human as the culprit."

"But I don't have the books," Dan protested. "How can I convince you?"

Dan was far more likely to play the hero than the villain. I shook my head. "I believe him."

Kyle shrugged. "Not exactly impartial, Slayer." And by the way he looked at Dan, I could tell he was liking the idea of Dan being the bad guy more and more.

Fang huffed. I'M NOT HATING IT, MYSELF.

Yeah, okay. I was still ticked at my former partner, but I couldn't let him take the rap for something I was sure he wouldn't do. He might stake Luis, if Luis gave him a good reason. But throw toxic material on a teenaged girl and dump her? No way. "In case you haven't heard, we're not partners anymore," I told Kyle.

"Okay, so prove his innocence like you did ours."

"I can't. I can't read his mind and Fang can't either."

Kyle looked at the dog in surprise. Oops, I probably shouldn't have revealed how we'd cleared everyone.

NAW, IT'S OKAY, Fang assured me. THEY KNEW I COULD READ THEIR MINDS, AND THEY WOULD HAVE PUT TWO AND TWO TOGETHER SOONER OR LATER.

Dan grimaced. "Don't you have someone else who can do some mumbo jumbo and prove I'm telling the truth?"

Micah looked mildly offended. "The Demon Underground is not anyone's personal magick shop. We also prize the privacy of our members. Even if we did have someone who could do 'mumbo jumbo' as you call it, I'm not sure I'd care to expose their powers to you. We prefer to keep that privileged information to ourselves." He thought for a moment. "But there is someone who could force you to tell the truth . . ." He turned to stare at me. "Someone whose powers you're already familiar with."

Oh yeah, Lola could do the trick. And she perked up at the thought of getting her hooks into Dan again. But I really didn't want to go there.

"No way," Dan blurted out, holding up both hands and backing away as if to ward me off.

METHINKS HE DOTH PROTEST TOO MUCH, Fang said wryly.

"Something to hide?" Kyle asked suspiciously.

"No. That's not it. I—"

He broke off, so I finished his sentence for him. "He doesn't want me to use my ability on him," I explained. "I have cooties."

NO, YOU HAVE POWER OVER HIM, Fang corrected me. POWER HE DOESN'T UNDERSTAND BUT SECRETLY ENJOYS. DAN HATES THAT.

So now the hellhound was an amateur psychologist?

Dan slanted me an exasperated glance. "Don't be ridiculous. But having that much control over men's minds isn't right."

NOT TO MENTION THEIR BODIES, Fang said with a leer.

I shook my head, feeling tired of the whole thing. But I knew Dan had a thing about being controlled after he was enthralled by a lustful female vamp a few weeks ago. "Don't worry, Dan, I'm not going to touch you. And neither is Lola."

"Then how is he going to prove his innocence?" Kyle persisted.

Dan looked like he was about to blow his top, but Micah made a calming motion again. "Please. Kyle has the right to ask, and I'd like to eliminate you as a suspect so we can move on. Lieutenant Ramirez would like that, too, I'm sure. Val has more control now, so the questioning would be very brief, then over."

"And I heard you owe Micah a favor," Kyle put in.

Dan glanced at me, looking torn. After a moment, he shook his head. "I do owe you a favor, but not this. I can't."

For some stupid reason, that hurt. I mean, I knew he didn't like being in Lola's clutches, but he should know by now that he could trust me, trust Micah. Guess he still thought of me as a thing . . . a monster.

WELL, SCREW HIM, Fang said.

I grinned. I could always count on Fang to be on my side. *Lola and I tried, but didn't get very far.*

Fang snorted, but luckily, the others didn't hear.

Kyle stared at Dan, his eyes narrowed. "You say you're innocent but won't do the one thing that would prove it one way or the other. Sounds like guilt to me."

Dan clenched his fists and glared down at the slight demon. "I don't need to prove myself to you."

"You do, actually," Micah said, looking suspicious now himself. "Or, rather, to the Demon Underground. With your known association with Val who had the books, your dislike of vampires and distrust of demons, plus your refusal to clear yourself, you are obviously a prime suspect." He raised his hand to stop Dan from interrupting. "You know that your lieutenant uses us to gather intelligence for him on the vampires in San Antonio. I'm afraid we might have to stop that if you are in the SCU and benefiting from any information we have to share."

I stared at him. "You can't be serious." If he threatened to cut Ramirez off, Dan might lose his job.

Micah shook his head. "I have to be, Val. I have to think of my people first."

Surprisingly, Dan seemed to understand that reasoning. "I get it, but I don't like it. I'll take some unpaid leave until you find the thief."

"I have a better idea," Micah said. "Why don't you and Val work as partners again? That way you can help find the thief and stop this damage, and Val and Fang will be able to keep an eye on you for us."

Kyle nodded. "Works for me."

Dan crossed his arms, but nodded as well. "I'll have to talk to Ramirez first, but if he agrees, it's a deal."

Well, crap. Didn't I get a vote? Why on earth would I want to take Dan on as a partner again? And what was Micah thinking? Was he trying to play matchmaker or something? This was soooo not what I wanted.

Chapter Fifteen

The next days fell into a pattern. I slept in the morning, questioned demons in the afternoon while trying to keep Shade and Lola from playing touchy-feely, and used the candle method to try to contain Lola. At night, I spent awkward times with Dan as he, Fang and I fruitlessly hunted the streets of San Antonio for misbehaving bloodsuckers. Not exactly like old times, except for the part where I had to concentrate hard to keep Lola from trying to feed on my partner.

It was a relief when Micah called and asked me to be present at a meeting with him and Alejandro. Thankfully, I let Dan attend the SCU briefing alone and arranged to meet him at my place afterward.

The vampires and demons met on neutral ground, in a hotel downtown. A really hoity toity place with a meeting room that looked like a men's club, or what I imagined a men's club to look like anyway—sleek brown leather, dark wood, shiny crystal and gold accents.

Fang paused in the doorway. SHEESH. KINDA MAKES ME FEEL GUILTY FOR SHEDDING ALL OVER IT. He shrugged and trotted in. OR NOT.

Alejandro brought two of his lieutenants with him—Luis and Austin—and Micah brought Ludwig, Fang, and me.

I LIKE THESE ODDS, Fang said. THREE OF THEM, FOUR OF US.

I grinned down at the small terrier. *Well, three and half, maybe.*

HEY, BABE, DON'T CUT YOURSELF SHORT LIKE THAT.

I shook my head. There was no way to win in a verbal contest with Fang, so I glanced around. The vamps looked at home, but the rest of us . . . not so much. It was a strange group to be facing each other across a polished cherry conference table. I glanced at the man mountain, wondering what kind of demon he was and why Micah had brought him instead of Tessa.

Probably for the same reason I figured he'd asked me to come—
to help control anything that got out of hand. Unfortunately, I was
having problems controlling myself right now. Or rather, Lola. She
remembered enthralling these three vamps before. Remembered it,
liked it, and wanted more. Keeping her under control and her hooks
out of Dan and Shade had caused me to go without feeding for far too
long. The hunger gnawed at me and Lola was constantly present,
urging me to slake her appetite with any available male. But I locked
her down tight. This was so not the time.

Alejandro steepled his fingers. In his tailored suit, crisp shirt, and
silk tie, he looked the very image of a Wall Street banker ... if it
weren't for his long flowing hair. And the fangs.

WELL, HE IS A BANKER OF SORTS, the hellhound reminded me.

Glad for the distraction, I smothered a laugh. Yeah, with a slightly
different currency.

"Thank you for meeting with us," Alejandro said. "I understand
you have been testing the blood from our banks. What did you learn?"

Micah nodded. "We have a medical technician among us who
tested the blood for water—in case it was holy water—silver nitrate,
and other foreign substances. He found nothing." He spread his
hands. "Then again, the bottles of blood you gave us didn't look as
though they'd been tampered with, so we can't be sure they were."

Alejandro's two lieutenants shifted as if they wanted to respond,
but deferred to their boss. "We sent a representative batch from both
locations where my people were poisoned. We did not find any breach
of the bottles' seal either. However, my people are also trained to
detect any tampering with the bottles. They would not have used it if
there was something wrong with the seal."

Micah leaned forward. "But people get lax, forget procedures. Are
you certain they didn't forget to check?"

"All five of them?" Alejandro countered. "I think not. And it is
beyond the bounds of reason to think that they drank the only
contaminated packages of blood in the bank. That would be too much
of a coincidence."

Micah nodded slowly. "I take it you didn't find anything in the
blood either."

"Nothing," Alejandro confirmed. "And none of our other bottles
appear to be tampered with. We tested one with ... a volunteer ...
who ended up in the same condition as the other five."

Fang snorted at my feet. WONDER WHAT THE POOR GUY DID TO

GET VOLUNTEERED.

Probably one of the vamps not in the Movement. I piped up. "Well, if the bottle didn't look like anyone messed with it, then maybe the contamination was in the human donating."

I was pretty proud of myself for that reasoning, but Luis sneered. "Did you really assume we would not think of that?"

"We did," Alejandro said with a quelling glance at Luis. "Each of our bottles is labeled with the donor's name, since some of my people have their favorite flavors."

Ew. That conjured up visions of a vampire tasting room, people lined up unconscious in glass coffins along the wall with tubes coming out of their veins and flowing into wine glasses. I suppressed a shiver. You'd never catch me donating blood.

Alejandro continued. "Since the labels were still intact on the bottles the mad ones drank, we tested a couple of donors to see if they were contaminated. They were not."

"Maybe it wasn't the blood," I suggested. "Maybe it was something else causing it."

"Such as?" Luis asked with a raised eyebrow.

"I don't know. Maybe they all visited someplace where they caught a rare disease or something."

Luis was too stuck-up to roll his eyes, but his nostrils flared in derision. "Have you never heard of Occam's Razor?"

"Huh?" Did anyone else think that was totally random?

Austin grinned at me. "Basically, it means the simplest explanation that is based on the facts is the most likely. Occam was the fourteenth century friar who came up with the idea."

Oh. Why couldn't Luis have just said that?

BECAUSE HE HAS TO FIND SOME WAY TO PRETEND HE'S SUPERIOR, Fang said. I BET HE HAS A TINY WEENIE, TOO.

Good thing I wasn't drinking anything or that would have caused an instant spit-take. As it was, I had to pretend I was coughing to cover the choking laughter. *You may be right, but I sure ain't checking his tighty whities.*

At least Fang's diversion allowed me to respond to Luis without anger. "Okay, let's assume it is in the blood in the bottles. If the bottles don't show any signs of tampering, how else is the poison getting in there?"

Luis gave me a tight smile. "Demon magick, perhaps? I notice there have been no more attacks on your kind."

Everyone around the table stiffened.

"I see," Micah said, sounding calm but looking as though he'd like to rip Luis's head off. "This is why you invited me here today."

Alejandro spread his hands. "If you have another explanation, I would be most happy to hear it."

Leaning forward menacingly, Ludwig bit out, "How about your people are faking it and using this so-called madness to revert to their real nature without consequences?"

Luis bolted up out of his seat. "How dare you!" He slapped his hands down on the table and practically hissed at Ludwig. "Demon spawn—"

The man mountain lunged across the table, his meaty paw headed for Luis's throat. Luis snarled back, fangs gleaming, and batted Ludwig's hand out of the way then leapt across the table . . . and the fight was on. Though the other men in the room tried to stop them, it was as if they weren't even there.

Oh, crap. Lola loved it, lapping up all that wonderful testosterone. This was not good.

AN UNDERSTATEMENT, Fang agreed. *DO* SOMETHING.

It was as if Fang had given Lola permission. My succubus shredded the barrier I had put up and burst forth, instantly sending surges of lustful energy into the men in the room and enslaving them . . . all but Micah, of course. "Stop," I yelled.

They obeyed me immediately, each man turning to look at me as if waiting for further orders.

Fang nudged me. UH, NOT EXACTLY WHAT I MEANT.

"Val," Micah said warningly, "what are you doing?"

Dumb question. He knew exactly what I was doing. But I was fighting too hard with Lola to answer him. She wanted to surge along the connection, stroke their chakras, suck up all that yummy energy. But though she had them thoroughly caught in her web, I wouldn't let her feed. It seemed like a violation of hospitality or at least a breach of our unspoken treaty.

"You haven't fed recently, have you?" Micah demanded. "Why didn't you use Shade?"

Since I couldn't answer him, Fang did. SHE'S AFRAID SHADE WILL BECOME TOO LOVEY DOVEY. SHE DIDN'T FEED ON HIM SO SHE REALLY NEEDS IT NOW, BUT SHE'S AFRAID TO LET GO AND TAKE ANYTHING FROM THE POOR LITTLE BLOODSUCKERS.

Traitor.

Micah watched me thoughtfully. "She has a good point—we don't want to offend our potential allies. Since your succubus doesn't work on my incubus, please feed on Ludwig." He glanced at the large man. "He should be punished for resorting to violence, anyway. At least, I hope he considers it a punishment."

I didn't want to feed on *anyone*, but Lola wouldn't give up her prey, and I wouldn't let her loose. Stalemate. Micah's solution was my only option—the only good one, anyway. Wonder if that was someone's razor, too.

I wasn't sure if I could separate him out from the pack, but I tried it, gingerly. Given permission to nibble on Ludwig, Lola surged into him and plucked all of his strings, making him vibrate with desire, forcing him to worship and adore the goddess that was Val. It was kind of sickening, actually. When he tried to embrace me, I forced him to stay where he was. As Lola hoovered up the energy he generated, I dialed it down from fire hose strength to more like a garden hose.

And now that Lola was occupied, I was able to disengage from the vamps. "I'm going to let go of the others now," I told Micah.

I gently released the vamps, and Alejandro immediately said, "Luis, no."

Good thing, 'cause he had my murder in his eyes.

"She didn't know any other way to stop the two of you without harming you," Micah told Luis quickly.

Alejandro nodded. "I know. She could have done much worse, but chose not to. We understand the pressures of the young newly coming into their powers. Do we not, Luis?"

Luis grimaced but Austin tried to hide a grin. Interesting. I wondered what the story was behind that. But Luis merely gave a curt nod.

"My apologies," Alejandro said with a slight bow. "The lack of an abundant supply of nourishment is making us all . . . testy."

Micah smiled back at him. "I should apologize as well. Ludwig is rather short-tempered." He glanced at the man, who was still in my thrall. "You can release him now, Val."

Oops. It had felt so good to feel satisfied again, the hidden wells of my body stoked once more, I had kind of forgotten I had Ludwig on a string. Lola was just playing with him now, getting him all hot and bothered. Luckily, she hadn't gone all the way to suck him dry. Embarrassed, I let him go. Now I kind of understood how the vamps felt after not feeding for awhile.

"Sorry," I told Ludwig.

No WORRIES, Fang said. HE ENJOYED IT ALL RIGHT, BUT FEELS SICK THAT HE HAD THE HOTS FOR A GIRL HIS DAUGHTER'S AGE.

True, he did look a little stunned and horrified. Good—it was a punishment after all.

Micah gave him a stern look. "It wouldn't have been necessary if you hadn't lost control." Then to everyone else in the room, he said, "Let's all sit down and see if we can discuss this rationally."

Luis and Austin took their cue from Alejandro and returned to the table. As everyone took their seats, Micah added, "After what happened with Lily Armstrong, we're all aware that one person's secret ambitions can have a devastating effect on an organization. But I believe both the New Blood Movement and the Demon Underground are united in wanting to find the culprit, whether vampire, demon, or human, and put a stop to the damage he or she is inflicting on both organizations."

"Very true," Alejandro murmured. "The organization should not be held responsible for the actions of one aberrant individual." He stared at Luis as if to bore that into his head.

NOT SURE THAT'S GONNA WORK, Fang muttered. HIS HEAD'S A BIT THICK.

"A change of subject," Micah proposed. "How are Lorenzo, Corina, and the others doing?"

"Better. But not entirely recovered yet. It may take some time for the poison to work its way out of their system."

Micah nodded. "Are they able to talk yet? Rationally?"

"Not yet. But when they are, we hope they may be able to shed some light on what happened." He spread his hands. "As you can see, tempers are growing short. Now that we've learned the donors are not the cause, we plan to reopen the blood banks for personal donations— no storage."

"Do you think that's wise?" Micah asked. "The banks may be a target."

Alejandro nodded. "We plan to add more security."

"I can add some of my people as well, if you think it will help," Micah offered.

YEAH, SINCE THEY'RE WATCHING THE VAMPS AT THE BLOOD BANKS ANYWAY.

Weird. Everyone knew it, but pretended like they didn't.

IT'S CALLED DIPLOMACY, BABE.

Alejandro nodded his acceptance. Well, at least the two leaders agreed, but I wasn't sure all their followers were totally on board. Not judging from their expressions, anyway.

"I assume this means you are not planning to come out nationally anytime soon?" Micah ventured cautiously.

Luis's mouth tightened but Alejandro quelled him with a glance. "For the moment, until this . . . issue is resolved. But we do plan to announce our existence. We would prefer to do it with you rather than without you, but either way, it will eventually happen."

Now Ludwig didn't look happy, but Micah merely nodded thoughtfully. "We have not yet come to an agreement, and some of the demons are very unhappy about it."

"And if these are the ones who are poisoning my people?" Alejandro asked with an arch of his eyebrow.

"Then I will ensure they are dealt with."

"How can we trust you to do that?" Luis asked skeptically.

"Indeed," Alejandro said. "What assurance do we have that you will do as you promise?"

Micah spread his hands. "What assurances would you accept?"

They all stood quietly for a moment, and I could feel the tension rise as both sides regarded each other with suspicion. Crap. Any moment now, they'd be at each other's throats again. Abruptly, I blurted out, "I'll be your assurance."

Everyone looked at me like I was crazy, so I added quickly, "If Micah breaks his word, or if any more of his people try to harm yours, I-I'll quit my job and work for Alejandro."

"Val, no," Micah said. "I can't let you take on my debts."

I raised my chin. "You can't stop me."

HEY, BABE, DID YOU THINK THIS THROUGH? Fang sounded worried.

Not really, but I had faith in our ability to make sure that didn't happen.

Alejandro glanced at me questioningly. "I have your word?"

I nodded.

A smile curved Alejandro's lips. "Then I accept. If the perpetrators of this outrage are not appropriately punished or if any more demons try to harm mine, the Slayer will work for me."

Micah frowned. "I assure you, we are doing all that we can to find the thief and stop this terrorism."

"Do more," Alejandro suggested. Then, without another word, he and his minions left.

"Whew," Ludwig said on an explosive breath. "Boss, you can't—"

Micah stopped him with an upraised hand. "Not now, Ludwig. This is a discussion for the entire organization. Would you wait outside for a moment . . . and try not to get into trouble?"

The big man nodded, looking like a guilty child, and stepped outside.

Now it was my turn. Micah turned to me. "What the hell were you thinking, offering yourself as assurance?"

Sheesh. It wasn't so amusing when he used that tone on me. "Do you know of a better way to keep his vamps from hunting for demon blood?"

Micah ran a weary hand over his face. "I guess not." But he wasn't letting me off the hook. "Do I need to say anything about you losing control there?"

"Nope. I get it. Bad Val. Bad Lola."

He raised an eyebrow. "That's not what I meant. I appreciate you helping to stop the fight, but I wish you had more control while doing it. You know that you can't go so long without feeding, Val. As you just demonstrated, the consequences are . . . not good."

Obviously.

Fang had to butt in. SHE'S AFRAID SHADE IS STUCK ON HER.

I glared at him and muttered, "Some friend you are."

HEY, KIDDO, I HAVE TO LIVE IN YOUR HEAD, TOO. YOU THINK IT'S FUN FOR ME WATCHING YOU GET MORE AND MORE WORKED UP WITH NO OUTLET? WHY DO YOU THINK I WAS SO GLAD TO FIND PRINCESS?

Oh. Sheesh, I hadn't thought about how my struggle would affect Fang and his libido. "Sorry."

"You need to come to an agreement with Shade or someone," Micah insisted. "As you can see, your lack of control is affecting everyone around you."

"I know. I'm sorry. I'll . . . figure out something." I had to. Micah was right. I couldn't keep losing control like this. One day I might go too far and suck the life out of someone. And that would make me no better than the vampires I slayed.

Chapter Sixteen

After I left the hotel, I went back home to get Dan. Gwen must have gone to bed or to work, Shade was sacked out on the couch with a demon watching him and reading a book, and Dan was spread out in Gwen's recliner, eyes closed as he listened to something on his ear buds.

I nodded at the demon watcher and decided not to disturb anyone else. As Fang went off to do ... whatever he did with Princess, I headed into my bedroom so I could have a few precious minutes alone for a change. I'd wanted friends, yeah, but sheesh, there was such a thing as too much togetherness.

I'd planned to collapse on the bed for a few minutes, but I saw a wrapped package sitting on it. There was a cute card with a note inside from Shade: "I missed your birthday, so consider this a belated birthday gift."

Emotions warred within me ... excitement—no guy had ever given me a gift before—and trepidation as I wondered what the gift was and what it meant.

I opened it and smiled. He'd found a couple of graphic prints with chocolate brown dogwood branches against an ice blue sky. Thank heavens, the gift wasn't too personal. I sighed in relief.

"Do you like them?" Shade asked from the doorway behind me.

I turned to smile at him. "They match the room perfectly. Thank you so much. But you shouldn't have."

He shrugged and leaned against the door jamb, his expression all swirly. "It's the least I can do after you've let me stay at your place."

I relaxed even more. That was a reason I could understand. "Well, since you insisted on taking the couch, how could I possibly mind?"

"Yes, but they could baby-sit me at my place just as well as here. I know Micah wants me here to make it look like I need more help than I really do, but ... " He paused, then asked abruptly, "Val, do you want me to leave?"

Oh, crap. I couldn't read his expression, but from the tone of his voice, I gathered he was maybe hurt or something. How the heck could I answer that? "Of course not—"

Dan stuck his head in. "Oh, sorry, am I interrupting?" Yeah, right, like he didn't know. "Thought you might want to hit the streets again while it's still dark."

Whew. Saved by the nosy partner. "Uh, yeah, sure," I told him. "Shade, I need to go to work. Can we talk about this when I get back?"

He nodded. "Sure. See you then." And he turned around and walked off.

Dan raised an eyebrow. "What was that all about?"

Ignoring the question, I said, "I'm ready. Let me get Fang and we can go."

Fang followed us to the truck Dan drove. Provided by the SCU, the silver Dodge Ram had an extended cab and doors reinforced with vampire-repelling silver. Fang leapt up easily—sometimes I swore that terrier had springs for legs—and I scrambled in after him. "So, anything good come from the briefing?"

Dan pulled out of the parking lot. "No. How about you? Anything come out of your meeting I should know about?"

"No."

WOW. SCINTILLATING CONVERSATION, YOU TWO.

I nudged Fang but didn't respond. I was tired of trying to act like everything was normal, like nothing was wrong. I turned to stare out the window, hoping to see some kind of fang to neck activity so I didn't have to spend another night locked up in this truck with a distant Dan.

After an hour of silence—well, except for the running commentary provided by Fang on Dan's probable ancestry—I finally had enough of it. "I don't like this any more than you do, you know."

Dan grunted but didn't say anything else. Too bad I didn't speak grunt. And I was sick of him treating me like a leper. "I don't want to be out every night with some guy who's afraid I'm going to rape him or something. I'm not exactly pining away for you like some lovesick kid, so just get over yourself, Dan."

FINALLY, Fang said with a heavy mental sigh. NOW CAN I GO DO SOMETHING MORE FUN? LIKE SHOVE A STICK IN MY EYE?

"I know," Dan said briefly.

He didn't even sound ticked. "What?"

"I know. All of that. You're right."

Well, yeah, but Dan hadn't actually been seeing eye to eye with me lately. "What's with the change of heart?"

He stared out the windshield as he drove the quiet streets of San Antonio. "Gwen lit into me. Told me I'd been acting like a jerk."

Go, Gwen, Fang said admiringly.

Dan continued staring out the front of the vehicle, avoiding my eyes. "I— I just—" He scrubbed a hand across his face. "Ah, hell. This is hard."

At times like these, I wished Fang could read his mind as well. But since he couldn't, I had to wait to see if Dan could find the guts to say what he's feeling. "It's okay, Dan. Take your time."

He nodded. A few minutes later, he said softly, "I wanted this to work out between us, I really did. But . . . "

Pain and regret rolled through me. I'd wanted it, too. "But . . . ?"

"But the age difference, the difference in our backgrounds, our working together, your super powers, Lola . . ."

"No. Nicole is a friend, nothing more."

"Yeah, I get that." At first, Dan had been impressed by my so-called super powers, but I understood how some guys could feel intimidated. I just hadn't thought Dan was one of those guys. "You're right, too. Maybe demons and humans should stay with their own kind." Less pain that way. Look what had happened to my father when he'd married a human.

He finally glanced at me. "Is that why you and Shade . . . ?"

"You and Nicole . . . ?" I mocked him.

Dan was deluding himself. The petite blonde obviously had a thing for my partner's hotness, whether he realized it or not. And he liked playing the big protective hero . . . which he couldn't do with me. A match made in heaven. But I doubted Dan would appreciate those insights, so I dropped the subject.

Dan, however, wouldn't let it go. "You and Shade . . . ?"

"What do you care, Dan?"

"I care. I may not want us to be together, but I do care about you. And hooking up with a shadow demon . . . not sure that's such a good idea."

"I am not 'hooking up' with him," I said, exasperated.

"So what was it when I caught the two of you in bed together?"

Fang snorted. For a guy who doesn't want you, he sure sounds awfully jealous.

I sighed. "Let me ask you this. What happens if you stop eating to the point where you starve yourself?"

He thought for a moment. "I die."

"Well, when Lola starves, someone *else* dies." I paused, trying to figure out how to explain it. "Look, if Lola doesn't . . . feed . . . often enough, she gets so hungry, it's all I can think about, all I can do to hold her back." It used to be easier, before I learned to let loose. Now I sometimes felt like a loose cannon, about to explode and blow everyone around me to smithereens. "Micah is trying to help me learn to control it by letting her out a little at a time under controlled circumstances. And Shade is . . ."

"The *feedee?*" Dan asked, a smile in his voice.

"You could say that. He's helping me learn to deal with my inner demon, that's all." And he didn't think of it as *rape*, like a particular cop of my acquaintance.

Dan pulled over to the side of the road near some park so he could look me in the eyes. "Okay, so what was all that tension about between the two of you before we left?"

Did I really want to talk about a possible new boyfriend with my ex-boyfriend?

Fang chuckled in my mind. Aw, GO AHEAD. I WANNA WATCH.

Why not? Dan was a guy. Maybe he had some insight or inside information on how the alien creatures thought. And the darkness helped make it a little easier, somehow. "He's allowed me to uh, practice on him, but . . ." I squirmed, not sure how to put it. "I think maybe he likes it too much."

"That's good, isn't it? You get what you need and he gets what he wants."

"It's not that simple. It's all mixed up with . . . other stuff." Other stuff I was *not* going to talk about with Dan. Oh, great, now I sounded totally lame. Maybe this wasn't such a good idea after all. "I've been avoiding him. That's the tension you sensed."

"You like him?" Dan asked quietly.

"No. Yeah. I don't know."

"But you feel like it's moving too fast."

My shoulders sagged with relief. "Yeah." That was it—he understood.

"Well, why don't you tell him that? If he's a decent guy, he'll understand."

"You think?"

"Yep."

Fang crawled into my lap. WELL, WHADDAYA KNOW? DAN CAME THROUGH WITH SOME GOOD ADVICE.

"Okay, I'll try it. Thanks." And I still needed to find the right time to ask him about Thanksgiving . . .

Standing up suddenly, Fang said, ROLL DOWN THE WINDOW. I THINK I SMELL ME SOME VAMPIRE.

I cracked the window and Fang's eyes flared purple. "Fang smells vamp," I told Dan quietly. "But I don't see anything yet. How do we play this?"

He unbuckled his seat belt. "Why don't we go for a walk in the park, just a guy, a girl and their dog?"

Okay, we were going to play bait. No problem. "Chill," I said quietly to Fang. "Your eyes are glowing."

He tamped down the purple and we got out of the car to stroll in the park. Fang put his nose down to the ground and followed the smells to a worn path into the trees. HE'S GOING THIS WAY. I THINK HE'S FOLLOWING SOMEONE.

I told Dan what Fang had said and we picked up our speed, trying to be quiet, but hoping to catch the bloodsucker before he could do any actual fanging. I palmed a stake and kept it mostly hidden behind my wrist. Dan pretended to put his arm on my shoulder while hiding a small crossbow behind my back. As for Fang, he was already armed with his weapons—teeth, claws, and the ability to talk anyone to death.

HEY, I HEARD THAT.

I grinned. *You were supposed to.*

Fang halted, one paw poised for the next step, and lifted his head. HE'S STOPPED.

I slowed and motioned for Dan to do the same. We crept up silently around a curve in the trail. Sure enough, there was a guy in a dark hat and cloak watching . . . a comely tavern wench?

MAYBE IT'S A UNIFORM FROM A BAR OR SOMETHING. Fang snorted. YE OLDE CAT HOUSE, LOOKS LIKE.

Weird. She did look rather . . . voluptuous. Maybe it was a costume from the Society for Creative Anachronism. Those people who dressed up like extras at a Renaissance Fair.

The vamp leaped out at her, she screamed, and I was on him in a second flat. I bowled him over and held my stake poised to strike, but the girl screamed again. "No, no. Don't hurt him."

Huh? When I paused, the vamp slammed his will into mine, trying to enthrall me.

Gotcha now, dude. "What's going on here?" I demanded.

The girl tried to reach for me, but Dan held her back. "Please," she said. "Don't hurt him. We were just playing a game."

I stared down at the vamp in dismay. She was right. From the memories in his mind and the marks on her neck, this husband and wife played Dracula and the Tavern Wench often.

Oh, crap. I scrambled up off him as Fang cackled in my mind. "She's right," I told Dan, pretending like I was brushing dirt off my sleeve but trying not to laugh.

"Who are you?" the wench asked.

"They call her the Slayer," Dan said with a significant glance at our wannabe Dracula, who looked more like the Prince of Geeks than the Prince of Darkness.

OH, LORD. SAVE ME FROM GAMERS, Fang drawled.

I didn't realize a vamp could pale even more than pasty white. He scrambled to his feet and retrieved his hat. "I didn't— I wasn't—"

"It's okay, I know." But maybe I could salvage something from this mess. "Are you part of the New Blood Movement?"

The vamp shook his head. "No, but I've heard of it." He glanced at his very human wife. "I don't need their blood banks."

No, he had his own portable one at home. Ick. But he didn't seem like a bad sort. He had gotten caught up in one too many role-playing games, was all. Unfortunately for him, one of those games had turned real, and he'd ended up in a permanent role as a creature of the night.

"Do you know anything about the poisoning going on at the blood banks?" Dan asked harshly.

"No . . . no! I don't go near those places."

I nodded at Dan. He was telling the truth.

"How about your bloodsucking friends?" Dan pressed. "Any of them know anything?"

"I-I don't have any vampire friends."

Strange, he was still telling the truth. I told Dan so. Dan looked exasperated, but asked, "Any clue whatsoever where we might find some unaffiliated vamps who might know something?"

The guy thought hard. "I've heard some rumors about a bar downtown where a group of vampires hang out in a private room, but that's all."

"Not part of the New Blood Movement?" Dan asked.

"No," the girl said and pulled her arm from Dan's grasp. "They sound like a bunch of poseurs. We avoid them but they hang at Club Gothique downtown."

"Okay, thanks," I said. "You can go now."

Giving us dirty looks over their shoulders, they hurried off to play their game somewhere else.

We couldn't afford not to check it out. Dan drove to the bar and as we got out of the truck, I glanced at the Club Gothique sign, the dark red script written in a blood dripping horror movie font. "Are they for real?" I asked incredulously.

He shrugged. "Maybe they figure hiding in plain sight is the way to go."

Dogs weren't welcome in most places that served food, so we left Fang outside. We entered the darkened bar, sullenly lit with red lights spaced along the walls. A live band played loud heavy metal music on the far end of the bar, and the denizens wore black, black, and more black, with touches of stark white, purple, dark red, and the glint of metal from multiple body piercings.

We didn't exactly fit in, as the hostile looks of the patrons testified.

Dan leaned down to shout in my ear so he could be heard over the music. "Sense any vamps here?"

I shook my head. "But that doesn't mean they aren't here." We'd have to find that private room.

Dan gestured with his head toward the bar. As we reached it, the band came to a crashing, screeching halt and announced they were taking a break. Thank God. My ears were ringing.

The bartender looked almost normal, with minimal body piercings and no black lipstick or make-up. Dan smiled and asked for the private party.

The bartender quirked a smile. "Sorry, it's by invitation only."

Dan flashed his badge. "Will this do?"

The barkeep's expression turned wary. "Hey, I don't want any trouble."

"And you won't get any, if you cooperate. We only want to ask them a few questions."

The man shrugged. "Hey, no skin off my nose. I just work here." He nodded toward a door at the opposite end of the bar from the band. "It's not locked. Go right in."

Dan glanced at me as we headed for the private room. "You ready for this?"

"Yeah. Let's do it."

Dan tensed then nodded to me and flung open the door.

I'd tensed up, too, but nothing attacked. A bunch of people, mostly in the eighteen to twenty-five age range, lay sprawled on red velvet sofas around the room, smoking, necking, and doing a variety of other things Lola was rather interested in, but I wasn't.

"Hey," one young man said. "Who invited you?"

Dan closed the door behind us, ignoring the question. "We're looking for vampires. Any here?"

The crowd parted to reveal a Morticia Addams look-alike, dramatically dressed in a black skintight dress trailing cobwebby fringe. She stepped from the back of the room, stood hipshot with her hands on her tiny waist, and opened her mouth in a snarl to reveal her "fangs."

Oh, spare me. "Filing your eyeteeth to points doesn't make you a vampire." Just sick.

"You're right," Morticia said with an annoyed smile. "But drinking blood does." She wiped a drop of something nonexistent from the corner of her blood-red lips.

Dan grinned. I had to agree. It was so . . . hokey. I couldn't imagine any real vampire wearing such constricting clothing. Not if they wanted to move fast.

"Any *real* vampires here?" Dan asked.

Morticia actually hissed. "Come closer and you'll find out."

I had to laugh. "Nice try. But you're nothing but a cliché."

Her eyes narrowed, but before she could say anything, one of her girlfriends interrupted, pointing at me. "I know you—you're that vampire killer who was at the rally on the Day of the Dead."

Morticia backed up a step, fear flashing in her eyes.

If there were any real vamps in the room, they would have either bolted toward me or away from me by now. Instead, they cringed back in alarm. I turned around and opened the door. "Don't worry, I only hunt real vamps. Not kiddie wannabes." On that note, we left the room and closed the door behind us.

Dan grinned at me. "Great exit line."

Three thumps hit the door one after the other, followed closely by the sound of shattering glass.

I shrugged. "Guess they don't think so." Crap. This whole night was a bust.

We got into the truck but before we could decide what to do next,

Dan had a phone call. After he hung up, he said, "That was Ramirez. There's been a possible burglary."

"What? There are so few vamps cruising that we've been reduced to checking out burglaries?"

"It's your parent's store. There's been a break-in."

Chapter Seventeen

Fear thrilled through me. "Was anyone hurt?" I demanded.

Dan shook his head and started the truck. "No one was there. But the fire alarm went off." He peeled off onto the road.

"Fire? There was fire?"

"I don't know. Calm down, Val. You'll see for yourself in a few minutes."

A few minutes? It felt like hours of worry and fear until we finally got to Astral Reflections. I barely waited for the truck to stop until I was out the door. Everything looked okay on the outside of the old two-story wooden building, and the fire trucks were just pulling away. Mom stood in the doorway watching them leave, hugging herself and looking shell-shocked and angry.

I came to a stop in front of her, not sure whether to hug her or not. So I stood there, feeling awkward. "What happened?"

Wordlessly, she stepped aside and gestured inside at the store. I gasped. It was totally trashed. Shelves were tipped over and books were strewn everywhere, with ripped pages scattered across the mess. Candles were broken, and delicate figurines that used to depict fairy, unicorn, and other fantasy creatures were smashed and lay in glittering shards everywhere. Rick stood in the middle of it, looking around helplessly as if he didn't know what to do or where to start.

"Careful," I told Fang. I didn't want him to hurt his paws on the broken pieces.

The terrier stopped at the door. I'LL WAIT OUTSIDE. YOU DON'T NEED MY HELP HERE.

Dan appeared at the door and took the situation in at a glance. "Have you called the police?"

Rick shook his head. "Just the SCU."

"Why the Special Crimes Unit?" Dan asked. "Do you think this was done by a vampire?"

"Maybe." Rick nodded at the counter. "See for yourself."

Dan and I crunched our way over to the counter, trying to avoid as many shards as possible. There, scrawled on the counter in large red block letters, it said, "Suffer the consequences, Slayer."

All the blood rushed from my head. Light-headed, I reached out to steady myself on the counter. "Is that blood?"

Dan leaned over and sniffed. "No, just a large marker of some kind."

"They attacked my *family*," I said incredulously.

"Indirectly," Dan said soothingly. "It doesn't look like anyone's hurt."

Not physically, maybe, but Mom and Rick both looked totally devastated. This store was their life. I turned a remorseful expression to Rick. "I'm so sorry—"

Rick enveloped me in a hug. "Not your fault, sweetheart."

Mom didn't say anything. What did her silence mean? That it was all my fault, that if it weren't for me, the store they loved wouldn't look like the "after" scene from a tornado? Unfortunately, it might be true. If I had backed down when I got the first note, this wouldn't have happened.

Rick squeezed me once more then released me. "We'll be okay. We have insurance."

But he didn't mention the fact that they'd also lose money while the store was closed for clean-up. And the height of the shopping season was coming up soon. "Can you open again after Thanksgiving?" It was only a couple of days away . . . and I still hadn't invited Shade yet. Guess I needed to do that soon.

"Sure, sure. Between your mother, me, Jen, and Joshua, we should get ready in no time. Besides, they didn't touch the new merchandise in the back that just came in. We'll be fine."

He started to pull out a chair, but Dan said, "Please try not to touch anything else. The SCU forensics unit should be here soon to see what they can find."

We exited just as the team drove up. The leader, a no-nonsense older woman with the name "Mahoney" embroidered on her police jacket, took charge. "What happened here?" she asked Dan.

"Looks like vandalism targeted at a member of the SCU, or possibly burglary." He nodded at Mom and Rick. "These are the Andersons, the owners of the store."

Mahoney nodded and gave swift instructions to her crew. As they headed in, she asked, "Is anything missing?"

Rick put an arm around Mom and spoke for both of them. "Not that we know of, but we haven't had a chance to look at everything."

She nodded. "Why the SCU? You suspect something out of the ordinary?"

Dan explained my involvement and the message scrawled on the counter. Mahoney looked thoughtful. "It's two o'clock in the morning. How did you know this happened?"

"The fire alarm went off, and the fire department notified us," Rick said. "But there was no fire—the vandal must have pulled the fire alarm himself."

Mahoney took a moment to tell her team to check the alarm for fingerprints, then asked, "Any idea how he got in?"

Rick's mouth twisted in a grimace. "The back door was broken in. He must have come in that way."

The policewoman glanced inside. "Your store is open to the public, so fingerprints may not tell us much. And given the nature of your merchandise, it wouldn't be unusual to find signs of nonhumans about. Our best bet is the door they broke into and the fire alarm itself. Any idea who did it?"

Dan shrugged. "We'll work the angle of who has a grudge against Val."

Unfortunately, that list was rather long. Damn it, I should have stopped when I got the first warning. I had no idea they'd come after my family.

Fang leaned up against me. IT'S NOT YOUR FAULT, VAL. IT'S THE FAULT OF THE LOW LIFE WHO DID THIS.

I squatted down to give him a hug. *Thanks, but if it hadn't been for me, this never would have happened.*

YOU KNOW BETTER THAN THAT, Fang said with a nudge. I'M GONNA CHECK THE SMELLS AROUND BACK.

As he trotted off, Dan drew me away from where Mahoney was talking to Mom and Rick. "Rick's right. It's not your fault."

I blinked back sudden tears. Anger and disgust were a lot easier to take than unexpected kindness. "That's what Fang said, too." But I wasn't sure I believed it.

"Do you think they were looking for the books here?"

"I don't know. Maybe."

"So what are you going to do?"

I rubbed my temples, trying to ease the sudden throbbing

headache this whole situation had given me. "I don't know." If I did nothing, more people could be injured . . . and by more than the thief. If we didn't find the culprit soon, the unresolved tension between the vamps and demons could escalate into a war. And if I continued trying to find the culprit, my family would be in more danger—the thief had proven he knew right where to hurt me. "It's a no-win situation."

"Okay, what do you *want* to do? Give up?"

The thought of doing that sent rage sweeping through me. "Hell, no. I want to catch the rat bastard who did this and hang him up by his *cojones*."

Dan winced at the thought. "Why don't you leave me to do the investigating?"

"And I should do what? Take up knitting?" Maybe Fang would like a nice knitted sweater and cap for the upcoming winter.

MAYBE *NOT*, Fang said with disgust as he came trotting up.

Just kidding, I assured him. I didn't think I could sit still that long. "Find anything back there?" I asked aloud.

NOPE. TOO MANY FEET MUDDIED THE SCENTS. THE PLACE STINKS OF THE BOOTIES THOSE SO-CALLED FORENSIC DUDES WEAR.

Well, they probably didn't have a forensic test for scents. At Dan's questioning look, I shook my head. "He didn't find anything."

"I'm not suggesting you take up knitting," Dan said. "But take some time off. You probably need it after everything that's happened lately. I'll talk to Ramirez, but I know he'll agree."

"And what about you? What if this psycho starts targeting you and your family? Like Gwen?"

"All the more reason you should stay home, so you can protect her."

"Are you suggesting we set ourselves up as bait?"

He looked taken aback. "No, that's not what I meant at all."

"Good." I wasn't worried about myself, but Gwen was another matter entirely. The thought of putting another friend in danger made me feel helpless and angry. I sighed. He was right. Staying home and twiddling my thumbs was probably the best thing for everyone. "Okay, I'll do it." I just hoped we'd find the culprit soon, or I wouldn't be able to vouch for my sanity.

I glared at Fang. *And no comments from you.*

He gazed at the sky, trying to look innocent. NOTHING HERE. NOPE, NOT A WORD.

"Good," Dan said, looking relieved. "I'll come by tomorrow,

check to see how you're doing."

"Why are you being so helpful?"

He shrugged. "Because until this is resolved, you and Gwen are in danger. And I want to prove to your friends that I didn't take the books."

Good enough. "Okay. Shall we go?"

He nodded and I headed back toward Mom and Rick. Mom was leaning against her husband, their arms around each others' waists and her head on his shoulder as they gazed at the destruction.

"Rick?" I asked gently. "Is there anything we can do?"

"No." He smiled wearily. "We'll start cleaning tomorrow, after they're done."

"Do you need some help?" After all, I wasn't doing anything.

Mom's expression hardened. "No. Just catch the bastards who did this."

Strange how such harsh words could soften my heart. Mom didn't blame me, didn't accuse me of doing it myself. Instead, she trusted me to find the people who had and punish them. "We will," I promised her.

As Mom turned back to stare into the devastation, Rick pulled me aside and led me to their car. "I was going to call you tomorrow. I've had someone looking into your genealogy, to find out whatever he could about your background." He opened the trunk and pulled out a small box full of papers. "This is what he found." As I took it gingerly, he added, "I didn't tell him we were looking for demons, but asked him to trace your ancestry back several generations and note anything odd that came up about them."

Wow. "I-I don't know what to say." Here I'd thought he'd forgotten to ask Mom about her background and instead, he'd gone out and gotten as much information as possible.

"You don't need to say anything. Consider it a Thanksgiving present. I just hope you find what you're looking for in there."

"Thanks, Rick." I gave him a hug and carried the box carefully back to the truck. Maybe this would help me figure out what other kind of demon blood ran in my veins. If nothing else, it would keep me occupied for awhile.

Dan dropped us off at the condo and I tried to be quiet, but it wasn't necessary. Gwen was at work and Shade was sitting on the couch in jeans and a T-shirt watching television in the dark. Princess was lying in his lap and his bare feet were propped up on the coffee table. Wow. The guy had no clue how gorgeous he was. Heck, even his feet were long, elegant, and pretty.

I glanced around. No one else was there. "Hi," I said cautiously when he turned to look at me. "Where's your babysitter?"

"All gone. We cleared the last of them. No thief."

"How are you feeling?"

"Bored. But I feel fine."

"No more blitzing in and out?"

"Very rarely. Princess seems to help." He petted her silky ears.

Oh, yeah. I just now realized I could see his expression. "She keeps you grounded, too, huh?"

He nodded and Princess glanced in my direction. I AM GOOD FOR MY HUMAN.

"I'm sure you are," I said, suppressing a smile.

Fang jumped up on the couch to touch noses with her. They shared some private communication then jumped off the couch and disappeared outside together. I shook my head. "Now there's a match made in someone's demented mind."

"Like us?" Shade asked softly.

Oh, crap. I felt my face heat. "Not what I meant," I mumbled.

"I know. But I think we should talk." He patted the cushion on the couch next to him. "Come, sit."

Emotions roiled within me. I really wanted to get to know Shade, but I was still so uncertain about everything. I needed to escape to my room until I knew myself better and exactly how I felt, but I had promised to talk to him. And maybe this would be a good time to take Dan's advice, too.

I carefully set the box Rick had given me on the coffee table and sat down next to Shade, perching on the edge of the cushions. He placed his hand on mind and I saw incredible sadness, longing, and regret in his expression. Pain twinged through me—I'd put that there. Lola was pretty satisfied from her recent feeding, so she wasn't as greedy as normal. Maybe I could get close without fighting my nature. I scooted back, toed off my shoes, and propped my feet up on the table, too. This way I wouldn't have to see his heartache, coward that I was.

He clicked off the television and twined his fingers with mine. I let him. It felt so nice, so normal. Like a real dating couple hanging out together. And why not? We might both be part demon, but a good chunk of us was still human. At least, I knew seven-eighths of me was.

I wasn't sure about Shade.

Maybe if I eased into this discussion, it wouldn't feel so difficult. Especially in the dark. A lot of things could be said in the dark that couldn't be revealed in the bright light. Leaning my head against his shoulder, I asked, "How much of you is demon and how much human?"

"Same as you," he said quietly.

Another thing we had in common. "I've been wondering . . . what exactly is a shadow demon?" I'd never gotten around to looking it up in the encyclopedia.

He laid his head on top of mind and snuggled me closer. "A full shadow demon can exist in more than one dimension at a time and phase in and out of them at will."

"And you?"

"I'm mostly human, so I stay in this dimension, but still have continuous contact with several others."

"Hence the swirling ribbons of light," I suggested.

"Yes, hence."

"Can you see those other dimensions? Do they look like ours?"

He hesitated for a moment. "Not like ours, but I can't describe it. I don't see them so much as I sense them. I exist in the shadows, sort of insubstantial. I can't interact with anything but the energy."

"What does a shadow demon *do*?" That part wasn't clear to me at all.

"We act as a conduit, to allow the energy to cross the boundaries of the dimensions. You remember how I pulled energy to heal Dan from one of them?" At my nod, he added, "That's what I do."

"So, there are other kinds of energy?"

"Yes. Many kinds."

His voice sounded final, discouraging me to ask more questions. But when had that stopped me before? "Like what?"

After a long pause, he said, "I'd rather not discuss it."

"Bad?"

"Yes, some are very bad."

And that proved what kind of a guy he was, that he hadn't allowed himself to use any of that, only the good energy. At least, that was all I'd seen him use. "What about this world's energy? Do you take some from here and send it to the other dimensions?"

"Every time I take energy from somewhere else, I exchange it for some here, to keep them in balance."

That made sense. "What kind of energy? And what does our energy do for them?"

"This world is very solid, or at least that's how it seems to me. I exchange that stability for things in the other places that we need."

"What if—"

"Please, Val, I'd rather talk about us, about what's going on between us."

"Sorry," I muttered. "But you're fascinating, you know?"

He kissed the top of my head. "You, too. But I'd like to know how you feel about me, about what Micah wants me to help you with. Is it . . . repulsive to you?"

"No, of course not." Hating that I'd put that uncertainty in his voice, I hugged him then flipped one of my legs over his so I could straddle his lap. Clasping his face between my hands, I said, "How can you think that? Couldn't you tell how much I enjoyed what we did the other day?"

He looked baffled and still a little hurt. "I thought so, but you've been avoiding me . . ."

And he looked so lost with those big sad puppy dog eyes, I couldn't resist kissing him. I tried to press my mouth to his, but I was still new at this, so I ended up smooshing our noses together. "Oops." Oh, yeah, what a seductress.

"Try again," Shade murmured.

He tilted his head one way, I tilted the other, and we fit together perfectly. I intended to give him just a short kiss and pull away, but Shade put his arms around me and I melted into him. The kiss went on and on, and when I tried to pull away for a breath of air, he slipped his tongue inside my mouth.

Oh, yeah. Now Lola was perking up and percolating in all the right places. But I didn't want this to be about Lola. I wanted it to be about me, the human me. Shade's hands roamed my back and we explored each other's mouths for a while until I felt too shaky to go on.

Pulling away, I collapsed next to him and tried to still my frantically beating heart as well as Lola's raging hormones. Oh, my. "Did that feel like I was repulsed by you?"

"No . . . " Shade pushed me gently down on the couch and pulled me into his arms until we were lying entwined together like one huge knotty being. I hoped he couldn't hear the fast thud-thud-thud of my heart against his chest. I didn't want to come across like some huge, inexperienced doofus or something. But this felt so special, so very right. I wanted to lie with him here forever, just like this.

"Okay, if you weren't disgusted, why were you avoiding me?"

I sighed. Truth time. And it was a little easier now that my head was lying on his chest and I couldn't see his face. "I'm still trying to understand what it means to be part lust demon, Shade. It's like my body is all gung-ho about experiencing all the lusty pleasures of life, but my mind and emotions haven't quite caught up yet."

"You mean you're not ready yet to uh . . . do the full Monty?"

I chuckled but nodded into his shirt, feeling embarrassed just talking about it.

He squeezed me tight. "That's okay, love. I don't expect you to."

Oh, wow. This was so totally stupid, but when he called me *Love*, I about melted into a big puddle of goo. Thank heavens Fang wasn't here to laugh at me. "You don't?"

"No. I know you're not ready yet. Losing your virginity is huge for a lust demon."

I sighed. He did understand. "Yeah."

"Of course, I don't really like waiting," he teased. "But I will. You're worth it."

Oh, my. Every time Shade opened his mouth, he made me feel even more special. Was this the perfect guy or what? But I didn't get it. Here was this totally hot guy who was nice, sweet, understanding . . . and could have any girl he wanted. Why me?

I didn't realize I'd said that last part aloud until Shade responded. "Why not you? You're strong, passionate, loyal . . . and really, really cute."

I wrinkled my nose. Cute. I'd never expected to be called that.

"Besides," he added in a softer tone, "you see me. Not the shadow demon, not the freak with the whirling interdimensional energy occupying his skin. You see *me*."

Oh. I felt all proud of myself, yet embarrassed that I felt that pride. "Well, you're something special," I assured him. And I knew quite well what it felt like to be treated like a freak. Speaking of which . . . "Uh, that reminds me. I kinda mentioned you to my mom."

"You did?" For some reason, that made a huge grin split his face.

"Yeah, and she wants me to invite you to Thanksgiving dinner."

He turned all still and quiet. "And you don't want to?"

"Of course I want to. It's just that . . . I'm not sure how they'll treat you. It might not be a great holiday."

He relaxed. "I know your family is important to you, and I'd like to meet them. Don't worry about me. I'm used to dealing with people's reactions to my weirdness."

I sighed—might as well face the inevitable. "Okay, but don't say I didn't warn you."

"I won't." He paused and ran a finger down the side of my face. "So you won't mind me helping you with your . . . with Lola?"

"No . . . but for now, can it just be you and me? She doesn't need you right now, but I do."

"Of course." He lifted my chin with his finger to bring my mouth to his.

We kissed softly and I lay my head back down on his chest as we snuggled. This was so nice, so peaceful. I resolved to relax and enjoy it while I could. Soon enough, we'd be back to hunting thieves, staking vampires, and soothing angry demons.

Chapter Eighteen

I woke in Shade's arms sometime late the next morning when Fang poked me in the side. GET UP, SLEEPYHEAD. TIME TO FEED YOUR FAITHFUL HELLHOUND.

I AM HUNGRY, TOO, Princess added. NOT DOG FOOD. I WANT GWEN FOOD.

"All right, all right." I disentangled myself from Shade and got up stiffly. It had felt nice lying in his arms all night, but the uncomfortable couch was no substitute for my own bed. Groaning, I staggered to the kitchen as Shade turned over and threw his arm up over his head.

I opened the refrigerator and surveyed my options. Hellhounds could eat anything without repercussions, but they preferred protein. Since bacon and eggs were something I knew how to cook, I put them on the stove. I was nowhere near as good a cook as Gwen, but at least it was edible, and the two hellhounds didn't complain.

The smell of bacon cooking woke Shade, and he joined us for breakfast. It was strange watching him eat. His food disappeared into the constantly moving boundaries of his face, but it was impossible to make out where his mouth was. I wondered if all the food he ate ended up in this dimension, or if some ended up somewhere else. If it ended up elsewhere, did that mean it was exchanged for food there? Ew. Ick. Didn't even want to think about that.

Neither of us were morning people, so we ate in silence for awhile until Shade said, "I haven't been to my place in awhile. I should probably go home now that I'm feeling better and we don't need to test anyone else." He stretched. "It'll be nice to sleep in a real bed again, too."

I nodded. I could understand his wanting to go home. And too much togetherness could be a bad thing. I didn't want us to get on each other's nerves before we'd even started a relationship. At least I hoped that's what this was.

He stopped eating for a moment. "Are you working tonight?"

"No." Realizing he didn't know what had happened the night before, I told him about the store, the warning messages, and Dan's suggestion to take some time off.

"Then would you like to do something together?"

Absurdly pleased by the thought of a real date, I said, "Sure. But can you . . ." I gestured at his general swirliness, which would make it difficult to appear in public.

"Not easily. But I thought we could go to my place or stay here, rent a movie, and order in."

I smiled shyly. "Sounds good. Why don't you come back here? I'd like you to be near Gwen when she's home, just in case."

"Cool." He rose and took the dishes to the sink, and even rinsed them off and put them in the dishwasher. He was well trained, too. "Where's your cell?"

I pulled it out of my pocket. "Here. Why?"

He took it from me. "To program in my number." He pushed some buttons then handed it back to me. When our hands touched, I saw a smile flash across his face. "In case you need to call me."

Did it make me a total dork that I thought that was incredibly cool and sweet, a real boyfriend-like thing to do?

He kissed me on the cheek. "See you later."

The two hellhounds, who had been dozing under the table after their meal, raised their heads. I WANT TO BRING FANG WITH US, Princess said. SHOW HIM MY HOME.

I glanced at Fang. "It's up to you. We won't be working today, so you're free to do whatever you want."

I GUESS I'LL DO WHAT PRINCESS WANTS, THEN.

He didn't sound all that thrilled, but the alternative was hanging out around here, waiting for trouble to come to us. Not exactly exciting. "Can you get them both on your Ducati?" I asked Shade.

"Actually, Micah took my bike home and brought back my car, so it should be no problem."

"Okay, good." Though it seemed strange that I didn't even know where he lived or what kind of car he drove.

The rest of the morning, I spent more time than I would like to admit daydreaming about Shade, but that wasn't productive, so I decided to get something done.

It took hours to read through everything Rick had given me on my ancestors. On my mother's side, I didn't find anything out of the ordinary at all. My father's side was a different matter. There wasn't a lot, mostly birth and death certificates, along with a family tree and some newspaper clippings, including obituaries.

Weird. The Shapiro lust demons didn't reproduce much. My great-grandfather was the full incubus demon in my family. He died at an unspecified age, estimated at twenty-five, and was killed by a jealous husband whose wife he had seduced. The obituary suggested he was a philanderer and the world was better off without him. His origins were unknown, and he didn't have any known family except for his only child, my grandfather.

My grandfather wasn't quite as bad, being only half incubus, but he was no saint either. He was widely known as a Casanova with the ability to charm any woman into bed. He died at the age of twenty-seven, killed by the father of a girl he seduced. He also had only one child—my father. And my father, of course, died at the age of twenty-three, having killed himself. He had only one child—me. No one commented on their unusual strength, speed, or healing powers, and the women in that line were totally normal except for carrying the offspring of incubi.

Confused, I set the papers down. Could I have more than one child? Did I want one at all? More importantly, should I try? I was too young to think about it yet, but I might want children some day. Having a child who was only one-sixteenth incubus or succubus didn't seem too awful, but what if I ended up marrying someone like Shade? What would happen if two different kind of demon genes mixed? A shadow lust demon? I wouldn't want to inflict that on any kid. Better look into birth control, fast.

Then again, would I even live long enough to have a kid? Life expectancy wasn't very long in the Shapiro demon line . . . Was this a curse of the Shapiros? To die an early death because of the demon inside them?

No. I wouldn't accept that. If my demon side was almost too strong for me to handle, imagine that doubled, quadrupled . . . No wonder my ancestors succumbed to the incubus within. Their deaths were a natural consequence of their inability to keep the demon zipped inside. Besides, hadn't Micah's father lived into his forties? Micah had never said what he died of.

Gwen said I could use her computer whenever I wanted, so I checked out the Internet. Lucas Blackburn's obituary said he'd died in a car accident at the age of forty-seven. Nothing supernatural about the drunk driver who'd killed him, and I couldn't find any mention of anything peculiar about Lucas anywhere else on the Internet. He knew how to keep his demon under wraps and had taught Micah to do the same. Maybe I *should* listen to Micah's advice.

Sighing, I pushed away from the computer. Another dead end. Frustration seemed to be the rule in my life lately. Frustrated in finding out where my extra abilities came from, frustrated in finding the books or the thief who stole them, and frustrated in . . . well, let's just say Shade had a lot to do with that last one.

My phone rang. Thank goodness—something to do. I answered it. It was Dan, checking on us, as promised. From the sound of the noise in the background, he was at the hospital. Since he didn't sound stressed, I assumed he was visiting Nicole again. I felt only a small pang of regret. Dan was better off with someone fully human, like himself. "Everything's fine here," I assured him. We discussed the possibilities for a few minutes and Dan asked, "You're sure this Andrew kid isn't the thief?"

"I'd like him to be, but Fang cleared him. It has to be someone else."

"Maybe."

"Hey, did the SCU forensics people find anything at the store?"

"No. Too many members of the general public had passed through there, and there were no prints on the fire alarm."

Well, crap. "Okay, thanks. I'll let you go." I couldn't help but rib him a little. "Tell Nicole I hope she's doing better."

"I, uh . . . oh, okay."

He sounded embarrassed and a little guilty for spending time with her. Well, I wasn't above feeling a little pleasure at his guilt. Grinning, I hung up.

Now what? I didn't have to stick around to wait for Dan anymore, and I wasn't sure what time Gwen would be home. I surfed the 'net awhile, shopping for stuff to go in my room and spending way too much money. So I was really glad when the doorbell rang, hoping whoever was there would provide a cure for my boredom.

Mood was there, her eyes glowing purple with distress as she supported Josh with one arm around his waist and the other holding his arm around her neck. His head lolled, and at first I thought he was drunk . . . until I saw the scrapes, cuts, and bruises all over him. "We need Shade," she said, sounding as upset as she looked.

I helped her half-walk, half-carry Josh to the couch. He collapsed there and groaned.

I knelt beside him. "What happened, Josh? Who did this?" Had the thief targeted another demon?

"Fault of . . . vamps," Josh muttered.

Oh, crap. "Do you know which ones?" I pressed.

But the effort must have been too much, for Josh passed out. Mood looked stricken. "Someone beat him up yesterday. It's really bad, and he won't go to the hospital. I'm afraid he's going to die." Her voice broke and the tears came, pouring silently down her face. She stared around the room. "Where's Shade? He has to heal Josh."

"He's not here, but I'll call him." This wasn't exactly what I pictured using his phone number for, but it was an emergency.

When he answered, I said, "Shade, can you come now? Josh is hurt bad and needs your help"

"I'm on my way."

Tears stained Mood's face, making her black and purple eye makeup blotch and run. "It's okay," I assured her. "Shade will be here soon."

He must not live far away, because he knocked on the door within fifteen minutes. I let him and the two hellhounds in. Fang and Princess slipped out the back, Fang muttering something about being in the way and finding some squirrels to chase.

I pointed wordlessly to the couch. Josh had regained consciousness, and though he couldn't—or wouldn't—tell us who had done this to him, he did open up enough to tell Shade where it hurt.

"I'm afraid there may be some internal damage," Shade said. "I can heal him, but it'll hurt quite a bit, Josh."

"Can't . . . hurt more . . . than it does . . . now," Josh gasped out.

"Okay. I'll need someone to use as a template, so the healing energies know how a healthy body operates."

"Me," Mood said immediately. "Use me."

"Are you sure?" Shade asked. "I'm only the conduit for the energy, but when you act as the template, you two will share a lot more than energy—thoughts, history, emotion. Are you ready to reveal everything about yourselves to each other?"

Mood turned even paler and glanced guiltily at Josh. I understood that look. The poor girl had a huge crush on him, and he wasn't even aware of it. "I can do it," I said softly. "I've done it before." It wasn't fun, but at least I didn't have any secrets to keep from the guy.

Josh recoiled, then grimaced at the pain. "No. Mood, please?"

She stroked the hair back from his forehead. "Of course, Josh. I'll do this for you."

Guess he didn't want to know the depths of the Slayer's heart. I couldn't blame him and, to tell the truth, it didn't hurt even a little to be unwanted. I just felt relieved that Mood was the one who would share everything with him.

Shade had Mood sit in a chair next to the couch and he knelt between them. "I'm going to place my hand on the back of your neck," he told them. "Are you ready?"

They both nodded. "Try to stay conscious and endure it as long as you can," Shade told Josh, then slipped his hands inside their collars to touch bare skin. He blipped into focus and I could tell when he started because Mood and Josh both stiffened. Josh's body bowed in agony and his mouth opened in a soundless scream. Mood looked stunned, apprehensive, and disbelieving all at once.

It was too painful to watch them, so I turned my attention to Shade instead. The last time he'd done this, *I* was the template and hadn't really noticed what was going on with the conduit. Once every second or more, Shade flipped to swirls, and harsh flickers of violet lightning pulsed through him, flashing from Mood to Josh. That must be the otherworldly healing energy he was using, but it looked like a raging storm inside the shadow demon.

Shade had told Dan and me it didn't hurt him, but the way he grimaced, his teeth bared and his head thrown back, it sure didn't look like a walk in the park. Then again, maybe it wasn't pain. Maybe he was just concentrating really hard.

I remember the whole process had seemed to take hours, but this only took a few long, agonizing minutes as Josh's wounds, cuts, and scrapes visibly healed. Shade released him abruptly. Josh fell back, passed out, but looked a hundred times better than he had before.

Mood put her hands over her face and burst into tears.

"It's okay," Shade told her tightly. "He's healed now."

Feeling I needed to do something, I said, "If you want to talk . . . "

But Mood just shook her head, then ran out the door, slamming it behind her.

Whoa. "I guess she learned exactly how Josh feels about her."

Shade stood up and slipped his hood up over his head. "He lost his girlfriend not too long ago. Hasn't gotten over her yet."

His voice sounded strained. "Are you okay?"

"Fine." But when he turned to walk, he staggered a little and caught himself on the couch.

"Yeah, right."

I hurried around the couch and tried to help him, but he jerked his arm away. "Don't touch me."

I backed away, palms out. "Whoa, dude. Just trying to help."

"I know." He bent his head and crossed his arms across his chest. "I'm . . . not stable right now."

What did that mean? I didn't remember this happening last time. Then again, he'd left pretty fast after he'd healed Dan, and I was far more concerned about other things then. "You don't look like you can walk, let alone drive. Why don't you lie down in my room?"

"Okay."

He stumbled toward my room and I went before him to clear his path and open the door. Though I was careful not to touch him, I couldn't help but wonder what the heck was going on. Once Shade was horizontal, and lying on his back, I closed the door and stepped toward the bed. "What can I do to help?"

"Nothing."

Well, that sounded final, not to mention rude. Now I was confused. After all, we were supposed to go on our first real date tonight, and this didn't seem like the Shade I knew at all. Then again, how much did I really know about the shadow demon? I thought for a minute, wondering what to do.

I should grant him his secrets.

I should respect his privacy.

I should leave him alone.

To hell with *shoulds*. I wanted answers.

Chapter Nineteen

I plopped down on the floor next to the bed. "I think I deserve an explanation."

"Go away, Val," he said, his voice sounding tight, like he'd gritted the words through his teeth.

I wished I could see his face, but it whirled with dark energy swirls. Strange. They were moving a lot faster than normal, and seemed shot through with virulent purple. "Not gonna happen. You helped me with Lola. The least I can do is help you with this." Whatever "this" was.

From the way my comforter bunched up under his fist, it looked like he was gripping it with all his might. I closed my hand over his fist and he popped back into focus, his face contorted into a snarling mask of demonic rage. I reared back for a moment, finally noticing the long, sharp blade in his other hand, pointed toward his own neck. What the—

I wrestled the knife away from him and tossed it into the corner, then clamped down on his fist again. I realized the rage wasn't directed at me. In fact, it looked like Shade was battling hard against something internal. Or against something in another dimension, maybe?

He tried to throw off my hand, but I wouldn't let him. Without letting go, I got up on the bed next to him. "Shade, what's happening? Talk to me." This was beginning to scare me.

He whipped his head away from me, trying to hide his raging agony in my pillow. With my other hand, I cupped his cheek, hoping to reassure him.

"Don't!" He sat up abruptly and shoved me off him, off the bed, and onto the floor. I could hear him breathing hard as he turned away from me and curled into a fetal position.

Stunned, I sat there for a moment on my aching butt. What the hell was going on? Whatever it was, I was pretty sure Shade wasn't in control of himself right now. Was this the shadow side of his demon? I could sympathize. When Lola took control of me, I wasn't always responsible for my actions either.

Speaking of Lola, maybe she could help him. Heck, she ought to be good for something. I got up and sat down gently on the bed, trying not to touch him and set him off again. Reaching down deep inside, I encouraged Lola to come out and play. She really liked Shade, so this should be a no-brainer.

My lusty demon was a little reluctant after we'd been thrown on our butt, but I ignored Shade's body language and reminded myself—and her—that he wasn't usually like this. He was usually nice, friendly, and, when he wasn't all swirly, hot enough to light anyone's fuse.

Oh, yeah. That did it. Lola reached out tentatively toward Shade. Whatever he was fighting, it didn't matter. He was still male, still helpless against Lola's lure. Thin tendrils of lust and need slipped in through him and slid up his spinal column, caressing his chakras along the way. I sent more wisps of energy to wind through his core, radiating out and down, touching all those sensitive, secret male spots and bringing them to his attention. I left him that way for a few moments, not wanting to do more that would force him to do my bidding.

"Val," he croaked in a warning tone.

"Shhh. Let me help you." I reached out to massage his shoulders. Boy, were they tense. "Relax. Just enjoy the sensations."

He let go of a tiny fraction of his tension, but he still wasn't feeling enough desire for Lola. Encouraged, I spooned against his back with my arm around his waist, hoping the touch of my body would finish what Lola had started. Oddly enough, instead of drawing energy from him, I was able to send energy into his body, stoking his pleasure centers with my reserves, stroking his nerve endings with a feather-light touch, helping him to feel human again.

Whoa. I didn't know I could do that. But it was sure nice to know I could give as well as receive.

He relaxed some more and unbent from his fetal position. Encouraged, I snuggled closer and let my hand wander up his chest, down his side to his hip and his outer thigh. He sighed in pleasure, and I let my hand move to the inside of his leg, the denim feeling rough against my fingertips. I squeezed his thigh and Shade rolled onto his back. "What are you doing?" he asked softly.

Ah, good. The strain was gone from his voice. Lola wanted me to let my fingers do a little more walking, but I wasn't bold enough to do that yet. I did want to see his face, though, so I pulled his T-shirt up and laid my palm flat on his warm stomach then gazed into his eyes. Pain resided there, along with shame and another emotion I couldn't name. "I'm trying to make you feel better," I said.

He sighed and closed his eyes. "It's working."

"Good," I whispered, then straddled his hips to run both of my hands up his bare chest, loving the hardness, the muscles, the ticklish feel of his chest hair. Very male. His lips parted as he watched me beneath hooded eyes, one lock of blond hair curled across his forehead. He was so gorgeous, so beautiful. I couldn't believe he was here. With me. Like this.

He reached out and clasped my hips, then raised his hands to lift my shirt up and over my head. He did it so fast, he caught me off guard. I froze for a moment, then realized that was all he planned to do for the moment. He clasped my bare waist, smiling as he gazed at me with a covetous look in his eye that Lola liked . . . a lot.

My body heated under his gaze and I fought the urge to cover my chest with my hands. True, I was still covered by a bra, but it was plain white cotton. Not exactly the sort of thing you wanted a guy to see the first time he saw you naked. I'd planned on something lacier and a lot prettier for our date, but hadn't had time to change.

"Beautiful," he murmured.

Embarrassed in the bright light, I slid down onto the bed and laid on my side. Shade sat up, shucked his hoodie, then pulled his T-shirt off over his head. He lay next to me and cradled me in his arms, bare belly to warm bare belly.

"This feels nice," he said as he hugged me and rested his forehead against mine.

Since he didn't seem inclined to do anything else, I wondered if he was still fighting . . . whatever. "Are you okay now?" I asked.

"I'm good."

I ran my hand down his smooth back, loving the feel of his chest against mine. I let Lola subside, since he seemed to be in control now. "What happened there, Shade?"

He stayed silent for a moment, then asked, "You sure you want to know?"

"Of course. I showed you my demon. Time for you to show me yours."

He chuckled at that then sighed. "I did."

"I know, and I want to understand it." Shade was so sweet, I wanted to help him any way I could. "You're not *just* a conduit for the other dimension's energies, are you?"

"Yes and no."

"Well, that helped. Not. Come on, share."

"I am a conduit . . . but I don't let all the energies through."

He stopped there and left me hanging. Sheesh, this was like pulling teeth. "I know you let through the healing energies, so what kind do you *not* let through? Bad ones?"

"You could say that."

"Come on, Shade. Spill."

He sighed. "Micah is the only other one who knows this. He's usually there for me, after the healing. But I didn't think about calling him when you called. I just came running."

This reluctance to talk was making me impatient, but I could tell this was difficult for him, and very important. "I won't mention it to another soul."

"I know." He squeezed me harder for a moment. "Okay. Shadow demons create a conduit between two dimensions. When I pull in healing energy from the other side, I send back other energy."

"You mentioned that before," I said encouragingly.

He nodded. "When it's going back and forth, it's not a problem. But once I stop . . . " He paused to take a deep breath. "Other . . . things . . . feel the disturbance and try to cross into this world. Through me. Your energy helped me stop them."

"*Things?* Like what?"

"Bad things. Bad . . . demons."

"*Demons* try to cross through you, through your body?"

He shuddered and nodded.

I had a sudden vision of Shade's body erupting with pustulant sores that became writhing monsters that grew from his body and fell off. That couldn't be right. "I assume we're talking full demons here. How is that possible?"

"As a conduit, I could channel their essence. Once it arrives here, they would take the form of one of the native species—humans, dogs, other animals."

"No wonder they were able to interbreed with us."

"Yes. Where do you think demons came from in the first place?"

"I never gave it any thought." But I did now. Good grief. It made sense. Demons weren't native to this dimension so they had to come from somewhere . . .

"Thank you," I said suddenly.

"For what?"

"For not letting any more through." A whole army of full-blooded demons? I shuddered. I didn't want to think about it.

"You're welcome." But there was an odd tone in his voice.

"There's more, isn't there?"

He sighed. "Yes. Did you ever wonder why you haven't seen more full demons?"

"Never thought about it." But now that I had, I was really glad I hadn't. Vampires were bad enough, but at least they'd been human once. Demons, not so much. "Why?"

"Because the last time they came through was in 1929. All you see now is their great-grandchildren, like us. That's why most of us have one-eighth demon blood. Unless we mate with another partial demon of the same type, the strain diminishes over time."

"1929? You mean the stock market crash, the depression . . . ?"

He nodded. "Caused in great part by creatures from another dimension. They see our world as a place to propagate freely in a safe environment. They can't help trying to destroy it at the same time. It's in their nature."

Stunned, I pulled away to stare at him. "You said the 'last time' they came through. I take it they've made it through before?"

"Yes, and each time with devastating effects on our world. That's why stories of demons go back throughout history."

"Why haven't we seen more of them? Not that I'm complaining, mind you."

"Because it takes a shadow demon like me to let them through. And I'll die before I'll let that happen."

Oh. "That's why . . . the knife?"

"Yes." He buried his face in my neck. "You see, though any full shadow demon can pass bodily through the dimensions, not every one can help their kind pass through the dimensions. Only a few special ones throughout history." He paused, then added, "Like my great-grandfather and everyone descended from him."

That bit of news hit me like a slug in the gut. "Ohmigod, Shade, it's not your fault," I hurried to assure him. "You're not responsible for the stupid things your great-grand-demon did." When Shade remained silent and unmoving, I added, "Besides, if he hadn't, neither of us would be alive today. Or people like Micah either."

"I know."

But he didn't sound as if it made any difference in his self-blame. "Can they come through at other times?"

"Maybe. If I get too angry." He gave me a wry grin. "You wouldn't like me when I'm angry."

So that's what Micah had meant. Images of a swirly green Hulk swam through my mind, but I dismissed them. To distract him, I asked, "So you know a lot about the different kinds of demons?"

"Some."

"Do you, uh, think it's possible that I have some other kind of demon in me?"

"No. Not possible. We can't interbreed."

No? Well, I guess that meant no shadowy lust demon rug rats were in the offing. Good to know. But I wondered why Micah didn't know it when Shade did. And what could explain me and my unusual strength?

Before I could ask, Shade said, "I don't want to talk about this anymore. Can we change the subject?"

"Okay," I said reluctantly. I'd ask him later, when he wasn't still shaken up by keeping back the demon horde. "What do you want to talk about?"

"Did you really offer to work for the Movement?"

Surprised, I pulled away for a moment. "Did Micah tell you that?"

"No, Fang told Princess."

And Princess, of course, never met a secret she didn't blab instantly. "Great spy she'd make," I muttered.

He pulled me back. "At least someone told me about it. You didn't really mean it, did you? You wouldn't work for the vampires?"

He looked so concerned, I squirmed a little. "Yes, I gave my word." But before he could say anything else, I added, "But only if another vamp gets poisoned or a demon tries to harm a vamp."

"Tries to . . . or succeeds?"

I thought back to our conversation, trying to remember exactly what I'd said. "Uh, I said 'tries to'," I admitted, "but I'm sure he knows I meant if he succeeded."

"I hope you're right," Shade said, but he looked like he doubted it. "They're dangerous, love. Very dangerous. And I don't care how civilized Alejandro seems, vampire nests have been known to chew up and spit out anyone who isn't just like them."

"I can take care of myself," I assured him.

"Against one or two, sure. But against many, some of whom hold your future in their hands?"

He looked a lot more worried than the situation called for. Soothingly, I said, "Don't worry. It won't happen. We'll find the thief, stop the bad guys, and all will be right with the world." Seeing he still looked skeptical, I kissed him to take his mind off the subject. "Can we not talk about this any more?" I asked, echoing his earlier words.

He shook his head, but seemed willing to drop it. Then, wickedly, he said, "Well, since we're both half naked and all . . . "

He kissed my neck and I dissolved into putty in his arms once again. Wow, that felt . . . awesome. Lola perked up again, glad it was time to play. Desire, warm and languid, played back and forth between Shade and me.

"Feed on me," Shade whispered between soft kisses on the swell of my breasts. "Make me forget I'm a shadow demon." He licked the curve of my breast along the line of my bra. "Take back the sustenance you gave me."

Oh, my. Suddenly, it seemed like we were both wearing too many clothes, and I ached in places that had never felt a guy's touch. I lost all control of Lola and she surged into him, wanting, needing, demanding. Lust curled between us, warm and thick as molasses, flowing back and forth and making me feel languid yet aching for a sensation I'd never experienced.

"Hold on a sec," he whispered. Shade let go of me and slid off the bed to lock the door. He removed his shoes, socks, knife sheath, jeans, then his boxers. Though he stood there, obviously totally naked, I couldn't see anything but his shadow demon swirls. They'd calmed down a lot but still obscured every part of his body, making him look like a hologram filled with eddying gray smoke. Oddly enough, the center of the swirls seemed concentrated right below his abdomen.

He reached out his hand and I gulped. Did I really want to see what was at the center? My face turned hot and I waffled mentally.

"It's okay, Val," he said softly. "You don't have to do anything you don't want to do."

Slowly, wondering what the heck I was doing, I extended my hand slowly until it touched his, bringing his body into sharp focus. This was the first fully nude man I'd ever seen, and I couldn't help but gape. And I'd thought he was gorgeous before . . . Oh, my. Heat spread through me, and I didn't know what to do. I wanted to see, but I didn't. Not understanding the sensations rushing through me, I stood up and propelled myself into his arms so I wouldn't have to look anymore. Sheesh, could I be any more idiotic?

"It's all right," Shade said, and I could hear the smile in his voice as he ran his hands down my back, soothing me. "No need to be embarrassed."

Oh, God. He already knew I was a virgin, but he hadn't known until now how very inept and dorky I could be. Embarrassed to see a naked man? Flushing with heat because I not only felt his desire for me through Lola's link, but also against my bare stomach? How stupid could I be?

Plenty. Then again, I didn't have to stay a virgin for long, did I? I eased off my jeans and kicked them aside, then leaned back into Shade's warmth. Since I was doing what Lola wanted, she was content to lie back and wait, letting me take charge.

I wasn't quite ready to take off my bra and panties yet. They were the last line of defense in case I changed my mind. Shade seemed to understand how I felt, for he didn't push. Instead, he pulled me gently back onto the bed, gathered me in his arms, and kissed me.

Wanting and need filled me and I kissed him back, feeling desperate to connect with this special guy. Oh, yeah. This felt right. But when he did nothing more than run his hands and his mouth over me, I asked, "Don't you want to . . . ?"

"Of course I do," he murmured in my ear. "But I won't until you're ready."

"Trust me, I'm *ready*."

He chuckled, low and sexy. "I don't mean that way. Losing your virginity is huge for a succubus."

Puzzled, I said, "You said that before. Isn't it huge for everyone?"

"Sure, but are you ready to lose everything else?"

Huh? "Like what?"

"You know." He trailed a finger down my cheek and kissed the hollow of my neck. "The other things that come with being a virgin succubus."

"What other things?"

He froze. "You mean you don't know?"

"No!" Was he about to reveal something horrible? Scared to know, yet even more frightened not to, I sat straight up and stared at him. "Tell me."

He propped up on one elbow. "When you came into puberty, you started developing unusual strength, speed, and healing powers, right?"

"Yes, but how does that relate?"

"You'll lose all that the first time you make love. Forever."

I sat back, stunned. So that's where those extra powers came from. "You're kidding me," I breathed.

"Afraid not. I'm sorry, I thought you knew. Micah didn't mention it?"

"No."

Shade frowned. "Well, maybe he didn't know. The male demons often lose theirs right away. He may not have been aware of the connection." He thought for a moment. "That would explain a lot. I don't think his father knew either."

Holy crap. If I made love to Shade, or anyone for that matter, I'd lose all the abilities that made me . . . me. No more being able to satisfy Lola's lust with the hunt, no more being the enforcer of the Demon Underground, no more job with the SCU . . . no more Slayer.

On the other hand, finally being able to make love, to become a real woman . . . to be more normal. Would it be worth it? I didn't know. They said your first time was usually painful, awkward, and possible all-around yucky. Not a good trade-off.

What the hell kind of choice was this?

Chapter Twenty

"Val?" Shade said tentatively. "Are you all right?"

"No. No, I'm not." How could I possibly decide between two such appalling choices? Especially since one of them was horribly, irrevocably final. It sucked dirty rotten eggs. "I . . . I have to think about it."

"I know," he said softly. He got up to slip his jeans back on then drew me back down to the bed to cuddle. "Don't worry, no pressure. You have all the time in the world to make a decision. And whatever you decide, it'll be right."

Well, in this case, *not* making a decision was actually making one. It made my head hurt.

I snuggled into his arms, needing comfort. That was all I intended, really, but Lola had been teased and left wanting twice this evening, and she wasn't about to let me get away with it a third time. She surged into him almost roughly, bringing him to instant lust and keeping him on the edge as she slurped up all that lovely energy.

Appalled by her greediness, I tried to cut her off, but it was like trying to stop a spewing fire hydrant with a wine cork. I wrenched myself away from Shade and flattened myself against the door, as far away as I could get, and fought to get her under control.

That worked, thank God. Lola released Shade, and I was able to slow the flow to a trickle until I was able to stop altogether.

"Wow," he said, unmoving on the bed. "That was . . . intense."

I was really glad I couldn't see Shade's expression right now. "I'm *so* sorry, Shade. I didn't mean to, but I lost control."

"I know. It's okay." He paused. "Maybe I should leave."

An excellent idea. I nodded. "Thanks for coming." Oh, crap. Could I say anything more stupid? A wave of heat suffused me and I turned my back on him to grab my clothes and put them back on.

Shade dressed slowly, retrieving his knife from where I'd thrown it. When he was done, he stood by the door, hooded and enigmatic. "We all have issues dealing with our demons, Val. Don't be so hard on yourself."

Sheesh. I'd practically drained the guy and he was all understanding and everything. I couldn't speak. What could I say? I just nodded.

I unlocked the door and he leaned forward to kiss me on the forehead. "We'll try this again sometime. A real date," he clarified.

"Sounds good," I whispered.

We searched for Josh, but he must have recovered and taken off on his own. Fang and Princess were lying side by side in the living room, strangely quiet.

After Shade and Princess left, I plopped down on the couch and covered my face with my hands. This night hadn't turned out at all like I'd wished. And though Lola had almost sucked Shade dry, it felt strangely unsatisfying.

Fang jumped up next to me and licked my hand. WHO LOVES YA, BABE?

"You do?" I asked with a smile.

YOU BET.

I hugged him to me, finding comfort in his small, fuzzy presence. "How much of that did you hear?" I asked into his fur.

PRETTY MUCH ALL OF IT. SUCKS TO BE YOU. But he cuddled closer to take the sting from his words and let me know he really did sympathize.

"Yeah." That covered it. Like being poised between heaven and hell. Either I chose to be a wimpy wanton woman, or a strong celibate slayer.

Heck, I couldn't be either right now. I had to stay home and twiddle my thumbs, wait for someone else to find a clue or the books, and hope my mysterious enemy didn't decide to take out any more frustration on my family and friends. It made me positively look forward to Thanksgiving dinner and the inevitable family drama.

The front door opened then and Gwen came in. Her schedule was so screwy, I never knew when she'd be home and when she wouldn't.

"You okay?" she asked. "You look like you just lost your best friend."

Fang barked and wagged his tail. NO. I'M RIGHT HERE.

She laughed. "Don't tell me. He just said *he's* your best friend."

"Yep." It should have made me smile, but I didn't feel like smiling right now.

Gwen shrugged off her jacket and dumped her stuff on a chair. "Okay, give. What's wrong? My big brother acting like a jerk again?"

"No. In fact, he's been really nice. He said you had a talk with him."

She nodded. "So what's wrong then?"

Hoping she'd have some good advice, I spilled the whole mess to her.

"Oh, Val, I'm sorry. I wish I could help, but I don't have any advice to offer. I don't know anyone else who's ever had to make such a tough decision . . . except maybe your mom."

"How do you figure? It was my father who was part-demon. Mom is fully human, like you."

Gwen shook her head. "No, I mean a decision between two awful choices. Like the one she had to make when she asked you to leave."

My laugh sounded bitter. "Yeah, right. Choose between the pretty blonde who looks like a clone of her and the uncontrollable lust demon who reminds her of her ex? Real tough."

"Do you think it was easy?" Gwen asked softly. "Think about it. She had to decide whether to protect your sister or keep your love. Don't you think that was difficult for her?"

"I doubt it. She was pretty mean, said some nasty things." Then again, so had I.

"Maybe she had to be mean. Maybe she had to be tough on the outside and keep you at a distance to be strong enough to do what she felt was right. That has to be a horrible choice for any parent to make." Gwen gave me a one-armed hug. "I've been thinking about this since I met her at the mall. I saw how she looked at you when you weren't watching. Like she regretted everything that had happened."

Fang nudged me. GWEN MIGHT BE RIGHT, YOU KNOW.

Strange. But if these two thought it was possible . . . After a few moments of reflection, I said, "She did seem nicer yesterday, when I saw her at the store." And though it hadn't been intentional, I had been a bad influence on my little sister. My demon "gifts" had led Jen to think I was special, and she wanted to be like me.

Gwen nodded. "So, if your mom was able to make such a horrible choice and survive it, maybe you can, too." She cocked her head at me. "And maybe you can survive Thanksgiving with her tomorrow, too."

I shrugged. Maybe. One really didn't have anything to do with the other.

"You can always come home with Dan and me. The Sullivans are a rowdy bunch, but we have fun."

Celebrate the holiday with someone else's family? I'd feel like an outsider, and Thanksgiving wouldn't be the same. Then again, it would never be the same at home either. How could it? "Thanks, but I'll try to be a grown-up and go home. Besides, I already invited Shade. Maybe I'll take a peace offering."

"Good idea." Gwen patted me on the arm once more. "Stop worrying so much and remember what Thanksgiving is all about—a day of gratitude for the good things in your life. Try to enjoy it." With that parting shot, she picked up her things and went to her room.

Don't worry, be happy . . . what kind of advice was that?

PRETTY GOOD IF YOU ASK ME, Fang said with a doggie grin.

"I didn't." But I knew he was only trying to help, so I kissed his fuzzy little head. Sighing, I stood up. "Maybe Micah has some wisdom to share."

I went to my room and called him, but Micah seemed shocked that Shade knew something about lust demons that neither he nor his father had a clue about. He hadn't known demons couldn't interbreed either, and worst of all, he had no idea about what I should do. "I'm sorry, Val, this is a decision you'll have to make on your own. But if you choose to uh, lose your strength, we'll help you find something else to do."

"Like what?" I had no other skills except helping Mom and Rick at the store, and I couldn't see myself in retail for the rest of my life.

"I don't know, but we'll find something."

Disappointment filled me at the whole conversation, but I didn't want Micah to feel bad, so I said, "Okay, thanks."

"Hey, if you decide not to go to your mom's house tomorrow, you can always come here. We close the club and have a pot-luck dinner here for anyone in the Demon Underground who's interested. Mostly singles like you and me."

It sounded tempting, but . . . "Have you found the thief yet?"

"No, I would have let you know if I had."

That's what I figured. "Then no. After those two warnings, I figure I ought to stay away from demons and vamps." Humans ought to be safe. "But I appreciate the invite."

"Okay, have a great holiday."

"Thanks."

I hung up and flopped backward onto the bed. The icy blue and brown of my room soothed me, yet made me feel like a fraud. Chic and sophisticated? Hardly.

Fang jumped up beside me to curl against my side, his small body feeling warm against my side. YOU'LL GROW INTO IT, he assured me. WHY DON'T YOU TAKE GWEN'S ADVICE?

I sighed. "It's hard not to worry." I didn't want to lose the very things that made me special. I'd always been defined by my strength, speed, and healing powers. If I lost those, who would I be? Just a girl with the ability to control men and make them feel horny. Oh yeah, great gift.

A LOT OF WOMEN WOULD ENVY YOU, Fang reminded me.

"None I'd like to know." What kind of woman would relish that kind of power? Sick.

But I was tired of moping and worrying. "Okay, let's go find a suitable peace offering."

ও • ঙ

Just after noon the next day, Shade, Fang and I stood at the door of my former home and knocked. Mom liked us to dress up for holidays, so I had on my best white blouse and prettiest vest, with make-up, tamed hair and everything. Fang had picked out my outfit and Gwen had helped with the face stuff and loaned us her car so I wouldn't ruin the look. I was determined to let Mom know that if she was willing to try, so was I. I'd even brought her favorite dessert, which Shade was holding for me.

He looked gorgeous as always, and had dressed in a nice sweater and slacks. I held his hand so no one would freak at seeing his demon side first.

Jen answered the door, grinning at the sight of us. "Oh, good, you came. And you brought your friend." I introduced them and she gave me a swift hug then glanced at Fang. "Just let me lock the cat up."

I CAN BE CIVILIZED, Fang said petulantly.

You can, but I'm not sure about the cat.

The hellhound seemed mollified at that, so we entered and I looked around. It looked pretty much the same as always, with maybe a few small changes. The delicious aroma of turkey cooking in the oven made the house smell wonderful. Mom came out, wiping her hands on a dish towel, and Rick joined us from the other room.

I introduced Shade, and I could tell they were all deliberately not noticing that we were holding hands. Might as well get it over with. Quickly, I explained about Shade and his swirliness, then let go of his hand.

Rick and Jen appeared fascinated, but Mom looked taken aback . . . like she wasn't sure how to react. Finally, she said, "I'm so glad you came." She looked uncertain whether to hug me or not, so I held out the bakery box. "Here. I brought this."

She glanced inside. "But you hate pecan pie."

I shrugged. "Yeah, but I know you and Rick love it."

Her expression softened. "And I made your favorite—apple."

I smiled. It was an excellent start, and I vowed to keep it that way for the rest of the day.

Like always, Jen and I helped Mom get ready in the kitchen while Rick set the table with the best china and crystal. This year, he went all out and decked out the table with store-bought decorations in a harvest and abundance theme. Shade helped him and I could hear them talking from the other room, wondering what the heck they could have to say to each other.

When we sat down to eat, Rick thanked the Goddess and asked everyone to say what they were thankful for, starting with himself. "I'm thankful for the goddess's gifts of our health, our prosperity, and for having my whole family together on this special day."

Did he mean me? The sentiment made me blink back tears.

"Val," he prompted. "Your turn."

We'd never done this before so I was caught a little off guard. "I, uh, I'm grateful for my job, my friends, Fang, and my family." Surprised, I realized that I hadn't had three of those last year at this time. I was more blessed than I realized.

Damn betcha, Fang said at my feet.

Shade pretty much said the same thing and Mom went on a little longer than we did, being much more global and politically correct in her thanks. Jen was more concerned with her narrow teenaged world, but they both expressed thanks for having me here today.

The rest of the meal went pretty well, with everyone trying to avoid sensitive topics and being on their best behavior. They didn't even object to me fixing a plate for Fang. I think it was the best meal I'd ever had in this house.

After dinner, we cleaned up then played Monopoly. That was safe, too, since there wasn't much about demons and vampires in the property acquisition game. Shade seemed comfortable enough and the others finally relaxed around him, especially since we tried to keep in skin-to-skin contact as often as we could.

For once, I did pretty good at the game. Rick usually won easily, but I had Fang to advise me this time. Who knew the cute little terrier could be such a ruthless real estate tycoon? But Rick won anyway and we ended up back at the table for dessert while Fang took a nap.

To keep Shade grounded, I slipped off my shoe and shimmied my bare foot up his leg. Sure, it might look like we were playing footsie, but I didn't care. This way he could look normal and we could both still have our hands free for pie. Since everyone was playing nice and we'd pretty much exhausted other subjects earlier, I asked, "Did the insurance cover the damage on the store?" Since Rick had said he was thankful for prosperity, it seemed like a safe subject.

Rick nodded. "We were surprised, but yes, they're covering most of it. Nothing was missing that we could see—just vandalized."

Jen piped up. "And we got it all cleaned up and ready to open for our big sale tomorrow."

Relieved that they hadn't suffered more because of me, I said, "Glad to hear it."

Mom, sounding tentative, asked, "Did you find any leads on who did it yet?"

"Dan and Micah are working on it, but I haven't heard anything yet." Apologetically, I added, "I'm afraid to do much more for fear they'll come after you."

Rick covered my hand with his. "We understand, honey. We appreciate everything you're doing."

It made me feel bad, 'cause I wasn't doing a darned thing. But there was one thing I could do. "Well, if you need any help tomorrow, let me know."

"I'd be glad to help as well," Shade offered.

"Thanks," Mom said. "But we should have it covered."

Jen rolled her eyes. "Yeah, if Josh shows up. He didn't bother to come to work the day of the break-in or the day after. Without any explanation, either." She glared at her parents. "No one else could have gotten away with that."

I shrugged. "If it's the same Josh I know, he couldn't. He was beaten pretty badly that day and wasn't healed until the following day. He was probably too embarrassed to mention it."

"How was he healed?" Rick asked. Shade and I exchanged an apprehensive glance, but Rick said, "Never mind. It's not important. Joshua did work yesterday."

Jen snorted, sounding a lot like Fang when he was disgusted.

"Yeah, but you didn't see the scene he and his friend had outside at lunch time."

"Jennifer," Mom warned. "Be nice."

"Come on, Mom. He and that Emo chick were yelling at each other about vampires and stuff . . . outside, where anyone could hear them. It's the only time I've ever seen her when her eyes weren't all creepy purple glowy."

Shade jerked, looking startled, and I gave him a questioning look, but he just shook his head.

"Were you eavesdropping?" Mom asked with a frown.

"No. I was just getting some fresh air. They were shouting so loud, anyone could have heard them."

Probably because Mood had confronted Josh about how he felt about her, though that wasn't my info to share. Trying to ratchet down the tension a bit, I said in a soothing tone, "He was probably upset because the vamps were the ones who beat him."

"No, they weren't," Jen said indignantly. "At least, that's not what he said."

"He didn't?" That was odd. Shade's expression turned grim for some reason.

Rick held up his hands. "Can we please not talk about this now?"

I gave him an apologetic look. "I'm sorry, but I think this might be important. Jen, can you tell us what they said?"

Looking pleased that she knew something useful, Jen nodded eagerly. "That girl yelled at him because he blamed the vamps when someone else really beat him up."

"Did she say who?" I asked.

"No. But he said it was really all the fault of the vampires because if they had saved his girlfriend like she asked, nothing bad would have happened to anyone."

Shade let out a noise as if he wanted to say something, but I beat him to it. "Saved his girlfriend, how?"

"I don't know."

"Did they mention his girlfriend's name?"

"Veronica," Shade said, pressing his fingers to his forehead as if he had a headache or was trying to hold something in. "His girlfriend's name was Veronica."

"Yeah," Jen said. "Is that important?"

"Very." Andrew's dead sister had also been Josh's fiancé. That meant he had a great motive for wanting vamps dead. And he'd tried to pin his beating on them. "Did they mention anyone else?"

"Just something about Josh not meaning to hurt a girl called Shawndra."

Shade rocked back and forth a little, looking pained. I peered into his face. "Shade, are you all right?"

He tried to tell me something with his eyes, but I wasn't getting it. "Not really," he managed.

My family looked worried. "He had a concussion not too long ago," I explained. "He probably just needs some rest." Or was having the same kind of epiphany I was and wanted to talk in private.

They all made sympathetic noises as I slipped my shoe back on and nudged Fang awake so we could head for the door. "Thanks for dinner," I said. "It was great."

"You're welcome," Mom said. "It was nice meeting you, Shade. I hope you feel better soon."

I fidgeted while they all did the polite good-byes and was able to keep my mouth shut until we got into the car and shut the doors. But then I couldn't keep quiet any longer. "Are you thinking what I'm thinking?" I demanded.

Chapter Twenty-One

"Probably," Shade said. "We have to get to Club Purgatory right away."

"Why?"

"Because that's where Josh is spending Thanksgiving, with the Underground."

I started the car and headed toward the club. "Yeah, looks like he's our guy."

HE CAN'T BE THE THIEF, Fang said in disbelief. I CLEARED HIM.

"Mood," Shade said curtly.

"Oh." The light dawned. "What color are her eyes normally?"

"Hazel," Shade said.

HUH? Fang sounded bewildered. THAT IS SO RANDOM. WHAT DOES THAT HAVE TO DO WITH ANYTHING?

Impatiently, I explained. "Whenever we use our powers, our eyes flash purple. But her eyes were purple *every time I saw her.* That's because she was controlling his emotions whenever she was around other people."

SO THAT'S WHY I DIDN'T PICK UP ON ANYTHING WHEN WE QUESTIONED JOSH, Fang said wonderingly. SHE HAD A LID ON HIM.

I sped up a bit more. "Was she in on this with him?"

"No," Shade said. "He was upset about losing Veronica and she was just trying to help."

I couldn't see Shade's expression, but his voice sounded tight and he was hunched over in his seat. "You okay?"

"Fine," he said. "I'm just . . . remembering things."

"Remembering what?"

"From when I healed Josh. It makes me dizzy."

"I thought you couldn't remember that stuff."

"Normally, I can't, but every time you or your sister mentioned something about what happened, I picked up flashes of his memory from when I healed him. Mood's too."

"How is that possible?"

"I don't know. I think it has something to do with you grounding me so soon after the healing."

WHO CARES HOW? Fang demanded. WHAT DO YOU REMEMBER? IS JOSH THE THIEF?

"Yes," Shade said. "He's a phase demon."

Whoa—news flash. A phase demon could phase in and out of solid objects . . . meaning he could walk through walls. Everything fell into place. Josh, the thief. It totally made sense.

Fang snorted. NO WONDER IT WAS SO EASY FOR THE LITTLE BUGGER TO STEAL THE BOOKS.

It was important to figure this out, but I was afraid to ask much more, afraid it would hurt Shade.

HE'S OKAY, Fang assured me. HE'S NOT HURTING . . . JUST TRYING TO STAY STABLE AND KEEP FROM GETTING TOO DIZZY.

Traffic had slowed to a crawl downtown so unfortunately, we had time for Shade to continue translating flashes of Josh's memories into something that made sense.

Desperate to cure Veronica's cancer, Josh had asked the vampires to turn Veronica into one of them. They refused without any explanation, which ticked him off, but he didn't do anything about it for awhile because Mood was keeping his emotions damped way down.

But when Mood jumped in to quiet the rumble at the club, she released him so abruptly that his anger at the vamps came back to him at once. He snuck out, phased through the office and the desk to take the books, then hid them inside the wall until he was able to come back and get them.

With the whiplash of emotions sawing through him, he wasn't really rational at the time. He'd planned to find out what the books said about vampires, then return them before we figured it out. Unfortunately, we found them missing too soon, so he couldn't. And . . . the books didn't *want* to be returned.

Whoa, again. I had to break in at this point. "Books can't feel," I scoffed. "You must have that part wrong."

NOPE, Fang said cheerfully, SHADE'S 'JOSH MEMORIES' ARE CLEAR ON THAT. THE BOOKS WHISPERED TO JOSH, WANTED HIM TO READ THEM AND USE THE DARK MAGICK INSIDE TO HURT HIS ENEMIES. Fang paused a moment. MICAH DID SAY THE BOOKS COULD BE

DANGEROUS . . . AND TESSA SAID SHE COULD FEEL THE MAGICK IN THEM.

Then why had I never felt it? I shook my head. That didn't matter right now. Shade continued to sift through his flashes, explaining that Josh had been so vulnerable that the darkness inside those books had sent him over the edge.

The books said vampires react badly to demon blood, so he drew his own blood and used his phasing ability to inject it directly into the supplies at the blood banks. He thought it would make the vamps sick, not knowing it would make them *crazy*. Apparently, he was either too grief-stricken or too stupid to figure out that they'd turned Veronica down *because* they couldn't drink demon blood.

"What was that bit Jen mentioned about hurting Shawndra?" I asked.

Shade shook his head and concentrated. "Shawndra found Josh with the books and wanted to help. Since you were getting too close to learning the truth, he wanted to discourage you and throw suspicion on the vampires at the same time. He thought if a demon got hurt, too, and they told you to back off, you'd stop looking at Josh."

It had worked, too. "So he dumped a bunch of weed killer on his friend?" What kind of creep *was* he?

"He didn't mean to hurt her. They used the page from the encyclopedia, and Shawndra splashed too much weed killer on her arm. She didn't realize how much it would hurt, but when she did, she made Josh leave her so Micah and Tessa could help her." Shade sighed. "That's why Mood was so mad at Josh, because he hurt Shawndra."

It all made sense. "Where are the books now?" I asked. "Maybe we should get them first."

"Can't," Shade said.

"Why not?"

Fang snorted, plucking the answer from Shade's mind. BECAUSE ANDREW FIGURED OUT THAT JOSH HAD THE BOOKS AND TRIED TO GET JOSH TO HELP HIM WIPE OUT THE BLOODSUCKERS.

Shade nodded. "Josh tried to tell Andrew they weren't at fault, but Andrew wouldn't listen. Instead, he beat on Josh, trashed the store looking for the books, then tore apart Josh's room until he found them."

"So Andrew does have them?" I asked in disbelief as I pulled up to the club.

"He does now," Shade confirmed.

"Then why are we here?"

"He might be here . . . or Josh might know where he is."

"And just how do you control a phase demon?"

"He can't phase through anything living, like people or live plants."

"Okay, you hold onto him and this time *I'll* beat the answers out of him."

We headed into the club and I slowed my step and smiled, trying not to let everyone know how hard my heart was beating. The party seemed to have wound down, and most people were gone. The only ones left were Micah, Josh, Mood, and Tessa, who were all cleaning up.

"Hey," I said lightly. "Did I miss all the good stuff?"

Tessa smiled. "Yes, sorry. I swear it looks like a pack of vultures swooped in and made off with everything."

"There might be some fruitcake left," Micah suggested with a smile.

"Uh, I'll pass." I doubted even Fang would eat *that*.

YOU GOT THAT RIGHT, BABE.

"Good decision," Micah said and raised his eyebrow, silently asking me what was up. Guess I wasn't as good at hiding my emotions as I thought.

I raised my voice. "Can everyone come here? I have some news."

They murmured questions but came to join us. Shade spoke into Josh's ear, then clasped Josh's wrist as if to ground himself. Good idea.

"What's your news?" Micah asked.

"I know who the thief is and why he did it."

Josh's expression didn't change at all, but while Micah and Tessa exclaimed, Mood looked apprehensive, her eyes glowing purple.

"Can you please let go of Josh's emotions?" I asked her.

"What?" She looked guilty and cast an apprehensive glance at Josh. "Why?"

Josh sighed. "It's all right, Mood. Let me go."

Mood looked uncertain but did as he asked. Her eyes gradually lightened to her natural color, and animation appeared in Josh's expression. I hadn't really noticed how dead it had seemed until now, when I saw him without Mood's control. His face turned heartbreakingly sad, as if he were experiencing his girlfriend's death all over again.

"Can you handle it?" Shade asked him.

Josh nodded and glanced ruefully down at Shade's hand on his wrist. "But there's no need for that. I gather the Slayer has figured out I took the books?"

"Val," Shade corrected, and didn't let go.

Josh looked confused. "What?"

"Her name is Val," Shade insisted, looking annoyed. "She's not a thing, not some monster you call the Slayer. Her name is Val. Say it."

How sweet. It kind of gave me warm fuzzies all over.

But the others just looked stunned. I was a bit, too—I hadn't expected Josh to admit his guilt so quickly.

"But why would you take them?" Tessa asked, looking bewildered.

I made an impatient gesture. "We'll explain everything later, but right now, we need to find Andrew. *He* has the books now."

Josh looked even more sad. "I-I'm sorry. I couldn't stop him."

"No, but I did," Mood said grimly.

Now *that* surprised me.

Josh stared at her, his mouth open. "What? How?"

"After . . . after Shade healed you last night, and I got all your memories, I tracked Andrew down. He was ranting about how the books told him he had the perfect way to kill a lot of vamps in one fell swoop. All he had to do was set the mansion on fire during the daytime and he'd roast them alive. They'd never be able to defend themselves." She grimaced. "He wanted to wait for Thanksgiving to make his revenge even more sweet, more to be thankful for."

Fang snorted. SO YOU DID YOUR HOCUS POCUS AND MADE HIM THINK HAPPY THOUGHTS?

"You could say that." Mood shrugged. "I had no choice. He was so crazy he wasn't worried about the war that'd provoke between us and the vamps or the danger to the rest of the neighborhood." She looked defensive. "I was going to tell Micah everything tonight, after the party."

The knowledge that Andrew was under lock and key didn't make Shade any happier. In fact, he looked even angrier. "Do you realize what would have happened to *Val* if Andrew had been stupid enough to go after the vamps? She almost had to go to work for Alejandro."

"No, what?" Mood asked, looking fascinated by Shade losing his cool.

She might not know, but I had visions of being locked inside Alejandro's mansion, slaving away in a house full of undead creatures, playing Renfield to his master vampire—and roasting alive with him.

No thanks.

"Never mind that," Micah said and gestured at Shade to calm down. "Where's Andrew now? He's obviously not currently under your control."

"I fed him some sleeping pills and locked him in my basement. He's not going anywhere."

"I don't know," Josh said. "He's stronger than you think, especially if he has those books."

"Not to mention *meaner* than we thought," I said.

Micah glanced at me. "You think the SCU could help with this, discreetly? He sounds dangerous."

"Hold on. I'll call Dan." He and Lt. Ramirez were the only ones I knew of in the SCU who wouldn't go off half-cocked.

Dan picked up on the first ring. "Sullivan here."

"Hey, Dan, it's a long story, but we've found the thief."

"Andrew, right? I've always suspected him."

"No, he didn't steal the books, but he got them later. He was planning to burn down the vamp mansion today. Kill Alejandro and all the others."

"Is he crazy? The other vamps would take revenge. There'd be all-out war."

"I know. The good news is, he's locked up in a basement right now. We need to take him into custody. Think you and Ramirez could help?"

"Hold on. I've got a call coming in. From Ramirez."

Silence. I waited anxiously while Dan talked to the lieutenant. When Dan came back on my phone he let out an expletive.

"What's wrong?"

"Andrew was spotted five minutes ago heading toward Alejandro's mansion. I can't get there in time. I'm on the other side of town."

I closed my eyes for a moment, wishing we could catch a break, even a little one. I glanced outside. It was still about an hour until sunset . . . plenty of time for Andrew to have himself some vampire barbeque. "I'm at the Demon Underground," I told Dan. "So I have folks who can help."

"Be careful, Val."

"Thanks."

I clicked the phone shut.

Shade, still holding on to Josh, looked appalled . . . and more than

a little ticked. " Andrew's rage, combined with the books' dark
magick . . .

NOT A GOOD COMBINATION, Fang said grimly.

No kidding. Andrew by himself was bad enough, but with the
addition of a powerful magickal influence . . . ? We were so screwed.

Chapter Twenty-Two

Micah took charge. "Tessa, call Ludwig and tell him to meet us there, then you stay here and watch Josh. Mood, come with me, and I'll pick up Kyle. Let's do this."

I headed for Gwen's car, then realized Shade wasn't following me.

HE TOOK OFF ALREADY, Fang said. ON A MOTORCYCLE.

That was strange. Why hadn't he just waited for me? As we sped toward the mansion, Fang said, YOU CAN'T LET SHADE GET THERE FIRST.

"Why not?"

MICAH'S WORRIED ABOUT SHADE. WHEN A SHADOW DEMON GETS ANGRY . . .

"I know, but he's been able to keep it together so far. And I'll be there to help him."

YOU DON'T UNDERSTAND. I CAN SENSE SHADE FROM HERE. HE'S REALLY PISSED THAT ANDREW WOULD HAVE SET A FIRE AT THE MANSION EVEN IF YOU WERE WORKING THERE, NOT TO MENTION PUTTING YOU IN THE POSITION OF HAVING TO WORK FOR THE BLOODSUCKERS, AND HE'S NOT LISTENING TO ANYTHING I SAY.

"Well, maybe he'll listen to me."

WITH ANDREW AND THE DARK MAGICKS EGGING HIM ON?

Oh, crap. Fang was right. I redoubled my speed and spotted Shade up ahead. But he managed to stay ahead of me the whole way on his more maneuverable bike. When we got to the mansion's gates I thought for sure he'd try to crash them, but instead, he slowed only enough to punch in the code and barely waited for them to open before he sped up the long driveway to the house. As I zoomed to a halt at the front door, several lengths behind him, I saw the two human guards come toward us, their hands stuck threateningly inside their jackets.

"Is Andrew here yet?" I asked Fang.

Fang sniffed the air. I SMELL HIM . . . AND GASOLINE. ON THE LEFT SIDE OF THE HOUSE.

Oh, crap. The side with all the trees . . .

"Talk to the guards," Shade said curtly as he took off running. "They know you. I'll take care of Andrew."

VAL, NO, Fang said. DON'T LET HIM GO.

Like I had a choice. Shade had already disappeared around the side of the house. The guards ran after him, guns drawn. Being shot wouldn't help Shade calm down any. "Wait," I yelled, jumping out of the car and waving at them to stop. "We're trying to help."

They slowed and one of them said to the other, "She's the Slayer. Alejandro did say she's a friend."

The other one glared at me, obviously wanting to disagree. "Talk fast and make it good," he barked.

I explained what was going on. "You go tell Alejandro, and we'll take care of the demon." I turned Lola loose on them a little, to get them under control. "Your first job is to get the vampires to safety, right? Move!"

The two men nodded and bolted inside the mansion. Fang yelled, COME ON.

He bounded to the left and I followed him around the side of the house. Shade and Andrew were slugging it out and the smell of gasoline was everywhere—on the grass, the trees, and even on the brick walls. With the assistance of dark magicks, Andrew might even be able to make *brick* burn. Crap. He was really determined to see everything go down in flames. And with the trees so close to this side of the house, it could spread to the rest of the neighborhood quickly.

I hurled Lola at him, but it did no good. He was too angry, too caught up in the wild, twisted magick, and Lola couldn't grab a toehold.

Andrew head-butted Shade, who fell backward, looking like he was about to explode at any moment. What would be worse? Andrew's fire magick or Shade losing control, then channeling every vicious demon who wanted a way into our world?

Andrew looked triumphant. I crashed into him, taking him down. At that moment, I seriously thought about staking him, even though he wasn't a vampire.

I wrestled with him, trying to pin him. But though I was stronger, he was bigger and wilder, thrashing in all directions, so that it was hard to hold onto him.

Finally, Andrew went rigid and glared at me. My skin began to grow warm. Heat swallowed me.

"Get off him, Val," Shade yelled.

"No!"

DO IT, Fang yelled. YOUR CLOTHES ARE SMOLDERING.

So that was why I felt so warm. Crap. I sprang away from Andrew. Tiny licks of flame ignited all over my clothes.

"*Roll,*" Shade said urgently, shucking his hoodie.

I rolled in the dirt as Shade beat out the flames with his jacket. Fang danced around, yipping with worry and anger.

Andrew scrambled to his feet. "Dirty vampire lovers," he shouted. He blasted a fist of flame at the house. The house and the trees next to it went up immediately, the flames licking greedily along the brick and bark, hungering for more fuel. Crap, crap, crap. I was no longer on fire, but everything else was.

I didn't have any power over the elements. Where the hell was Micah?

"No!" Shade yelled.

CONTROL HIM, Fang barked.

It hadn't worked before, but maybe it would now. I gathered my wits together and dug down deep then thrust Lola's needs into Andrew, who was raising his arms and dancing like he'd just scored a touchdown.

This time, I caught him with his magicks down, so he froze in place.

NOT HIM, Fang said. SHADE!

What? I glanced at Shade and saw him standing stock still, his arms spread wide, fists clenched, and head thrown back as if he were straining against something. His ribbons of light whirled faster than I'd ever seen them, and purple flashed so that it looked like the mother of all lightning storms going on inside his body.

Oh, no. And when Shade's anger opened up the doors between dimensions . . .

WE'LL BE BUTT-DEEP IN DEMONS, Fang said. STOP HIM.

I pulled half of Lola's attention away from Andrew and slammed it into Shade. She wasn't as needy, wasn't as strong since she'd already fed, and the energy seemed to disappear into him, out the other side to . . . somewhere else. Another dimension?

No, no. This couldn't be happening. I pulled some of the energy from Andrew and fed it into Shade. It helped slow the whirling energies a little, but not enough. Ignoring the raging fire behind me that had now leapt to a couple of trees, I threw myself at Shade and wrapped myself around him, hoping the bodily contact would help.

Shade's face was distorted in agony. "No," he screamed. "Kill me!"

"No," I shouted back. I siphoned more energy from Andrew, but it still wasn't enough. If I let go of Andrew, he might set fire to the whole city. He looked crazy enough to do that. But if I didn't focus all of Lola's energy on Shade, Shade would kill himself rather than let a herd of demons into our world.

No way. Not going to happen.

Hoping like hell I could capture Andrew again after Shade was under control, I released Andrew and concentrated Lola's entire attention on Shade. Wrapping myself even tighter around him and dragging him down to the ground, I kissed him hard. I forced even more energy into his body, letting the tendrils fill him up with lust and longing, grounding him as much as I could in this world, in this body.

Slowly, it worked. I felt Shade relax as he gradually gained full control of himself. I knew he was okay when his arms went around me and he returned the kiss.

"Dude," Kyle said above us. "This is so not the time."

Shade pulled away and laid back on the ground, looking wiped out. "Thanks, I'm okay now. Go get Andrew."

I scrambled up and saw Micah and Mood had arrived with Ludwig and Kyle. Ludwig was using his massive fists to punch huge geysers of water at the fire. So *that* was his talent. He was a water demon.

"Mood, can *you* control Andrew?" I called.

She shook her head, looking strained. "I've been trying to reach him, but he's too strong. I can't . . . " She slumped. "I lost him."

"Can you help me with Shade? We really, really need Shade to stay calm."

"Sure," she said, looking glad for something to do.

I glanced around. The sun was setting, and I couldn't see Fang anywhere.

I'M OVER HERE, came Fang's voice. ANDREW IS HEADING FOR HIS CAR.

I ran through the woods. The hellhound was smart enough to stay out of Andrew's sight, but he'd followed him after the coward had run off.

I caught sight of Andrew at a distance, as he was about to climb the estate's wrought iron fence. I wasn't sure if Lola could reach him, but I had to try. I slammed Lola into him with all my might. "Stop, right there!"

It worked. Andrew froze with one foot on top of the fence and the other on this side. A dazed expression replaced the fury on his face. I walked slowly toward him, debating what to do. I could tell him to impale himself on the fleur-de-lis decorations on top and claim he'd done it to himself on accident. Who would know?

YOU WOULD, Fang reminded me.

"Yeah, well, it was only a fleeting thought." I sighed. "Andrew, get down from there and come face the music."

With Lola suffusing every part of his body, Andrew had no choice but to follow me back to the house. He looked almost groggy, as if I were the Pied Piper and he was a hypnotized rat. I was glad to see that Ludwig had put the fire out, but there was a loud argument going on between demons and vamps at the front of the house. Alejandro and his two lieutenants were outside, now that the sun had set.

Shade hung back and stayed out of it, thank heavens, but the rest were having a shouting match amid the stench and smoke. Mood looked too tired to control anyone but Shade.

When Austin saw us, he flashed his fangs at Andrew and snarled, "Fire demon."

Everyone turned and surged toward us, but I held up my hands. "Stop unless you want to end up in thrall like him."

I let them have a taste of Lola, just to remind them what I could do. They simmered down, but Luis, for one, still looked murderous. Even Alejandro glared at Andrew.

"He's just a stupid kid," Micah said.

"He's adult enough to try to kill everyone in this house," Luis bit out. "Justice demands that you hand him over to us for vengeance."

"He wasn't totally responsible for his actions—the dark magicks in the books had a lot to do with that," Micah said. "But he'll be punished, I promise you."

"How?" Luis sneered. "In the human courts?"

"No, by us," Micah said. "I *promise* you, he will be appropriately punished."

Alejandro made an impatient gesture. "Can we trust you?"

Micah stiffened to his full height, and Ludwig ranged himself alongside his leader, clenching and unclenching his fists. Damn. Looked like a fight was about to erupt again.

"Stop it," I insisted, pushing a little with Lola to make my point. "Alejandro, Andrew isn't the one who poisoned your blood. Another demon did that."

"Demons," Luis spat. "I knew it."

I felt like slapping him but stared down Alejandro instead. "It was *your* fault, Alejandro. You didn't warn the others. You didn't tell them the truth."

"What are you talking about?" came Alejandro's furious question.

"Andrew was angry because the vamps refused to turn his sister to save her life."

This news made the other vamps trade frowns. Austin looked taken aback. "We can't turn demons."

Alejandro nodded. "There is a prohibition against it."

"Because . . . ?" I prompted. I knew the truth about demon blood making vamps sick, but I wanted *him* to tell his people, not me.

Alejandro's nostrils flared. "That is a private matter for our kind only."

Oh, he *knew* all right. But he was keeping it secret from the others. I was beginning to hate secrets.

"Alejandro. Don't you understand what I'm getting at? This explains what happened to Lorenzo and the others. What made them go mad."

Alejandro's expression changed as my point sank in. "So *that* is what happened to my people."

"Yes. The donated human blood was mixed with a demon's and that is what made your vamps crazy."

Austin and Luis looked stunned.

"*His* blood?" Luis asked, pointing at Andrew.

"No, someone else's," I told him.

"The books told you of this?" Alejandro asked. "The books with the dark magicks?" At my nod, his eyes narrowed. "Where are they now?"

Good question. "Andrew?" I asked.

He shook his head. Still under Lola's control, he had a zombie expression. "I don't know."

"What do you mean, you don't know?" Everyone stared at him in shock.

"They didn't want to burn in the fire, so they told me to hide them, and I did . . . but I can't remember where."

HE'S TELLING THE TRUTH, Fang said in disgust. THE MAGICKS

HAVE CLOUDED HIS MEMORY.

"They must be found and destroyed," Alejandro insisted. "They could be very dangerous in the wrong hands . . . to *all* of us."

No kidding. "*Secrets* are dangerous in the wrong hands," I reminded him. "If the fact that vampires couldn't drink demon blood was common knowledge, Veronica would have known the vampires couldn't turn her, and so would Andrew, and this never would have happened."

Micah spoke. "This settles it. Andrew was a victim of vampire secrecy."

I turned on him. "You're no better."

He looked taken aback. "What?"

"Always with the damned secrets. Ooh, let's not let anyone else know what makes us vulnerable, let's not let anyone know what the encyclopedia can do, let's not let anyone get close enough to help us." I knew I sounded like a drama queen, but I didn't care. "Who died and made you keeper of all the demon secrets?"

"Well, my father did, actually."

Fang snorted in amusement, but I ignored him. "If the Demon Underground hadn't kept secrets even from their own, kids like me wouldn't have to grow up feeling like freaks. And we might have figured out that Josh is a phase demon long ago, and— " Alejandro made a negating gesture. "Some things should be kept confidential, for our very survival."

"Maybe. But at what cost?"

"You can't really expect us to reveal *all* our secrets," Micah protested.

"Okay, maybe not. But at least you can think about it and see what makes sense to share."

Alejandro and Micah both looked stubborn, but I was glad to see I got them thinking about it.

"What about these two criminal demons?" Luis asked. "The fire demon and the phase demon must pay for what they did to our people."

Before they could start arguing again, I asked Alejandro, "Are the poisoned vamps doing better?"

"Yes, Lorenzo and the others are almost fully recovered."

That was a relief. "Then why don't you and Micah decide the punishment *together?*" They were the most level-headed of this bunch, and it would help to set a precedent for inter-species cooperation.

They looked at each other. Micah frowned. "Providing he remembers that Josh and Andrew were crazed with grief, influenced by dark magick, and believed that your people were responsible for Veronica's death."

Alejandro inclined his head. "And providing you are able to keep the two under restraint until a decision is made."

Micah nodded decisively. "Val, if you would please put Andrew to sleep?"

I let Lola surge deeper into him. "Andrew, go to sleep."

He slumped down to the ground, passed out.

Micah nodded. "Good. Kyle, if you would keep him there until we are ready to deal with him?" To the others, he explained, "Kyle is a dream demon."

Wow. He was sharing secrets and everything. Progress.

Micah held out his hand to Alejandro. "I apologize for what my people did. I hope we can make up for it somehow."

Alejandro took his hand and smiled. "By agreeing to be by our side when we come out, perhaps?"

Micah winced. "I'll have to think about *that*. Shall we talk later, after everyone has had a chance to cool off?"

Alejandro nodded.

As Micah and Alejandro discussed the arrangements, and Ludwig and Kyle hauled Andrew off, the other vamps went back into the house. Shade came up behind me to sling an arm around my shoulders and murmur, "Great job."

AW, SHUCKS, Fang complained. WE DIDN'T EVEN GET TO KILL ANYTHING.

"That means she's getting better at controlling situations," Shade told him with a grin.

I leaned into him, loving the feeling as his arms closed around me. "Thanks."

"Sorry I was more of a hindrance than a help."

I pulled away to look into his face. "No, you weren't."

"Yes, I was, and without you, San Antonio might be on fire or overrun with demons right now. Thank you for stopping me . . . without killing me."

"Hey, I couldn't kill you just when I'm getting to know you. And thank *you* for helping me with Lola. I have much more control now."

He grinned and kissed me on the nose. "So we're good for each other. You help me control my demon and I'll help you control yours.

Like we're destined to be together or something."

Fang rolled his eyes. OH, GAG ME.

Shade laughed and lowered his voice. "Even without making love in the usual sense of the word."

I felt myself flush at the thought. That was a decision for another time. Too much had happened today to think about that. For now, I was happy to just be with my new boyfriend. I sighed in contentment. I'd learned where my strength came from, caught the thief, and, even though I hadn't retrieved the encyclopedia, at least no one else could find it, for now.

I was learning to get Lola under control, and had even improved my relationships with Dan and my family. Now that I could sit back and let Micah and Alejandro take all the responsibility, make all the decisions, and keep the hotheads under control, life was good. But not too boring, I hoped.

"Val," Micah called. "Can you come here a moment?"

I reluctantly peeled myself away from Shade.

"Alejandro reminded me of your agreement to come work for him," Micah said.

Uh-oh. I hoped he'd forgotten that. Shade rejoined me and hugged me hard with one arm. Though he didn't say anything, I knew he was urging me to get out of this any way I could. Luckily, it looked like Mood was keeping an eye on his temper still.

I smiled brightly, as if my cheeriness would hold back the darkness about to descend. "But no one else was hurt, so the agreement is null and void."

"Not exactly," Alejandro drawled. "I believe you said if someone else *tried* to harm my people, you would come to work for me. Andrew did try."

"That wasn't my intention and you know it. Besides, we just helped you avert a grisly death by fire here. You owe us."

Alejandro regarded me thoughtfully. "Perhaps. Shall I suggest a compromise?"

"Like what?"

"You come along to all of the discussions our two groups have together. You seem to have a knack for helping people to see reason, and for ending conflicts as well as starting them."

Relieved, I said, "Okay, I can do that."

But Alejandro wasn't finished. "*And* you work for me for a short period of time."

"How short?" I asked apprehensively.

"Let's say . . . until the books are found and dealt with, and we have revealed ourselves to the world."

"Don't do it," Shade whispered.

But I had no choice. I'd given my word. Besides, I had to find those books, no matter who I worked for.

"Can we put this in writing . . . in a contract?" This time I wanted it spelled out exactly how long I had to work for the creatures I was accustomed to slaying and exactly what I was to do.

He smiled. "Of course."

I didn't trust that smile, but I'd make sure I had a damned good lawyer to help me put that contract together before I signed away my life. "Okay, deal," I said and shook his hand, wondering if I was making a mistake.

THE QUESTION ISN'T *IF* YOU'RE MAKING A MISTAKE, Fang informed me. THE QUESTION IS, HOW BIG IS THE MISTAKE GONNA BE . . . AND HOW MUCH IS IT GOING TO HURT?

I glanced at him. *You really think it'll be that bad?*

He looked gloomy. UNFORTUNATELY, YEAH. BUT AT LEAST YOU'LL GET YOUR WISH.

What wish?

YOU WON'T BE BORED.

A Note From Parker Blue

Dear Reader,

Thanks to all the fans of *Bite Me* who asked me for more adventures with Val, Fang, and the others. I have to say, I didn't expect Shade to be such a major character in the series. He showed up in *Bite Me* as a throw-away character, but he fascinated me so much I gave him a bigger role in that book than I had planned.

As you can tell, he fascinates Val, too, and will definitely be around for book three of the Demon Underground series. I continue to learn more about the characters as I write them, so I'm as eager to know what happens next as you are.

To learn more, please visit my website at parkerblue.net.

Parker Blue
Colorado Springs, CO

Where Val's Adventures Began
BITE ME, Book One,
The *Demon Underground* Series

The vampire jumped me again, but this time I was ready for him. We fought furiously, Jason determined to sink his teeth into my neck and rip my throat out, and me just as determined to stop him. Unfortunately, he liked close-in fighting, and I couldn't get enough space to reach the stake I had tucked into my back waistband.

I grabbed his throat and squeezed, but he wrapped me in a vise hold and wouldn't let go. He slammed me up against a brick wall, intent on crushing me. *Trapped.* Worse, the power I tried so hard to keep confined was able to reach him through my energy field in these close quarters and I could feel the lust rise within him as he ground his hips against mine. Pervert.

Though I was able to hold off his slavering overbite and incredibly bad breath with one hand, my other hand was caught between our bodies. He couldn't get to my neck, but I couldn't get to my stake either.

Stalemate.

Time to play dirty. Remembering even vampires had a sensitive side, I kneed him in the crotch.

He screeched and let go of me to bend over and clutch the offended part of his anatomy. That took care of the lust. I hit him with an uppercut so hard that he flew backward, landing flat on his back on the sidewalk. Whipping the stake from its hiding place, I dropped down beside him and stabbed him through the heart in one well-practiced motion.

His body arched for a moment, then he sagged and lay motionless—really and truly dead.

Now that my prey had been vanquished and the demon lust sated, the fizzing in my blood slowed and stopped, leaving me feeling some of the aches and pains I'd inflicted on my body. It was worth it, though.

But adrenaline pumped once more when I heard a car door open down the street. The light was dimmer here between streetlights, but I was still visible—and so was the body I crouched over. "Who's there?" I demanded.

"It...it's me."

Damn it, I recognized that voice. Annoyed, I rose to glare at my younger half sister. "Jennifer, what the hell are you doing here?"

She got out of the back seat of the beat-up Camry, white-faced. "I told you I wanted to come along."

"And I told you not to."

She shrugged, displaying defiance and indifference as only a sixteen-year-old could. "That's why I hid in the back of the car."

Stupid. I should have checked. I usually drove my motorcycle—a totally sweet Honda Valkyrie—but on nights when I went hunting, my stepfather let me borrow the old beat-up car since it had a convenient trunk. Unfortunately, it was too easy for my little sister to creep into the back seat and stow away there. Obviously.

And I should have known Jen would try something like this. I'd made the mistake of telling her about my little excursions, even giving her some training on how to defend herself in case she ever encountered one of the undead. She'd been eager to learn everything she could, but Mom had gone off the deep end when she found out, especially when Jen had come home sporting a few bruises.

Mom had forbidden Jen to talk about it again and had threatened me with bodily harm if I even mentioned vampires around my little sis. Lord knew what Mom would do if she found out about this.

Jen stared down at the dead vamp and grimaced. "I've just never actually seen one of them before."

"A dead vampire?"

"Any kind of vampire."

Was that censure in her voice? "That's what he was," I said defensively. Mom was right—Jen was far too young and innocent for my world. I had to find a way to keep her away from all this. "I don't stake innocents."

"I know. I saw."

"Dammit, Jen, you shouldn't have come. It's dangerous." And if one hair on her pretty little head had been harmed, Mom would have *my* head on a platter.

"Yeah, well, we can't all be big, strong vampire slayers," she said. She tried to make it sound sarcastic, but it came out sounding more wistful than anything.

I sighed, recognizing jealousy when I saw it. I knew Jen envied my abilities—my *specialness*—with all the longing of a teenager who wanted to be something extraordinary herself. Of course, it was the demon inside me that gave me advantages she didn't have. All of my senses were enhanced far beyond normal, including strength, speed, agility, rapid healing, and the ability to read vamps' minds when they tried to control me. Unfortunately, my little sister had no clue as to the price I paid for those advantages.

And she also had no idea how much I envied *her*. Fully human, with All-American blond good looks and plenty of friends, she had everything I had always wanted and could never have—true normalcy, not just the appearance of it. With my Jewish/Catholic, demon/human background and the melting pot that went into my heritage, I felt like a mongrel next to a show dog. My lucky half sister had managed to avoid the bulk of my confusing heritage since we shared only a mother.

But I couldn't say any of that—she wouldn't believe it. "Help me get the body in the trunk," I said tersely.

I usually had to do this part by myself, but why not take advantage of Jen's presence? Besides, participating in the whole dirty business might turn her off for good. I unlocked the trunk and opened it.

She hesitated. "I thought—"

When she broke off, I said, "You thought what? That he'd turn into a neat little pile of dust?"

She shrugged. "Yeah, I guess."

"I wish it were that easy." I took pity on her. "And he'll be dust soon enough—when sunlight hits him. Come dawn, I'll make sure his ass is ash."

Jen grimaced, but I wasn't going to let her off that easily. It was her decision to tag along—she'd have to pay the price. I grabbed the vampire's feet. "Get his head."

She stared down at Jason's fangs and the small amount of blood around the stake in his heart and turned a little green. "Can't you just leave him in the alley?"

I could, but then Jen wouldn't learn her lesson.

Well, damn, I sounded like Mom now. Annoyed at myself, I snapped, "We can't just leave him here for someone to trip over. What's the matter? Too much for you?"

She shrugged, trying to act nonchalant. "No, I just thought Dad might not like it if you got blood in his trunk."

"He's used to it." Besides, the blood would disintegrate along with the rest of the body when sunlight hit it.

Jen gulped, but I have to give her credit—she didn't wimp out on me. I'd expected her to blow chunks at the least, but she picked up his shoulders and we wrestled the body into the trunk.

Jen wiped her hands on her jeans and stared uneasily at the casket. "Is he really dead?"

"Mostly," I said, then grinned to myself when Jen took a step back. There was still the remote possibility Jason could heal if the stake was removed from his heart. But for that to happen, his friends would have to rescue him before dawn, tend him carefully for months and feed him lots of blood. Not likely.

I shrugged. "But the morning sun will take care of that." I closed the trunk.

Just as I locked it, the headlights from a car blinded me and a red light from its dashboard strobed the street.

"It's a cop," Jen said in panic.

Not good. But it didn't have to be bad, either. "Relax. Let me handle this."

The plainclothes policeman exited the unmarked car. "Evening, ladies," he said, obviously trying to sound friendly, though he came across as wary and suspicious.

"Evening," I responded.

Though he tried to appear like a guileless rookie, I wasn't fooled. He might only be in his mid-twenties, but he had the watchful alertness of a pro. He hooked the thumb of his right hand in his belt, making it easy to draw a weapon from that bulge under his left arm.

As he came closer, I could make out his features. He was about six feet tall with short brown hair, a straight commanding nose, and a solid bod. Totally hot. I might even be interested if he were a little younger and lost the suspicious attitude.

The demon inside me agreed, wondering what it would be like to enthrall him, get him all hot and bothered, feed on all that lovely sexual energy. That was the problem with being part succubus lust demon— ever since I started noticing boys, the demon part of me had been lying in wait, urging me to get up close and personal, wanting to compel their adoration, suck up all their sexual energy.

I'd given in once, and the poor kid barely survived. But not this time. Not again. I beat back the urges, which was pretty easy since I'd just satisfied the lust by taking out the vamp.

"What are you doing here?" he asked.

"I'm sorry, Officer...?"

"Sullivan. Detective Sullivan." He flashed his badge at me.

I smiled, trying to look sheepish. "My little sister snuck out of the house to meet her boyfriend, and I was just trying to get her back home before Mom finds out."

"In this part of town?"

"Yeah, well, she doesn't have the best of judgment. That's why she had to sneak out."

Jen gave me a dirty look, but was just smart enough to keep her mouth shut.

He didn't look convinced. "Got any ID?"

"Sure—in the car." I gestured toward the front of the vehicle to ask permission and he nodded. Shifting position so he could watch both of us, he asked Jen for her ID, too.

I retrieved my backpack and handed my driver's license to the detective along with my registration. He glanced at them. "Your last names are different."

"Yeah—we're half sisters. Same mother, different father. We have the same address, see?"

He nodded and took both IDs back to the car to speak to someone on the radio.

"Ohmigod," Jen said in a hoarse whisper. "What if he finds out there's a body in the trunk? We'll go to jail. Mom and Dad will be so pissed."

"Just relax. Everything should come up clean, so there's no reason for him to even look."

Sullivan finished talking on the radio then handed our IDs back.

"Can we go now?" I asked with a smile. "I'd like to get Jen home before Mom finds out she's gone."

"Sure," he said with an answering smile. "Just as soon as you tell me what's in the trunk."

Oh, shit.

"Nothing," Jen said hastily, the word ending in a squeak as she backed against the trunk and spread her arms as if to protect it. "Just, you know, junk and stuff. Nothing bad."

Oh, great. Like that didn't sound guilty.

Still casual, he asked, "Would you mind opening it for me?"

Yes, I did. Very much. Swiftly, I mentally ran through the options. I couldn't take him out—I didn't hurt innocents. Besides, he'd just called in our names so they'd know we were the last to see him. Taking off wasn't an option, either—he knew who we were and where we lived.

Demon lust fizzed in my blood, the succubus part of me that allowed me to enthrall men, bend them to my will and make them willing slaves. *You could take control of him, force him to let you go,* a small voice whispered inside me.

Heaven help me, for a moment, I was tempted. But I couldn't do that. I couldn't take advantage of humans like that. I'd promised the parents—and myself—that I'd never do it again.

My only choice was to do as he asked and hope he'd give me time to explain. Crap. This was so not going the way I planned.

Gently, I moved Jen aside, unlocked the trunk, and braced for the worst.

He lifted the lid and stared down inside. He didn't even flinch. Good grief, was the man made of stone? Expressionless, he asked, "Vampire?"

This was so surreal. I relaxed a little, hoping I might even be able to come out of this without getting into major trouble. "Uh, yeah. The bloody fangs are a dead giveaway."

He gave me a look. The kind that said I wasn't out of trouble yet and he didn't appreciate smart-ass comments. "Why did you stake him?"

Why? He was staring down at the dead undead and he wanted to know *why?*

Jen blurted out, "Because he was drinking some guy's blood." She shifted nervously. "I saw it all."

The cop nodded. "So did I."

I gaped at him. "You did?"

"Yeah, I was just calling for backup when you waltzed up and tapped him on the shoulder."

Crap—I'd been so self-involved I hadn't even noticed the unmarked car. Note to self: *pay attention!*

If you love Val Shapiro, you'll love Allie Emerson
The *Unbidden Magic* Series
Marilee Brothers
Book One: MOONSTONE
Book Two: MOON RISE
Coming in 2010, Book Three: MOON SPUN

MOONSTONE

**Allie Emerson is destined to fight evil and save the world.
But first she has to survive high school.**

Chapter One

One minute, I was on a ten-foot ladder adjusting the TV antenna on the twenty-four-foot trailer behind Uncle Sid's house, where I lived with my mother, Faye. The next minute, I sailed off the ladder, grazed an electric fence and landed face down in a cow pie.

Swear to God.

Though groggy and hurting, I rolled onto my back. A window in the trailer cranked open and I heard my mother scream. "Allie! Ohmigod! Somebody call 911!"

I was surprised Faye managed to open the window. She'd spent most of the last two years in bed since, at age thirty one, she Retired From Life. But really, call 911? We had no phone and I was the only other person in the area. Who was she talking to? Blaster the bull? I smiled weakly at the thought of Blaster in a phone booth, punching in 911 with one gigantic hoof.

Okay, technically, I landed in a bull pie, not a cow pie. The mess dripping off my face was compliments of my Uncle Sid's prize bull, speaking of which . . .

It was then my wits returned. I felt the ground vibrate, heard the rumble of hooves. I reared up to see a half-ton cranky bull racing toward me, head down, mean little eyes fixed on my prone body.

Faye continued to scream shrilly. I moaned and crawled toward the fence, looking over my shoulder at Blaster who bore down on me like a runaway train. When I tried to stand, I slipped in the wet grass and landed on my belly. Oh God, he was just inches away. I wasn't going to make it! I rolled into a ball and screamed, "No, Blaster! Go back! Go back!"

Laying on the wet grass, trembling with terror, I watched as Blaster stopped on a dime, blew snot out of his flaring, black nostrils and released a thunderous blast of flatulence—that's what my teacher, Mrs. Burke, calls farting—and, of course, is the reason Uncle Sid named him Blaster.

"Back off, Blaster," I said between shallow, panicky breaths. "Good boy."

I hoped the "boy" comment wouldn't tick him off, what with his fully-developed manly-bull parts dangling in full view as I lay curled on the ground looking up. Yuck!

Suddenly my vision narrowed and grew dark around the edges. It was like looking down a long tunnel with Blaster front and center, bathed in light. A loud buzzing filled my head. The next moment, Blaster took a tentative step backward, then another, walking slowly, at first, then gradually picking up speed until he was trotting briskly backwards like a video tape on slow rewind.

Mesmerized by the sight, I sat up and watched Blaster's bizarre retreat back through the tunnel. At that precise moment, I should have known something strange was going on. But hey, I was a little busy trying to save my life.

As I crawled under the fence, my vision returned to normal and the buzzing faded away. I stood and swiped a hand across my sweaty face. At least, I *thought* it was sweat until a trickle of blood dripped off the end of my nose. Surprised because I felt no pain, I touched my face and found the blood was oozing from a puncture wound in the center of my forehead.

I glanced up at Faye, who continued to peer out the trailer window, her pale face framed in a halo of wispy blond curls, her eyes wide with shock. She inhaled sharply, and I knew another scream was on its way. I held up a hand. "Come on, Faye, no more screaming. You're making my head hurt."

"But, but, the bull . . . he, he . . . " Faye began.

I wasn't ready to go there. "I know, I know."

I staggered around the end of the trailer and banged through the door. Two giant steps to the bathroom. I shucked off my clothes and stepped into the tiny shower.

"You okay, Allie?" Faye asked.

She peered through the open doorway, paler than usual. Her right hand clutched the locket that held my baby picture, the one that makes me look like an angry old man. The only time she took it off was to shower.

"I'll live," I muttered.

"Weird, huh? Blaster, I mean. I heard you yell at him. Bulls don't run backward, Allie."

When I didn't answer—what could I say?—she waited a beat. "Use soap on your forehead. Did it stop bleeding?"

"Yes, Mother." I reached over and slid the door shut.

Deep sigh. "You don't have to be snotty. I told you to be careful."

The TV blared suddenly. Oprah. Not that I'm a spiteful person, but I blamed Oprah for my swan dive off the ladder. Late last night, a sudden gust of wind knocked over our TV antenna. When I got home from school today, Faye insisted she had to watch Oprah. Like that was going to change her life. I finally got tired of hearing about it and borrowed Uncle Sid's ladder. Moral of story: Never wear flip flops on an aluminum ladder.

I turned on the water, stood under the weak stream and checked for damage. Other than a slight tingling in my arms and legs and the hole in my head, I seemed okay.

I toweled off my curly, dark-brown hair and pulled it back into a messy ponytail. When I wiped the steam off the mirror, I saw a dark-red, dime-sized circle the size in the exact center of my forehead. I touched it gingerly, expecting it to hurt. But it didn't. Instead, a weird sensation shot through my head, like my brain was hooked up to Dr. Frankenstein's machine, that thing he used to make his monster come alive. I must have given a little yip of surprise because Faye said again, "You okay, Allie?"

"I'm fine," I said. "Just a little sore."

"Did you check the mail?"

"The first's not until Friday. Today's the twenty-ninth," I said.

"Sometimes it comes early."

The welfare check *never* came early. The state of Washington was very reliable when it came to issuing checks.

"Yeah, okay," I said, not wanting to burst her bubble.

Wrapped in the towel, I took two steps into the living room/kitchen, reached under the table and pulled out the plastic crate containing my clean clothes. I dug around and found clean underwear, a tee shirt and a pair of cut-off shorts.

I slipped into my bra, once again thinking how cool it was I finally needed one. Though I hoped for peaches, I'd managed only to grow a pair of breasts roughly the size and shape of apricots. Oh, well, apricots are better than cherries. Our valley is called "The fruit bowl of the nation," hence, my obsession with naming body parts after produce.

I slipped into my treacherous flip flops, headed out the door and spotted Uncle Sid darting behind the barn. Faye says Uncle Sid is not a people person but I thought he was just trying to avoid Aunt Sandra and her constant nagging. That woman's voice could make a corpse sit up and beg for mercy.

I trotted down the driveway, stopping suddenly when I spotted a pair of denim-clad legs sticking out from under the Jeep Wrangler parked next to Uncle Sid's house. Legs that belonged to Matt, Uncle Sid's son and older brother to spoiled brat, Tiffany.

How can one kid—Tiffany—be so annoying and the other—Matt—so totally hot? I tried to avoid Matt because of the way I got when I'm around him. Though I'm normally loquacious (last Wednesday's vocabulary word that I copied and vowed to use at least three times,) one look at Matt and I lost my power of speech. My jaw dropped and my mouth went dry. There's just something about him—sleepy blue eyes, light brown hair that usually needs combing, a crooked grin and a sculpted, rock-hard body.

It wasn't some creepy, incestuous thing since Matt and I weren't real cousins. Sid was Faye's step brother. Nope, we didn't have the same blood coursing through our veins. Matt's was probably blue, while mine came from the mystery man Faye refused to talk about.

I tiptoed past the Jeep to spare myself further humiliation. I'd almost made it when he rolled out on one of those sled thingies and grabbed my ankle. "Hey, kid, how ya doin'?"

The warmth of his hand against my bare skin turned my normally frisky brain cells to mush. Sure enough, my lower jaw was heading south. "Uh, just great, Matt," I said, averting my eyes and licking my suddenly parched lips.

He released my ankle and stood up. "Good," he said. "Your mom still got that . . . whaddaya call it?"

"Fibromyalgia." As I said the word, I felt my upper lip curl in a sneer. "So she says."

"She getting better?"

"She's trying to get social security benefits, you know, the one for disability."

The words tasted bitter in my mouth.

"Oh yeah," Matt said. "I saw Big Ed's car here the other night. He's her lawyer, right?"

My hands automatically curled into fists. I narrowed my eyes and studied Matt's face, looking for a smirk or maybe a suggestive wink. Even though I didn't want to punch him, I could and I would. I knew how to punch. Faye had made sure.

No problem. He'd moved on. Wonder of wonders, he was looking at me. I mean, really looking at me with those sexy blue eyes. His gaze lingered for a long moment on my chest. Whoa! Was he checking out my 'cots? I was suddenly aware I'd outgrown my shorts and tee shirt. Not knowing what else to do, I shoved my hands into the pocket of my cut-offs and took a step back.

"Well, hey, I gotta go check the mail. See ya, Matt."

His voice followed me as I headed down the driveway. "Hey, kid. If you ever need a ride somewhere, let me know. I got the Jeep running real good."

Because my mouth had fallen open once again, I settled for a casual wave of acknowledgement even though I wanted to pump a fist in the air and scream, "YES!"

As I trotted to the mailbox, the late April sunlight warm on my shoulders, I pondered this strange turn of events. Even though he called me "kid," clearly Matt had noticed a couple of new bulges on my formerly stick-like body. Hmmm. Had my tumble off the ladder, followed by the electric fence zapping, released some sort of male-attracting hormone?

In spite of my mini-triumph, Matt-wise, a dull headache began to throb painfully at the back of my skull. I opened the mailbox and, as predicted, Faye's check had not arrived. There was, however, a familiar tan envelope from the Social Security Office of Adjudication and Review. Probably another form for Faye to fill out asking questions like, "Are you able to push a grocery cart?" And, "Can you walk up a flight of stairs?" Questions Faye had already answered "No" and "No."

When I handed her the envelope, Faye sighed and dropped it, unopened, onto the pile of similar tan envelopes stacked between the bed and wall.

"Big Ed's coming tomorrow. I'll let him deal with it." She looked pointedly at her watch.

I took the hint. It was time for Fay's nightly ritual, two slices of peanut butter toast and two cans of Busch Light. The menu varied only on Thursday night. Big Ed night. He always brought burgers, fries and a fifth of Stoli. Not that I'm around on Thursdays. No way. But, when I come home on Friday, the place smells of grease and vodka.

Let me make this crystal clear. Big Ed was Faye's lawyer, not her boyfriend. That was what Faye said. He'd been working day and night on her case for two years. That was what Big Ed said. Me? I had my doubts.

Later that night, I heard the sound of Faye's rhythmic breathing and tiptoed back to the bedroom. I gathered up the empties and the plate littered with peanut butter-smeared crusts and tossed them in the garbage.

Tomorrow was Thursday, Big Ed night. I'd be staying with Kizzy Lovell, the town witch. That was what a lot of kids called her. Since I wouldn't be home until Friday, I made sure I had clean underwear in my backpack.

As the evening wore on, my headache grew steadily worse. At ten, I turned out the light. I pulled the curtains back so I could see the night sky, a brilliant canopy of far-flung stars and a full-faced moon. I held my hand up to the window. Bathed in moonlight, my palm looked washed in silver, its tell-tale lines carved in dark relief by the unknown maker of my fate. I thought about the times Kizzy studied the lines on my palm and said, "You're a special girl, Alfrieda. Like it or not, you have the Gift."

Every time I'd say, "What gift?" Kizzy would smile mysteriously and say, "You'll see," which really irritated me because, clearly, the only gift I had was the ability to get all-A's on my report card. Even that wasn't a gift, since I hated Algebra and had to work my butt off.

I had no sooner wrapped up in my faded pink quilt and snuggled into the couch bed when I remembered the aspirin and glass of water I'd placed by the bathroom sink before I brushed my teeth. I groaned and switched on the light. The bathroom was only a few steps away. But in my present state—cotton-mouthed and head pounding with pain—the distance seemed as vast as the Sahara Desert. I swung my feet to the floor and turned my head slowly toward the bathroom. I could see the glass of water perched on the counter like it was taunting me, "Come and get me, Allie."

I reached out a hand, thinking, *It would be a whole lot easier if you came to me*, and it happened again. The whole dark-around-the-edges, tunnel-vision, buzzing-in-the-head thing. The glass teetered back and forth, danced a little jig across the counter and shot into the air for a moment before it slammed onto the floor and shattered into about a jillion pieces.

"What the hell's going on, Allie?"

I looked up to see my mother standing in the narrow hallway. My hand, still extended toward the glass that wasn't there, shook violently. "I dropped it. That's all," I said. "Go back to bed. I'll clean it up."

Faye's eyes narrowed in suspicion but finally, she turned and trudged back to the bedroom. When I opened the door and stepped outside to fetch the broom, I was greeted by a symphony of night music. Strangely, the pain in my head was gone. The soft spring air was alive with a chorus of crickets backed by a full orchestra of spring peepers, their mating songs accompanied by the tinkle of wind chimes.

But, hold on. We didn't have wind chimes. We'd never had wind chimes. I walked to the back of the trailer and stared up at the gnarled old apple tree next to Blaster's pasture. Nudged by a gentle breeze, long silver tubes bumped together, creating a melody with subtle variations as the air around them ebbed and flowed. It was stabilized by a dangling iridescent glass ball whose surface caught and held the moonlight.

Must be some prank of Matt's. Vowing I'd figure it out in the morning, I grabbed the broom, opened the door and froze. A woman sat on my couch bed. A woman with flowers in her long, dark hair, wearing a pink-and-yellow, tie-dye dress embellished with a blazing purple sun. A woman, smoking what looked and smelled like weed. I opened my mouth, preparing to scream so loudly and shrilly the shards of glass on the floor would shatter into even smaller pieces.

The woman said, "Hi. I'm Trilby, your spirit guide. Guess what? You just passed your first test. Isn't that groovy?"

Chapter Two

I stepped inside and whisper-screamed, "Are you nuts?" while fanning the air and glancing back toward Faye's bedroom. Thank God, the door was closed. "Out!" I said. "I don't care who you are. Get out!"

All I could think was, *Grounded for Life*. Trust me, it's no picnic being grounded in a twenty-four-foot trailer.

Trilby giggled. "Oh, you're worried about Mom. It's okay. She can't hear me." One of her fingers shot up. "Or see me." A second finger joined the first. She got through "smell" and "taste" then stopped, looking puzzled. "I know there're five senses but I'll be damned if I can remember the last one."

"Who cares?" I jerked my thumb toward the door. "Outside," I ordered. My voice was shrill with panic.

"Allie," my mother called. "Who are you talking to?"

My heart leaped into my throat then settled in my chest, banging so loudly I was sure Faye would hear it and ask who was playing the drums. I flapped my hands at Trilby, frantic to be rid of her. She blew out air in disgust and rolled her eyes but rose from the couch and, in a blur of color and a blast of frigid air, disappeared.

"Nobody's here, Faye," I said. "I have to memorize something for school. I'll go outside." I backed out the door reciting, "We, the people of the United States, in order to form a more perfect union . . . "

"Cool, huh?" Trilby said from directly behind me.

I whirled around. "This isn't happening! I'm sound asleep in the middle of some stupid dream."

But then Trilby fluttered her fingers in my face—and I do mean *inside my face*—and said, "Neato. I didn't know I could do that." She passed her hands through my body. "Wooooo! Are you scared?"

I jumped back, trying to wrap my mind around the fact I wasn't dealing with a flesh-and-blood woman, a living, breathing human being, but an apparition, a spook, a wraith. Swear to God, Trilby was a ghost! Not a particularly scary ghost, but most definitely a ghost.

I said the first thing that popped into my mind. "Scared? I don't think so! Look at you! Your lipstick is on crooked, your eyes are bloodshot, you're higher than a kite. And that 'wooooo' thing? It went out about a hundred years ago."

"That's just mean," Trilby said, pouting. She plopped down in a lawn chair. "I'm trying to help you and you're messing with my groove."

I sat in the other chair and pointed at the wind chimes. "Yours?"

"Yeah, my signature touch. Nice, huh?"

I sucked in a shaky breath. "This is probably a dream, but why are you here? What do you mean, I passed the first test?"

Trilby straightened her shell-and-bead necklace then touched the peace sign painted on her wooden bracelet. She leaned toward me and narrowed her eyes. "You're my ticket out of a bad scene. If we do this right, I get to go up there."

She pointed at the sky.

I sniffed in disapproval. "Smoking weed can't help."

"Listen, little girl. I've been stuck in the SeaTac airport since 1971. Talk about hell!"

My mind swam with confusion. "SeaTac?"

"Yeah. Some of us aren't quite ready for the big crash pad in the sky. So we get to hang out at Concourse A, watch the planes take off, sleep on the floor, drink coffee and wait for 'the call.' You're it. So, cooperate, okay?"

"Focus, Trilby. What test did I pass?"

"*At journey's end I lie close to her heart, the maid who is strong of mind,*" she quoted. "You know, as per the prophecy. That one."

Trilby had to be in the middle of some sort of drug-induced hallucination. I wasn't sure how to deal with her but then, I reasoned, she *was* a ghost, so maybe this was typical ghostly behavior. I needed more information. "I have no idea what you're talking about."

"Hmmm," she said, rolling her eyes heavenward. "I'm trying to remember my instructions. Today's the thirtieth. Right?"

"No," I said. "It's the twenty-ninth. At least for another hour."

"Oh, damn, my timing sucks! You don't have it yet," Trilby said. "I blew it."

Her lower lip quivered and she blinked hard to hold back tears.

Chagrined, I thought about poor Trilby, trapped forever in SeaTac Airport, Concourse A. I'd never been there but it didn't sound much like paradise.

"Okay, so it's the wrong day," I said. "Maybe that's not so bad."

She brightened. "Do you really think so?"

"Tell me everything you remember about your instructions, starting with this thing I'm supposed to have."

Trilby started to answer then pinched her lips together and shook her head. "No," she said. "If you don't have it, that part will have to wait."

"Have what?"

She fiddled with her beads. "I said, IT WILL HAVE TO WAIT!"

"Okay, okay." I cast a nervous glance toward Faye's window. "You don't have to shout. Just tell me what you can."

"You have the sign on your palm, right?"

I thrust out a hand, palm up, and turned it toward Uncle Sid's yard light. She leaned toward me and traced a finger across my palm. Her feathery touch left a trail of light, and I gasped in surprise.

"Yep, you've got it."

She touched the tiny red mark in the middle of my forehead. "And you had an unusual experience today."

I told her about Blaster running backward and the flying glass.

"All right!" She pumped a fist in the air. "I'm not totally screwed. TKP. Telekinetic power. The ability to move things with your mind. You did it. You're 'the maid whose mind is strong.' Oh, this is so groovy!"

I still didn't understand. "What's next?"

"Oh, it gets much better. See ya around, kid. I gotta get back."

"Wait! Wait!" I said as she started to fade away. "Next time write the instructions down. That's what Mrs. Burke makes us do in English class."

Too late. Trilby was gone.

Chapter Three

The next morning I stood out by the road with Mercedes and Manny Trujillo, waiting for the school bus and thinking about Trilby and wondering if I'd dreamed her. The wind chimes were gone. I checked. Maybe she took them with her to wherever . . . SeaTac airport if you can believe a ghost. Or, maybe it didn't happen at all.

I almost told Manny and Mercedes about the night. But they believed in things like vampires, werewolves and wendigos, whatever those were. Manny and Mercedes thought that stuff came from the devil. I was afraid they'd think the devil had paid me a visit, and they'd stop hanging out with me. I didn't have *that* many friends.

I had to talk to Kizzy and find out what the heck was happening to me. Was this the Gift she kept talking about? And, more importantly, could I get rid of it? Maybe there's an exchange counter where a person can go to return special gifts, like I returned the hideous pea-green stocking cap Aunt Sandra gave me for Christmas.

Before I could get answers to my questions, I was faced with a more pressing problem. Namely, protecting Mercedes and Manny from our arch enemy, Cory Philpott. The Trujillos lived on Uncle Sid's property. Their mother, Juanita, cleaned Aunt Sandra's house and Pedro, their dad, ran the Mexican crews that did all the hard work in the orchard.

Manny and Mercedes were way too nice. With seven kids and two parents sharing a three-bedroom house, it seemed like they'd know how to defend themselves. They didn't. Apparently that was my job. Cory Philpott lived to torment Manny and Mercedes.

At exactly 7:45, the bus rolled to a stop and the doors opened with a groan and hiss. We formed a single-file line. It was always the same. First me, then Mercedes, then Manny.

Patti, our vertically-challenged bus driver, used a booster cushion, had big hair, dagger-like fingernails, and a deep, raspy voice due to the pack of unfiltered Camels tucked in her shirt pocket. She greeted us as she always did, with high fives and our special name.

"Hey, Gorgeous Green-eyed Girl," she said to me. (Sometimes

just "G.")

"Sweet Cheeks!" she exclaimed as Mercedes plodded up the steps.

"There's my Stud Muffin," she said to Manny, whose moon face split in a broad grin.

We made our way down the aisle as Patti ground the gears and lurched out onto the road. As usual, the only seats left were next to Cory Philpott, whose evil, troll face brightened as we approached. I gave him a squinty-eyed glare as Mercedes slipped into her spot next to the window.

He looked away from me and hissed at Manny, "Hey, beaner boy. Your backpack full of tacos? Do you share with your big-ass beaner sister?"

Okay, here's the deal. I was fed up with Cory's bullying. More importantly, I had a plan. Last fall, our science teacher trapped a black widow spider in a fruit jar. He passed the jar up and down the rows so we could get a good look at its shiny black body, long, long legs and the red hour glass on its belly. When I turned around to hand the jar to Cory, he levitated about a foot in the air. Beads of sweat popped out on his forehead, and his hands were shaking. He may have even wet his pants. I didn't check, for obvious reasons.

What good is secret information if you don't use it? The time had come. I rose in my seat, my eyes wide with horror as I gazed at the top of Cory's head. "Oh, my God! That's the biggest black widow spider I've ever seen. Cory! *It's in your hair!*"

Ashen-faced, Cory screamed like a little girl and scrambled into the aisle, jumping up and down and clawing at his hair with both hands. "Is it gone? Is it gone?" he yelled.

After a brief flurry of excitement—most of the kids were still half asleep—somebody from the rear of the bus spoke up. "Come on, dude, she's playin' ya. There's no spider."

Patti glanced over her shoulder. "This isn't even black widow season. Get your ass in the seat!"

Hoots of laughter echoed through the bus. Cory collapsed back into his seat then turned to glare at me. He'd pretty much stopped harassing me after I punched him in the face the past January, when he said something gross about Faye and Big Ed.

Mercedes leaned close and murmured, "Cool. I told you he was into you."

She thought Cory had a secret crush on me, that the purpose of his bullying was to get my attention. Mercedes was a total drama queen who saw unrequited love in the strangest of circumstances. She taped every episode of *General Hospital* and watched them on Saturdays.

"As if," I said in Mercedes-speak.

The bus pulled up in front of our pathetic excuse for a high school. John J. Peacock H.S. had exactly eighty-seven students in four grades. The Peacock school district was like a rich family's poor relative—sorta like Faye and me—jammed between two prosperous districts to the north and south.

All the rich kids who lived in Peacock Heights, located on the hills above Peacock Flats, went to Hilltop Christian School. They wore WWJD buttons—What Would Jesus Do—and the teenagers got blitzed every weekend. I don't think Jesus was a big party guy, but then again, he did turn water into wine. Even though Matt and Tiffany lived in the flats, they went to Hilltop. Aunt Sandra wouldn't allow them to go to public school.

After Patti's usual send-off—"You blockheads behave. See ya later, taters—" we poured out of the bus and into the old brick building, down a narrow hallway and through the ancient cafeteria, whose support beams were wrapped in thick insulation to keep the asbestos from seeping out. At least that's what our principal, Mr. Hostetler told us.

I had the perfect opportunity in English class to test out my new super powers. I sat at a perfectly level table with the perfect cylinder, a number two pencil. Could I make it roll horizontally across the desk? I glanced around to make sure nobody was watching before I tried. And tried. And tried. Couldn't do it. All right! Goodbye, super powers. Or maybe my mind was too cluttered with Mrs. Burke's multi-cultural lesson of the week.

Mrs. Burke was big on us learning about other cultures. Each week, we had a foreign phrase to use. This week it was French.

"When I call your name," she announced on Monday, "you will respond by saying, "*C'est moi, Madame Burke,*" which she told us meant, "It is me."

Sometimes she had to call roll three or four times before everyone cooperated. Today was no exception. Cory Philpott, still surly from our encounter on the bus, kept mumbling, "This is bullshit," under his breath and refused to answer.

Finally, Junior Martinez, who's two years older than the rest us due to his unfortunate incarceration for carving up a rival gang member, turned around and told Cory, "Say it, you little piss pot."

He did.

A lot of the girls at Peacock H.S. had the hots for Junior. He had smooth, olive skin, a deep dimple in his right cheek, and he drove a low rider to school. Rumor had it he was trying to nail every girl in the freshman class and he was right on schedule. Except for me, of course. Faye may not be Mother of the Year, but she told me everything I needed to know about sex. Sometimes more than I wanted to know. Manny saw Junior pushing a kid in a stroller, so apparently he's already reproduced. Extremely uncool.

After I punched Cory—and got kicked out of school for a week—Junior started calling me "Home Girl" and "One Punch." Not that I would ever be part of a gang but it doesn't hurt to have Junior on your side. Mercedes, of course, saw it differently.

"Ohmigod!" she exclaimed. "Junior totally likes you."

After school I stayed on the bus when Manny and Mercedes got off. When Patti stopped in front of Kizzy's house, Cory just had to get in one last shot.

"Oooo, you're staying with the witch tonight. You gonna boil up a couple of little kids?"

I slung my back pack over one shoulder and started down the steps before I answered, "Nope, but we sure could use a big old hunk of white meat. Want to stop over later?"

"Good one, G," Patti said. "That boy never learns."

"Pick me up here tomorrow, okay?"

"Damn straight," she said with a jaunty wave.

The doors slid shut and the big tires spit gravel as Patti tromped on the gas pedal.

As I approached Kizzy's house, I felt my heart beat a little faster. The house could barely be seen from the road. It was hidden behind a humungous hedge that ran all the way around her property. The only way to get in was through the iron gate set in middle of the hedge. I never approached the gate straight on. I cut over to the hedge and sneaked up on it because of the eye. The gate had this spooky eye painted on it. Swear to God, no matter how hard I tried to avoid the eye, it watched me, its glaring black pupil tracking my every move. A falcon's eye, Kizzy told me. A symbol used to ward off evil.

In spite of what Cory said, Kizzy was not a witch. She was a Romany gypsy, and apparently there was a difference. Who knew?

With an involuntary shiver, I averted my gaze from the eye, slipped through the gate and trotted down the walk toward the hulking, two-story house. The porch, with its overhanging roof, wrapped all the way around both sides of the house. A *veranda*, Kizzy called it.

"Alfrieda, you're here!"

Kizzy stood at the top of the stairs and held out her arms. She was the only person who called me by my hideous real name. Thanks to Claude, Faye's dad, I was given the name Alfrieda Carlotta Emerson. Faye ran away from home at seventeen. A year later, stuck in the hospital with a baby she didn't want (me) and no visible means of support, she struck a deal with Claude. In exchange for paying the hospital bill, he got to name me after his beloved, long-dead mother, Alfrieda Carlotta Emerson the First.

"Hey, Kizzy!" I slipped off my back pack and stepped into her embrace. She smelled of incense, lavender and Virginia Slims. Not that I'm a fashion expert but Kizzy always looked like she was dressed for a photo shoot in case a photographer from *Vogue* magazine was hanging around Peacock Flats.

Today, she wore a silk, turquoise dress the same color as her eyes. Her long, dark braid, sprinkled with gray, was draped over one shoulder. Three silver bangle bracelets encircled each wrist. Silver hoops hung from her ears. She'd replaced the rune stone she usually wore around her neck with a pale blue gemstone in an ornate silver setting. The stone was the size of a large marble. A shimmer of light danced on its surface. Strangely, I felt a strong need to reach out, touch it, hold it in my hand and stroke its glistening surface. I clasped my hands together tightly to resist the urge.

Kizzy studied my face then gently touched the mark in the middle of my forehead with a manicured fingernail. "Ah, I see the third eye has awakened. Come. Sit"

She led me to the porch swing.

Okay, sometimes Kizzy creeped me out. Wasn't it bad enough I lived in a travel trailer and wore clothes from a thrift shop? I mean, nothing screamed "Loser," like a third eye popping out in the middle of your forehead. I rolled my eyes in disgust.

"Should I start wearing bangs?"

Kizzy's tinkling laughter reassured me. "It's not a real eye, Alfrieda. The third eye is located deep within the brain. It's called 'the seat of the soul,' the link between the physical and spiritual worlds. Tell me what happened."

I took a deep breath and the words tumbled out. The only thing I held back was my visit from Trilby. When I told her about Blaster and the glass, I watched Kizzy's face carefully, looking for something negative, maybe a flicker of amusement or doubt. Instead, she clapped her hands in delight. Her clear, turquoise eyes danced with excitement.

"Oh, but that's wonderful! Don't you see?" Once again, she reached out and touched the tiny mark in the middle of my forehead. "You hit your head in the exact spot where the third eye is located. And the headache you had? The awakening of the third eye causes pressure at the base of the brain. It's all as it is supposed to be, darling girl."

Impulsively, she drew me in for another hug. Normally, I'm not into touchy-feely stuff, but as Kizzy stroked my hair and patted my back, I felt hot tears stinging my eyes. When there's nobody to talk to, things build up in your mind until you feel like your brain will explode. I mean, what do you do with all that stuff? It bounces around in your head and makes you crazy. In spite of the whole "third eye" thing, at least one person thought I was okay.

"What about the electric fence?" My voice came out muffled, since I was still pressed against the front of Kizzy's silk dress.

She released me and, without thought, I took hold of the gleaming stone that hung around her neck. It felt warm in my hand. "The jolt of electricity in combination with the bump on your head probably gave you a jump-start, so to speak."

I giggled and stroked the smooth blue stone.

She tapped a fingernail against her front tooth, something she did when she was deep in thought. "Hmm, yes, I'm sure of it. The telekinetic power—when you made the bull run backward —was a manifestation of the two phenomena working together. And the buzzing sound and tunnel vision? It's called an *aura*."

"But I can't do it anymore," I said. "I tried in English class. I couldn't even move a pencil." I added hastily, "Not that I want to."

"You weren't motivated," Kizzy said. "The power will return."

The sun slipped beneath the veranda's overhanging roof. I held the pendant to the light and gasped as sunlight sparkled and danced on its opalescent surface. "It's beautiful," I said. "What do you call it?"

"A moonstone," Kizzy said. "It was my mother's. Her name was Magda." She leaned forward and looked deep into my eyes. "What do you see when you look at this house? When you see the way I live?"

Whoa, was there a right answer here? I loved Kizzy for the good person she was. But I was pretty sure her question wasn't about that. I remembered my mother saying, "Look at that house! She has people to drive her around, cook for her, clean for her. Where do you get dough like that?"

"Well," I said, clearing my throat and looking away. "You seem to be pretty rich."

"Exactly!" Kizzy's eyes filled with tears. She dug around in the pocket of her dress and pulled out a tissue. She dabbed at her eyes. "But my mother was the saddest person I've ever known. She said it was because of the moonstone."

I dropped it like it was a burning ember. "Why?"

Kizzy shrugged. "She claimed she was being punished for misusing its power."

Oh great, I thought, looking at the pendant. *More magic B.S.*

"She wanted more children, but my father died when I was four. It was just the two of us in that big house in Seattle, surrounded by riches my mother could not enjoy."

"How did she misuse the moonstone?"

"She said she'd done something shameful, that she'd been greedy. She blamed herself for my father's death. Somehow, in her mind, it was all connected. The moonstone, the money, her loneliness."

"That's all she told you?"

Kizzy nodded. "I didn't know about the moonstone until Mother was dying. She told me to keep it safe until I met the right person."

"But what about your daughter? What about Carmel?"

Kizzy and her husband had adopted Carmel as a baby. The only thing she'd told me was she and her daughter weren't close and that Carmel hung out with a rough crowd. Kizzy always rolled her eyes and murmured, "Bad blood," when I mentioned her daughter. Today was no exception.

"Not Carmel," she said firmly. "She's not the right person."

"Right person for what?"

"Someone with the Gift. Someone pure of heart who would use it for good, not evil."

"Oh," I said. "Somebody like you."

Kizzy took my hand. "No, my dear. I don't have the Gift." She looked at my palm, traced the arc that circled what Kizzy called "the lunar mound," and ended below my little finger. "Mother had a line exactly like this, but you have something she didn't."

I rolled my eyes. Not this again. "Yeah, right," I mumbled and tried to pull my hand away.

Kizzy tightened her grip and pointed at a tiny constellation of whorls and hatch marks in the center of my lunar mound. "Look," she said. "A perfect star."

I jerked my hand away. "Everybody has that."

"No."

Kizzy showed me her palm. No star. No line. I shook my head in denial, suddenly uncomfortable with the whole spooky business.

Kizzy slipped the moonstone pendant from around her neck. Once again, she took my hand and turned it palm up. I knew what was coming and felt powerless to stop it. I watched, hardly daring to breathe. She dropped the moonstone onto my palm, the glistening silver chain pooling around it. She gently closed my fingers.

"And now, it's yours."

Breinigsville, PA USA
09 March 2010

233871BV00002B/159/P